Low Down
and Dirty

Low Down and Dirty

A NOVEL

VICKIE M. STRINGER

ATRIA BOOKS

New York London Toronto Sydney New Delhi

ATRIA BOOKS

A Division of Simon & Schuster, Inc.
1230 Avenue of the Americas
New York, NY 10020

First Atria Books hardcover edition March 2012

ATRIA BOOKS and colophon are trademarks of Simon & Schuster, Inc.

For information about special discounts for bulk purchases, please contact Simon & Schuster Special Sales at 1-866-506-1949 or business@simonandschuster.com.

The Simon & Schuster Speakers Bureau can bring authors to your live event. For more information or to book an event, contact the Simon & Schuster Speakers Bureau at 1-866-248-3049 or visit our website at www.simonspeakers.com.

Manufactured in the United States of America

10 9 8 7 6 5 4 3 2 1

Library of Congress Cataloging-in-Publication Data
Stringer, Vickie M.
Low down and dirty : a novel / Vickie M. Stringer
    p.   cm.
    1. African American women—Fiction. I. Title. II. Title: Low down and dirty.
  PS3569.T69586L69 2012
  813'.54—dc23   2011046471

ISBN 978-1-4516-6086-9
ISBN 978-1-4516-6089-0 (ebook)

To my mother-in-law, Norma Berry.
I love you!

"Vengeance is mine saith the Lord."

Red's new mansion was a $2 million, 7,000 square foot, adobe style hacienda, nestled on two acres of landscaped desert in Scottsdale. The home boasted six bedrooms, five and a half baths, a five car garage, a home theatre, two dining areas, two living areas, a game room, and separate casita. Marble floors ran throughout the home, while granite kitchen countertops, a luxurious master bath, and a barrel tile roof finished up the home's luxury.

Red strolled across the marble floor of her family room and headed outdoors to her swimming area. She unwrapped the towel around her waist and slid into her steaming hot tub and relaxed.

She had a bowl of fruit next to the hot tub, as well as a bottle of Cristal. Red lifted the Cristal and poured herself a full glass of champagne. She was already enjoying her new life in Scottsdale. The malls there were like nothing she had seen before. Most were high end, and brimming with luxury shops. It was going to take her a year to hit all of the shops and the malls in Scottsdale. She had already explored one, and had been hit on by two black physicians during the course of her brief shopping excursion. Rich men were falling out of the sky in Scottsdale. It was that kind of place. A far cry from Detroit, where she grew up without a pot to piss in.

Red sipped at her champagne and thought about her life, and what had happened to her. She didn't want to think about her mother, and speculate whether or not Bacon had sent his boys to her house yet. Bacon was an ex-boyfriend that was sugar to pure shit. He was bitter over a Dear John letter, dangerous and foolish. Worse, harder than bed bugs to get rid of. She had hardened her heart and accepted the fact that her mother wasn't going to be in her life one way or the other. Deep down, Red hoped that they would be attacked at night, when her mother was at work, and her stepfather, turned child molester, Jerome was there by himself. That would be the best scenario. She could imagine, one day she would drive to Las Vegas, grab a burn-up cell phone and call. Hopefully her mother would answer and tell her that Jerome was dead. But that was in the future. Right now, she just wanted to relax and get settled.

And then there was Detective Thomas who had internal affairs after him for a rape charge supported with the evidence on a video tape that may well have been Red's masterpiece.

She had set him up perfectly. She'd recorded their lovemaking, and saved his cum from the last time they had sex. He would have a hard time explaining why she had his DNA inside of her. The report from the doctors at the clinic definitely sealed the case. She could just see his face when he read it. They extracted the semen from her vagina. Red threw her head back in laughter. *Bruised pelvic area, rough abrasion signaling forced entrance.* Too bad the detective had a big dick. *They weren't always a good thing to have, especially when a bitch was accusing you of rape,* Red thought. She laughed again.

Then there was Bacon and her childhood ex-boyfriend named Blue. Two assholes for the price of one. She could just see the look on Bacon's face when the police pulled that side panel down, he probably shitted himself. Yeah, he had better get himself a prison girlfriend this time, because there would be no coming out of this one. This time, he had been caught red-handed. *Bacon and Blue would hopefully be cell mates. So they could hump each other,* she thought.

And then there was Terry and Kera. Kera was going to be going away for a long time. Red had set her up cold. *The stupid, greedy bitch,* Red thought. She couldn't just leave well enough alone. She always acted all religious and high and mighty, and then stealing anything she could get her hands. *Hopefully they'll put her in a cell full of big-ass dykes.* She could just see Terry's face when Child Protective Services showed up at her door. That bitch was probably in shock therapy by now.

Red took another sip of her champagne and laughed. She still had the recording of Terry admitting to shooting up her house and trying to kill Kera. She would wait a couple of months, and then send that recording to the police as well. That way, just when that bitch thought her troubles were over, she would get hit with the biggie. Mekel, the love of Terry's life and Kera's baby daddy, would probably leave that bitch just to keep from paying any more of her legal fees! Red broke into laughter at the thought of it.

She had taken care of all of her enemies. She had been living high on the hog in Scottsdale for more than a week, and she didn't have a care in the world. If only she had Q, the only man that she ever wanted for all the right reasons. She'd left Q behind, and he may be the only man she regretted saying that about. He'd been too angry to reason with at that time, and she'd had to put her desire to reconnect with him on hold. She wished he were here with her in the hot tub. Being free and clear and getting away from Detroit with her own money had always been her dream. But she always thought that she would be doing it with Q.

A wind blew across the desert, and Red looked up into the star-filled sky. The desert wind reminded her of Mexico, and she made a silent promise to herself to go there.

Thinking of Q brought to mind Chass Reed—what a bitch. She was all over Q, and Q was acting like she was something special. She would have to get rid of old Chass in order for Q to see clearly. In Red's mind she was the only woman for Q, and Q was the only man for her. He just needed to be reminded of that. Sometimes an extra bitch in the picture complicated things. Red planned to check on him in a few months to see if Q had come to his senses yet. Her ringing phone on the ledge of the hot tub interrupted her nostalgia.

"What the fuck?" Red eyed her phone. *No one had this number,* she thought. Who the fuck could be calling?

The phone kept ringing. Red answered it. "Hello?"

"Hey, Red."

"Who the fuck is this?"

"Who the fuck you think this is?"

"Catfish?"

"That's right, bitch! I told you, you can run, but you can't hide."

"How the fuck are you calling me?" Red panicked. "How did you get this number?"

"Somebody should have told you, Red. The thing about legit money is that it's easy to track. Somebody also should have told you, I bury bodies in the desert."

Red hung up the phone, jumped out of the hot tub, ran inside of her house and locked the door. Her breath had rushed out of her body, and her heart palpitated. She nervously scanned the interior of her mansion, afraid to move, afraid to go upstairs, afraid to grab her keys and run for the garage. Despite his grotesque appearance, he still managed to find himself on top. Red, on the other hand, found herself pressed up against the wall and falling to the floor in tears. Catfish had found her.

CHAPTER ONE

*T*he oak front door of Red's hacienda may have muffled Catfish's threat, but Red still heard it loud and clear.

"You can run, but you can't hide!" She lay on the floor of the front hallway defeated, still soaking wet from her hot tub, trying unsuccessfully to control her tears. The taste of the Cristal she'd been enjoying just minutes earlier suddenly turned bitter on her tongue as she wondered why she hadn't been more prepared for this day. She'd planned for it, put most of the pieces in place, but she still had a few things left to do. Like buy a gun. God almighty, why hadn't she at least gotten a gun?

The one loose end she'd left hanging out there was Catfish, and that nigga was now standing on the front step of her spacious new home in Scottsdale. But how? Her getaway had been clean. She knew that. And Catfish was a scraggly, bottom-feeding muthafucka. He'd be the last person who could have tracked her. "Legit money is easy to trace," he'd echoed in her head.

She didn't understand how he'd gotten onto her money, legit

or not. Yeah, there were business licenses, but nothing with her name on them. Everything was under the name Go 2 Holdings. Even Gomez Realty was under the holding company on paper. And there were businesses called Gomez Realty in cities all over the United States. Why would Scottsdale stand out?

That was the other part of her plan—go someplace that nobody who knew her would ever think she'd go. Leaving Detroit was a given. What would Catfish think she'd do? She had contacts in New York and knew the town. That'd be the first place a dumb muthafucka like Catfish would look. Maybe he'd think she'd want someplace like Detroit, only bigger and better. Then Chicago would fit the bill. If she was really on the run maybe he'd think she'd want to leave the continental United States— hell, she was a boricua and spoke Spanish like one. Why didn't homegirl just go to Puerto Rico? Or even Florida would be a logical choice. She could have had Miami wrapped around her little finger. Thinking ahead she didn't go to any of those places. She went to Scottsdale. How the fuck had Catfish figured to look for her here?

She heard a tapping at the door. Not knuckles. Something else. Hard. Knocking. Like metal. Like the barrel of an automatic. "Bitch, I hear you whimpering in there," said Catfish in an artificially sweet voice. She could tell his face was right up against the doorjamb. "Pull your shit together and open up. This door look strong, but you know I'm 'bout to come through it. One way or another."

Red sat up on the floor, swiped at her tears, and wiped the snot from under her nose with the back of her hand. *He's right,* she thought. *Get it together. If you gonna get ruined, it can't be by a low piece of shit like Catfish.* She thought about pieces of her plan she had working for her. She still had the stashed money. She had accounts in a number of different banks, and a hundred grand in cash in a safe deposit box in one of them. And she had a go kit upstairs—an old, beat up canvas bag containing a passport, a credit card, some clothes, and ten grand in cash. But the chances of her being able to run upstairs, grab the bag, and get out of the house before Catfish came in shooting were not good.

Then there were the false trails, fake letters and e-mails in her desk, phony memos that would make somebody think she was moving one way, when she was going another. But what good was any of that if she couldn't get Catfish to at least nibble at the bait.

The tricks she used on Bacon wouldn't work on Catfish. Things such as flattery, remorse, asking for another chance. There was never anything between Catfish and Red but pure, unadulterated hatred waiting for revenge. Catfish, on the other hand, would come through the door pulling a trigger. And the stupider the nigga, the harder he was to reason with.

She had to give him something to wrap his little brain around. She pushed herself to her feet and straightened the bottom of her Parah Noir bikini. Then she sniffled, took a deep breath, and dealt the cards. "All right, now—now listen, Catfish. I know there's a couple things you want right now."

"A couple things?"

"Well, I'm guessing one of them's to just pop one in my head."

"Huh. Really? You think? What's the other one?"

"You talking about legit money, so I guess you mean the movie, since that's the biggest. But I'ma tell you right now, you ain't got no part of that. I worked my ass off for that."

"The what?" said Catfish. "Bitch, you . . ."

Red rolled her eyes. *Come on,* she thought. *Use that scraggly head of yours. Two plus two equals what?*

"Nah!" said Catfish, catching up with it. "You got a movie deal for *Snitch Nigga, Bitch Nigga*?"

Hell, the book had been a bestseller that told the authentic story of the game on the streets of Detroit and the hustlers who played it. It wasn't too much of a stretch that somebody in Hollywood might be interested in it. But now Red had to slow it down. Catfish was dumb, but he was also streetwise. He wouldn't fall for a sloppy play. "Look! Whatever! You ain't got no part of nothing I got going."

"How much?"

Red stayed quiet.

"Open this muthafuckin door, bitch. You and I got some talking to do, but I got to see your eyes when you talk."

Red put the palm of her hand on the door and breathed heavily. This is it, she thought. *Open the door, and play the hand.* She kept calm. "Catfish?"

"I'm standing here."

"I'ma let you in, but you got to be cool."

Catfish slapped the door, it sounded like with the palm of his hand, like he would slap her if the door weren't there between them. "Bitch, I'm coming through this door one way or the other. You know that." Damn.

"All right, all right," she said, revealing the actual fear in her voice.

She opened the door and stepped back.

CHAPTER TWO

*C*atfish stood on the front step, grinning. He lowered his gun hand and stepped inside onto the Italian marble, surveying the house top to bottom as he did.

"Mmm! You done raised yourself up out the streets right this time, bitch. I mean, I know your crib in Motown was nice, but this place the shit." He stepped close and bulged his bug eyes inches from her face. He leaned in and he sniffed at her like a dog. "What you been drinking, girl?"

Red blinked and leaned back from him. "Cristal."

"Yeah, that sounds good. Go ahead and pour me some of that."

She waited a beat, then turned and walked toward the back door.

Catfish took a couple of quick steps after her. "Where the fuck you think you going?"

"The bottle's on ice out by the hot . . ." She caught herself when she realized what kinds of ideas Catfish might get.

"By the hot . . ." He bounced on his toes. "Tub? Is that what you was trying to say? Damn. You know how to make a nigga feel right at home, huh?"

Oh no, she was not getting into a hot tub with a slimy Catfish. She was about to tell him to just wait, and she'd get him a glass. On the other hand, he was too cozy with that Glock. If she could get him to put it down, she might be able to make a move for it. If she shot some raggedy ass nigga from Detroit in her home or on her pool deck, one with a record like his, it wouldn't be too tough to sell it to the cops as self-defense. She knew what words to use—*intruder, attempted rape, feared for my life.*

She led the way through the living room and out onto the pool deck. Red let her bikini-clad ass do the work, and when she glanced over her shoulder Catfish was scratching his dick with the gun and smiling. She lifted the bottle of champagne out of the ice bucket and turned to him.

"What, I don't get a glass?" he said.

She picked up the flute off the tile next to the hot tub. "Share mine."

Catfish eyed her for a sec, then shook his head. "You a fine-looking bitch, Red, but you scandalous as hell. You ain't trying to play me with this shit about the movie, are you?"

She did her best to look flustered. "Look, maybe there is a movie, and maybe there isn't. But either way, you ain't part of that deal."

Catfish's eyes got big and he tensed, waving the gun around. "Oh, yeah, I think I am part of that deal. You know I know that story like the back of my hand."

"You just don't listen, do you?"

Red bowed her head and shook it.

"Come on," said Catfish. "Where you keep your papers and shit at? I need to check you out. And I know you all about contracts and signatures, little Miss Legit." He put the side of the

Glock's barrel on her upper arm and shoved her toward the interior of the house again.

Red gathered her advantages where she could find them. She now had a weapon in her hand—the heavy champagne bottle—and she wasn't about to let it go. She carried it with her through the house into her study. One wall of the room was lined with shelves, which held books on real estate, business, interior design, and finance. A Queen Anne desk stood facing inward in front of a large window, a matching chair behind it. Two leather chairs on either side of a coffee table completed the room.

"Damn," said Catfish. "You even got like a den up in this bitch."

"It's called a study."

"Oh, a study. Right, 'cause you all the time studying on how to rip niggas off."

He walked past her toward the desk, grabbing the bottle of Cristal out of her hand on the way.

Damn, she thought. She held onto it long enough to make Catfish do a little stutter step, but she knew she had to let it go.

He took a swig from the bottle as he rounded the desk and settled into the chair. Then he set the bottle on the desk.

"Have some respect and use a coaster," said Red, and she rolled her eyes.

Catfish paid her no mind. He rifled through a stack of papers on the corner of the desk. Then he opened the drawer and started digging around in there with one hand, the other still holding the Glock.

Red crossed her arms in front of her chest and took a casual step forward. The champagne bottle was now within arm's reach.

Catfish settled on a document of several pages stapled together. "Mou?" he said.

"M-O-U," said Red.

Catfish sneered at her. "I see how to spell it, bitch."

"No, it's . . ." She rubbed her forehead with her fingertips. "It's pronounced M-O-U, Catfish. It stands for memo of understanding."

He thumbed through the pages until he got to the signatures at the end. "Oh, this like a contract, huh? There your signature." He studied it for another few seconds. "And who this other dude who signed it? Que-en . . . Tar-an . . ."

Goddamn, you dumb, she thought. *Can't you even read, you sorry ass muthafucka?*

Then Catfish got it. He slapped the palm of his hand down on the desk. "Oh, my God. Quentin Tarantino?" He looked up at Red and gave her a stupid grin. "You got Quentin Tarantino into your shit?"

Red took another step forward. Now her thighs were right up against the front of the desk, and the bottle was in easy reach.

"How much?" said Catfish.

Red hung her head as if beaten. "Check page three."

Catfish frantically began thumbing through the pages, finally putting down the gun in frustration. He started reading page three, lips moving the whole time. Then his lips stopped moving and turned up at the corners. "Two million? Two muthafuckin million?"

He threw the papers down, unconsciously covering his gun with them. "All right, bitch. 'Bout half that mine. At least."

Red shook her head. "That money's mine, muthafucka." It was a risky thing to say, but she had to play it real or he'd never buy it.

Catfish rose up out the chair, eyes on her, groping for the gun under the papers, then pointing it at her.

"What I'm saying is . . ." She held up her hands.

"What?"

"What I'm saying is, maybe I can hook you up with your own money on this thing."

"My own money?" He still had the gun pointed at her.

"Well, like you said, you know all about the story. You know the streets. You lived that life. Maybe I can get you a gig as a technical advisor on the movie."

He sneered. "Technical advisor? That don't sound like no high-paying job to me."

"You get to hang out with the actors, show them around Motown . . ."

Now she had him thinking. "Yeah," he said, looking up at the ceiling as he set the gun on the desk again. "I could see that. There's gonna be some fine bitches in that movie too." He looked at Red. "You gonna get that Eva Mendez?"

"Eva Mendez? Uh, what part would she play?"

"What, bitch? I don't give a fuck what part she play."

Red raised an eyebrow at him. "I can talk to some people about it."

"Yeah," said Catfish, nodding thoughtfully. Then his attention snapped back to Red. "And I'm still gonna need half that two mil. In fact, how much of that you got in the house? Just lying around. Like in the cookie jar."

Hell no. He was not going to go rummaging around in the house and find her go bag, her ten grand, all her bank account numbers, her credit cards.

"Where the cookie jar at, Red?" He started to push himself up from the desk using both hands. "Let's go look for it."

CHAPTER THREE

*H*er heart started to pound as she reached for the bottle on the desk. She grabbed it by the neck with both hands and swung it like a baseball bat at Catfish's whiskers.

The blow split his lip and knocked him back into the chair. Champagne sprewed everywhere.

"Don't put no damn bottle on my Queen Anne desk!" yelled Red. She swung the bottle again.

This time Catfish was ready for her. He raised his left arm and took most of the impact on his wrist. He winced from the pain, but saved himself another blow to the face. Red brought the bottle down from above her head, crushing Catfish's fingers. In addition to the glass's watermark, the poor desk was now awash with champagne and blood.

"You muthafucka, Red!" yelled Catfish. "I'ma kill you, bitch."

She needed one more good solid swing at his head, but she wasn't going to get it. Now she had an angry Catfish to deal with, and that was dangerous. He was on his feet, and even with his broken right fingers, he upended the desk, practically throwing it at her. With the desk came everything that had been on top of it—papers, lamp, and the Glock. She thought of diving for it, but if she didn't grab and fire clean, he'd be on her, and that would be just about it. She was no match for him hand to hand. She screamed and threw the bottle at his face. The glancing blow didn't stop him, but it might have been just enough to give her half a step.

She turned and ran. Through the living room, out the back door, and into the desert. No go bag, no car keys, no shoes. Just a black to-die-for bikini and her life.

CHAPTER FOUR

*U*nder the circumstances, Detective Thomas was as confident as he could be, going into a hearing where everything seemed stacked against him. Red had filed a complaint of rape, backed up with as much rape kit evidence as he'd ever seen in his career in the Detroit Police Department: pubic hair, semen, some bruising, and a videotape of the event. Before leaving home, he changed clothes at least three times, unsure which of his suits said, "I'm not a rapist."

Detectives Robinson and Lynn of the Internal Affairs Division would be there, but this was more than just an IA investigation. It was criminal, so there was bound to be a detective present who was involved in the criminal investigation that might eventually land before the State of Michigan.

Still, as he made his way down the corridor toward room 300D of Detroit Police Department Headquarters, he knew he'd done all he could to prepare. With the help of Roylon Shaw, his police union lawyer who now accompanied him, he was as ready

as he'd ever be. The two men's shoes clicked along the green lino-
leum floor, making Thomas feel like he was marching into battle.
And he didn't think he could have picked a better guy to have in
his foxhole.

Shaw had been a cop himself for twenty-five years and had
earned his law degree at night during the last six of those. He'd
started his career on the DPD back in the days when a black cop
had to fight for every bit of respect he was due. Thomas knew the
older man had seen his share of administrative ass-fucking. He
liked the fact that the guy wasn't afraid to brawl with the brass.
Shaw had the face of a fighter, but his navy blue Brooks Brothers
suit, red striped power tie, and alligator briefcase left no doubt
that he was a legal badass.

When they stopped outside the door marked 300D, Shaw put
his arm around his client's shoulder and pulled him in close.
"Okay, now their favorite weapon in this kind of hearing is hu-
miliation. They're going to try to demoralize you. They're going
to try to anger you. They're going to fuck with your head. Just
remember, when it comes time to dance with these muthafuckas,
you let me lead. We're going to go through it point by point, just
like we talked about. We're going to make 'em see they ain't got
shit on you."

They walked through the door at exactly 9:59 A.M. for the ten
o'clock hearing, and Thomas immediately felt like he was walking into the arena with the gladiators. Detectives Robinson and
Lynn were seated at the table that ran the width of the room in
front of the window. Standing at the window looking out was
Detective Marquez Nuñez, the lead investigator on the rape
charge and the man who had literally taken Thomas's shield
from him at the time of his arrest. Nuñez wore a tailored, silver
gray suit with a razor-sharp crease in the pants, and a gold watch
peeked out from under the white cuff inside his coat sleeve. He
turned and gave Thomas a condescending smile. Thomas didn't

smile back. Nuñez stood a whole five feet, five inches tall and weighed only 120-pounds soaking wet, but he carried himself like he was the biggest man in the department. No doubt he saw himself making commissioner before he was fifty.

Seated at the table next to Detective Lynn was a deputy commissioner who would supervise the hearing. Next to him was a court reporter sipping coffee, relaxing until kickoff. In a chair off to the side was a man Thomas didn't recognize, dressed in a neatly pressed, but off-the-rack suit. He was a black guy in his late twenties with close cropped hair and a baby face.

The ranking officer rose from his seat. "Detective Thomas, Mr. Shaw," he said. "I'm Deputy Commissioner Conrad. I'll be hearing preliminary IA statements today, as well as responses. You gentlemen can be seated right there." He pointed to a small table that faced the much larger one and the window behind it. Then he looked over his shoulder at Nuñez. "I believe we're ready to get started, if everyone will have a seat."

Nuñez pulled out a chair and sat at the administrative table, not hurrying, not caring that he was holding things up.

You're just cool as a porcelain toilet, huh, bitch? thought Thomas as he adjusted himself in his chair.

Roylon Shaw leaned close to Detective Thomas and tilted his head toward Nuñez. "That's a Brioni suit my nigga's wearing," he whispered. "On a cop's salary? IA should be looking into *his* shit."

The deputy commissioner cleared his throat. "We're on the record in the matter of the Internal Affairs Division inquiry into the actions of Detective Thomas, subject of a rape complaint by Raven Gomez, a woman alleged to have had knowledge of certain crimes the detective was investigating. In the room are Detective Thomas, and his union attorney, Roylon Shaw. Also present are Detectives Robinson and Lynn of the Internal Affairs Division, as well as Detective Marquez Nuñez, who is assigned to investigate the criminal charge of rape. Special Agent Marcus Holt of the FBI is in attendance. Complainant Gomez is not present. And would someone like to explain to me why that is?"

Thomas whispered in his attorney's ear. "What the fuck are the feds doing here?"

Shaw shook his head.

Lynn and Robinson both leaned forward and looked down the table at Nuñez, waiting for him to answer the deputy commissioner's question.

Nuñez nodded. "All right, I'll take that one. Sir, Ms. Gomez's whereabouts are not known at this time." He shot a glance at the FBI agent. "However, that information is being developed even as we speak. And in lieu of her presence, we do have her sworn statement, and physical evidence of the crime, including a video of the act itself." Then he pointed at Thomas without looking at him. "Mr. Thomas is—"

Thomas shifted in his chair. "*Detective* Thomas, if you don't mind."

"Deputy Commissioner, the subject of this investigation doesn't deserve to be called *Detective*. He is a rapist and a disgusting—"

"I'm not a rapist," said Thomas. "We're here to discuss those charges. Nothing's been proven, and nothing will be."

"—animal who is better suited to wearing a Department of Corrections number than a badge. His filth, his abhorrent behavior—"

"You want to see some behavior," said Thomas. "I'ma behave on you in about two seconds, muthafucka, and stomp your short ass even lower to the ground!" He tried to rise, but his lawyer put a big hand on his shoulder and held him down.

Nuñez just smiled.

"You pint-sized piece of shit," said Thomas. "Grinnin' muthafucka."

"All right," said the deputy commissioner. "That's enough from both of you."

"Deputy," said Attorney Shaw, "Detective Nuñez's comments are completely inappropriate and do nothing to further the purpose of this hearing. I move that they be stricken from the record."

"I'm not going to strike them from the record. They're not evidentiary, but I am going to advise Detective Nuñez to proceed with decorum from this point on." He turned and glared at Thomas. "As for you, Detective Thomas, you do realize you're here to answer to charges of a violent crime. Do you really think committing a violent act during the hearing is going to help your case?"

Shaw leaned over and whispered in his client's ear. "That ain't the way to dance in this dance hall. I said, let me handle it."

Thomas looked at the deputy commissioner. "No, sir. I understand. But if I may, I'd like to state for the record that I don't appreciate Detective Nuñez's characterizations of me."

Deputy Commissioner Conrad chuckled. "I believe you've made that very clear on the record."

Others in the room laughed. Shaw patted Thomas on the back.

"And I'll remind you again," said Conrad, "that you're in danger of losing not only your job, but also your freedom. You have a very competent attorney here representing you. I suggest you let him do the talking."

"I understand, Deputy Commissioner. I'll—Yes, sir."

"Detective Nuñez," said Conrad. "Do you have anything else you'd like to present at this time?"

Nuñez smirked and tugged at his cuffs. "Sir, we do, in fact, intend to bring charges against Mr.—the defendant—"

"Wait a minute," said Shaw. "For the record, Deputy Commissioner, my client is not a defendant yet. The department may intend to bring charges, but they haven't brought charges yet. Any charges. Of any kind."

"Yes, yes," said Conrad. "He's the subject of an investigation only. We know. And the charges pending against him are extremely serious."

Shaw shook his head. "Ah, but Detective Nuñez seems not to know this."

Conrad batted the statement away with his hand. "Come on, Roylon. His job is not to be impartial."

Thomas felt his heart sink into his stomach. He didn't expect the brass to be on his side, but Deputy Commissioner Conrad was leaning away from him.

"Now let's cut through the bullshit." Conrad turned to Nuñez. "Detective Nuñez, go on. You intend to bring charges against the subject of this investigation. Yes? Yes?"

"Yes, sir. The charge of rape being the most serious, but also conduct unbecoming, inappropriate sexual relations with a potential witness, and intimidation of a potential witness."

"And the witness, also the complainant, is being sought. I assume our federal brother over here has something to do with that?"

No one said anything.

"Agent Holt?" said Conrad. "Anything you'd like to add?"

"We have—lines in the water."

Conrad raised his eyebrows. "A fishing metaphor. I have to tell you, Special Agent Holt, that doesn't sound promising."

Holt didn't seem rattled. "We feel we're close. We'll know more in a couple of days."

"And, Mr. Shaw, do you and your client have anything you'd like to present?" said Conrad.

"Yes, we do, sir. I have some things I'd like to enter into the record, and my client would like to make a statement."

Deputy Commissioner Conrad thought for a moment. "Well,

since the FBI feels it's close to a development in the search for Ms. Gomez, let's see where that goes. Obviously, I'd like to include her in this inquiry. Let's reconvene in three days and see if Agent Holt can produce Ms. Gomez at that time, or if he can enlighten us as to his progress. Perhaps he'll let us know what kind of bait he's using, and how many hooks."

On the front steps of the headquarters building, Thomas breathed in deeply and loosened his tie. "Was there anything good that came out of that?" he said.

"Yeah," said Shaw.

"What?"

"You ain't in bracelets."

Thomas laughed and shook his head. "Well, hallelujah!"

Shaw laughed too. "Praise be."

"Yeah, praise be to Raven Gomez for keeping her muthafuckin' head down. Man, what was all that FBI bullshit?"

"Yeah, the feds are slippery little bitches. If they know something, why aren't they saying what it is? If they don't know anything, what the fuck they doing here?"

"Indeed," said Thomas.

Shaw took the Ray Ban aviators out of his pocket, held them up, and blew the dust off the lenses. "Look, let me make some inquiries, see what I can find out about what they have going." He slipped the sunglasses on. "In the meantime, will you please chill, muthafucka? You did *not* impress the Deputy Commissioner. You want him to think you're some kind of Omar Little? All you're doing is making my job harder."

Thomas chuckled as he shook his attorney's hand. "All right. I got you. I'ma let you do your thing."

As Shaw strolled down the sidewalk, Thomas stood on the steps a moment longer, gathering his thoughts.

"Roylon Shaw," said a voice behind him.

He turned to see Marquez Nuñez a couple of steps above him, watching the back of Shaw's head.

"Now there's a tough cop from the bad old days. Gotta figure he was into some serious shit."

"Damn!" said Thomas. "You just see evil everywhere you look, huh? The whole world's gone wrong and you the nigga gonna make it all right."

Nuñez stood two steps above Thomas, looking down into his eyes. "I know a bad cop when I see one."

"I bet you wish you could go through life standing two steps above everybody, pygmy muthafucka."

Nuñez took two steps down and looked up at Thomas. "I don't need to be two steps up to be a bigger man than you."

Thomas balled up his fists but kept them at his side. "You want to square off on me?"

"What are you gonna do? Wrinkle my clothes?"

Thomas felt his shoulders tense. *Not now,* he thought. *When this is all over and I'm working the streets again, I'll cross paths with this muthafucka.*

CHAPTER FIVE

*R*ed sat on the bench outside an old-fashioned gas station a half mile from her home and checked the bottom of her feet. They'd been blistered and cut by her 150-yard sprint into the desert, and then aggravated by her limping, hurried walk the rest of the way to the first patch of development behind her subdivision. Catfish hadn't been right on her heels. Maybe she'd hurt him worse than she thought. That idea even made her smile a little. Still, there was no way she was going back to check on him. Her home—the beautiful home she'd built after all her hard work dealing with niggas like Catfish and Bacon and Zeke, Detective Thomas, Kera, all those fucks—was now blown.

She put her feet back on the sidewalk, looked up, and wiped sweat from her face with both hands. As she glanced around, she noticed the looks people were shooting her from the pumps and from the station's counter inside. She was a black woman wearing nothing but a black Parah Noir bikini in an upscale, 98% white part of Scottsdale. Yeah, she was out of place, but that was only part of the reason people were looking at her. Bitches stared because they knew she was too fine to compete with, and men stared because they wanted something she had.

That last part was going to save her, because those men had something she wanted, too. She sat for a few more minutes until she'd come up with just the right tale to tell. Then she scouted out the potential victims, eventually settling on a fat, balding, forty-something man pumping gas into his Escalade. Perfect. He was wearing loafers, a white polo shirt, and Hugo Boss slacks with a golf glove still sticking up from his back pocket. It must have been a frustrating eighteen holes, judging by the scowl on his face and the unkempt wisps of hair flying around his head. Best of all, in the back window of his ride was a decal that proclaimed him the proud father of a Mesa High School honors student.

Red lifted herself off the bench and smiled, ignoring her painful, barefooted steps across the concrete to the pumps.

"Excuse me, sir," she said as she got within earshot.

The man looked up from the gas nozzle he was holding, frowned for a moment, and then smiled broadly. "Yeah?"

Red kept the smile going, but dialed it down to shy. "This is really embarrassing, but, uh—well, my girlfriend and I were on our way to the lake and she, uh . . ."

"She what?" said the man, curious and obviously ready to get his flirt on.

"Well, she kicked me out of her car. And now I need—I'm so embarrassed. I've never done this before, but I need cab fare."

The man chuckled. "Whoa! Now, why would your girlfriend kick you out of her car?" He finished pumping and hung the nozzle back on the pump.

"I confessed something to her, and I guess I was a little too—you know—forthcoming."

"Uh-oh," said the man. "Were you naughty?"

Red withdrew a step and put her hands on the hot, sweaty skin above her breasts. "It wasn't my fault. I swear! Her boyfriend came over to *my* house. It wasn't like I invited him. He just showed up."

"I don't blame him. And let me guess. You were very hospitable to him?"

She feigned a deepening embarrassment and bowed her head. "I—it was just that . . ."

"Relax, relax," said the man. Then he looked around to make sure no one was listening. "I understand. But I gotta tell you, I'm not really in the habit of just *giving* money to strangers." He looked around again and licked his lips. "Now, if we knew each other a little better . . . You know, maybe if we took some time to . . ."

Muthafucka, thought Red. She'd planned on using what she had to get what she needed—some skin, a wink, a smile, some sweet words in a honeyed voice—but she hadn't planned on stumbling across someone completely greedy. Still, she didn't miss a beat. "I've been told I make friends easily."

He gestured to the passenger door. "Climb in. There's a hotel just up the road."

"Oh, darn," she said. "I don't have that much time." She looked over her shoulder at the gas station, then back at the man. "If you want to know the truth, I've got another confession. I've never done anything like this in a public men's room, but it's always been a fantasy of mine."

The man laughed. "Oh, you're a bad girl, aren't you?"

"No, I just—"

"Let me pull my car into a parking space. I'll meet you over there."

"Oh, God," she said, a big smile playing across her face. "I can't believe I'm doing this."

She strolled over to the side of the gas station where the

men's and ladies' rooms were. By the time she got there, the man was out of his car and hurrying to join her.

"You know," she said as he drew near, "in my fantasy I—I mean, it, uh, I like it a little, you know, forceful."

She could actually see the bulge in his pants as he considered what she was saying.

"Well, this being your first time and all, I don't know how I could deny you your fantasy." He put his hand around her upper arm, ushered her into the bathroom, and locked the door. He'd squeezed her arm firmly, but he needed a hell of a lot of practice before he came close to being forceful.

The small room smelled of piss and puke. The floor under her bare feet was sticky in some places, slick in others. She hated the thought of putting her knees on it, but she was going to get what she needed from this fat little bitch boy. But the guy just stood there looking at her, like he had no idea what to do.

She realized she was going to have to write the whole damn script for him. "You're not going to make me get down on my knees to suck you hard, are you? To suck your big, mean cock so you can slam it into my tight cunt?"

The man was breathing hard now and had that serious look that teenage boys got when they were about to get some for the first or second time. "Yeah, that's right," he said. "Uh, get down on your knees and suck my cock." And as an afterthought he added, "Bitch." Then he unzipped and pulled his white, miserable cock out of his pants. It was throbbing and twitching as it went from half staff to fully erect in just a few seconds.

At least the fucker don't need Viagra, thought Red as she lowered herself to her knees. She sat back on her heels, away from him, and looked up with mock fright in her eyes. Then she whispered, as if not to break the spell, "You're too tall for me. Spread your feet apart so I can reach your dick with my mouth."

The weak-ass bitch did as she instructed him. For a moment

she considered how passive he was and wondered if he'd let her tie him up. That would work. Still, the moment was at hand and she didn't have time to fuck around anymore. And she had no need, either.

She grabbed his stiff dick with her left hand. She made her right into a fist and brought it up from between his knees into his balls as hard as she could.

He groaned and dropped, almost in slow motion to his knees while she scrambled to get out of his way so he didn't fall on top of her. "What the fuck?" he said, his voice strangled with pain.

"You know what sucks?" said Red. "I mean besides the fact that I just cracked your muthafuckin' nuts? Attempted rape. That's what sucks."

Now the man fell to his side and pressed his cheek to the piss covered floor, speechless.

"You know they got a security camera out there. And it's gonna show you grabbing me by the arm and dragging me into this shitty men's room. How's that going to look to the cops? To your boss? Your friends at the county club? Your wife? How's it gonna look to your honors student and the other kids at Mesa High School?"

"What the fuck do you want?"

"Are you really so stupid I gotta tell you to give me your wallet?"

"Okay, okay." The man reached behind him and pulled out his wallet.

Red snatched it from his hand and rifled through it. Seventy-eight bucks in cash and an ATM card. She left the credit cards. His wife might get in his shit over that. She didn't want any wild cards. Next, she reached for his cell phone held in a plastic side holster.

"Hey," he shouted as he tried to bat her away.

"Relax, Butch. I ain't trying to molest you. I just need your phone." She snapped the leather holster and pulled the phone out.

"What's the ATM code?" she asked.

The man was breathing deeply now, the pain easing up a bit. "I can't give you that."

"Then I start screaming. And with the way you grabbed my arm, the bruises are gonna look real good in the rape kit photos." She doubted he'd squeezed her hard enough to bruise her, but it was easy to sell him on how macho he was, even while he was lying on a nasty men's room floor with a pair of swollen balls and a limp dick. "You probably didn't think black folks bruise, but we do."

"All right, all right," he said. "The password is 1949."

"1949?" said Red. "That's the year your wife was born?"

"Yeah. How'd you know?"

"Helpless pricks are always predictable. Enjoy your recovery.

"And on that note, I'm gone," said Red. She took a step toward the door, then looked back. "Just remember, we'll always have Scottsdale."

$\mathcal{W}$ith her new money and cash card stuffed down the front of her bikini bottom, Red hobbled along the shoulder of the road, looking back from time to time for Catfish or her golfing buddy, her new money and cash card stuffed down the front of her bikini bottom. A quarter mile later she wandered into a strip mall and did some quick shopping. She considered Ann Taylor Loft, but figured she'd better stick to a tight budget until she got a few things working for her. She hit a shop called She-She and quickly made her selections—a Nike warm-up suit (with pockets), Nike flip-flops, and a Nautica cap. It ate up almost her whole cash take. She asked the shocked and suspicious clerk to cut the price tags off, slipped into her purchases right there in front of the counter, and went to find an ATM.

Fifty yards down the sidewalk she found one. Pulling the cap down over her eyes, she stepped in front of the surveillance camera and shoved Golfing Buddy's card into the slot. She tried to take $400 and got a message saying the daily limit was $200. She figured it'd work like that, but the larger score was worth a try. She pocketed the $200, sat down on a nearby bench, and used her new (yet temporary) cell phone to dial up a friend—maybe the only friend she had left in Detroit.

The phone rang six times, then went to voice mail. Red waited for the beep. "I know the caller ID says some fucked up name you never heard of, but this is me, Red. I need your help, girlfriend. Call me back."

A minute and a half later the phone rang and Red flipped it open. "Quisha?"

"Red?" said Laquisha Denny. "What you doing using a phone with a name like Fred Lindenburg?"

Red slumped on the bench, almost breaking down in tears at the sound of her friend's voice. "Damn, Quisha, it's good to talk to you."

"What's wrong, Red? I can hear the stress in your voice and that ain't like you."

"Girl, I'm in all kinda trouble. I guess you heard Bacon took a fall during that New York trip. Got pulled over behind his running buddies who were in a truck full of drugs."

"Bacon, Blue and those other two niggas. 'Course I heard. Trap still trippin' bout that shit. Him and Bacon was just gettin' into some good business. Some muthafucka snitched on they asses. Rolled 'em up good."

A smile tugged at the corners of Red's mouth as she recalled how she'd set up Bacon and Blue one of their drug runs to New York. "I'm still trying to figure out who coulda done them like that. Somebody needs to clean that shit up, 'cause I got left alone and now I'm in trouble."

"What's happening with you, girl?" asked Quisha.

"I had to go on the run behind some shit Bacon did. He had him some serious enemies. Now the muthafuckas coming after me."

"Where you at, Red?"

"Believe it or not, Arizona."

"Arizona? You in some witness protection gig or something?"

"Yeah, of my own design. But it ain't working out too good."

"Who's coming after you?"

"That boy Catfish. He chased me right outta my crib. I got nothing but the clothes on my back, and even them I had to scam to get. But I'm trying to figure out how Catfish got out of prison and how he tracked me down."

"Girl, you know I got my ear to the streets in Motown. I'ma see what I can find out about that shit."

"Quisha, you're such a good friend to me. I do need whatever info you can get, but what I also really need is clothes and cash." Red took a deep breath. She knew it was a lot to ask. Quisha's man, Trap, was a smart hustler and she'd have to make some moves to get any real cash behind his back and hit the road with it. And asking her to roll up out of her cushy life was a big thing anyway. But Red had no one else to turn to. "Quisha, I need your help. I need you to come out to Arizona."

Quisha said nothing for a moment, then it was as if she had to search for the words. "Ariz—girl I—what? You serious?"

"I am, Quisha. I need you."

"I ain't too big on this kinda cloak-and-dagger shit."

"Quisha, I got nobody else I can trust. I could call my mom and my stepdad, but . . ." Red knew her mom and Jerome had to have been done in by that time, but she could still play it out for Quisha if the girl needed a little push. "After what that man did to me when I was a little girl, I just . . . And my mom just let him."

"What he did to you? What you mean? He do some nasty shit to you?"

Red let herself cry into the phone a little.

"Oh, hell no," said Quisha. "You ain't calling them."

"Can you come out here? Just bring me some cash and clothes. Just to get me over till I can figure this out."

There was silence for a few moments, then Quisha sighed. "Don't they have Western Union, American Express, Money Gram or anything that we can use?"

"Those things are traceable. I'm not walking into any place collecting money. I can't chance that." She paused.

"All right, girl. You need your girlfriend. I'll be there."

"Quisha, you're the best," said Red.

"Where should I meet you?"

"There's a place in Phoenix called the Barrio Café. Mapquest it and meet me there in two days."

"Two days?" She scoffed. "Oh, well, as long as it ain't like tonight. I mean, I got two whole days to come up with some cash, go out and get you some clothes, make travel arrangements, and come out there."

"I know it's short notice, but I'm out here on my own now. I don't know how long I can last."

There was silence on the line for a long moment. Then Quisha sighed. "All right, girl. I got your back."

"Quisha, I promise, this gonna come back around for you one day."

CHAPTER SEVEN

*K*era lay on her side in the upper bunk as her cellmate, a dark-skinned girl named Giselle, stood at the bars and shouted conversations with other inmates on the block.

"My private life of luxury is over," said Giselle.

"I don't know why the fuck they putting some new bitch in with you," said an unseen woman on the block. "Don't they know you ain't got no social graces?"

Several women howled with laughter.

"Not only that," said Giselle. "She ain't even done nothin' real. You know what she in here for?"

"What she do?" asked a third woman.

"She forged some checks."

"Least she got paid," responded the same woman.

"Walked into a bank to rob it, didn't even use no gun," said Giselle.

"She must be one of them brainy bitches," said the first woman.

Giselle looked over her shoulder at Kera. "No doubt," she sneered.

They talked about her like she wasn't even there. As far as Kera was concerned, they could just continue to ignore her forever. But she knew that wouldn't happen. She couldn't just be invisible. That fact became all the more painful as she looked across the tiny cell at the metal toilet in the corner. She had to take a shit. She could hold it for a few more minutes, but, eventually, she'd have no choice but to climb down off the bunk, pull her orange jumpsuit down to her knees, and sit on that disgusting, bare metal thing. In front of Giselle.

She didn't even know the proper prison etiquette. Was she supposed to tell her cellmate that she was going, or just go?

"Shit, Giselle," said another inmate. "She brand new. Be gentle with her."

Everyone laughed again.

Kera told herself they were just messing with her. Just fucking with the head of the new girl. No big deal. The CO's in intake had told her that the first few days would be rough, but that she'd settle in. As she swung her legs off the side of the bunk and eased herself down to the hard, gray floor, she couldn't imagine ever settling into this place.

She stepped to the toilet, glancing at her cellmate as she did. The ugly bitch was still leaning against the bars talking to her friends. Kera pulled her jumpsuit down and sat on the cold, steel, seatless rim. She quickly pushed out a log, then cringed as it made a loud plop in the water. She'd hoped she could do this without attracting any attention.

"Yo, bitch," said Giselle, looking right at her now. "Don't be using no twenty sheets of my paper, now. And flush that nasty pile before it stink up the whole place. Damn! I smelt pepper spray sweeter than that."

Other inmates laughed. And then they all went back to their conversations.

Kera wiped her ass, flushed down, and climbed back up into her bunk, feeling like a dog with its tail between its legs. *What the mother fuck did I do that was so wrong?* she wondered.

She'd been good to Mekel, had given him a child. And she didn't care what the crazy-ass doctors said, she had nothing to do with Mekel Junior's problems. She drank a little in the beginning of the pregnancy, smoked a little chronic, but she wasn't the only woman to do that. Terry was the bitch who physically assaulted the baby. And in the end, Mekel had chosen to be with her instead of Kera.

Red would say Kera had wronged her, when Kera skimmed a few bucks from that bitch's massive and ill-gotten bank deposits. But Kera believed it was only what she was due. She couldn't imagine why God would trash her whole life for something like that. Just a few mistakes—a few misunderstandings—had taken away the nice life she was building as she struggled to recover from the wrongs Mekel and Terry and Red had done to her. Now she was in this hole with these raggedy-ass bitches.

She rubbed the scars on her forearm where she'd cut herself repeatedly. At first she'd done it in an attempt to atone for her sins. At least that's what she'd told herself. But during the weeks that followed that first cut, she'd done it whenever she was stressed. It had become a habit. Lying there in the prison bunk she moved her right hand down her left forearm to the scars across her wrist. Those were no mystery. She knew exactly why she'd made them, and so did anyone else who happened to see them. She rolled over in her bunk, faced the wall, and let go of her tears.

Q sat on the edge of his bed in the rehab center, held up the cane, and turned it under the light, watching the black polished wood shine and the silver handle sparkle. "So, this is my new pimp stick," he said without a smile.

Chass stood over him and clicked her tongue. "Come on, now," she said. "This is a getting-out present. I just thought you deserved to leave the rehab center with a somewhat more stylish cane than that cheap, hospital-issue aluminum thing." She pointed to the plain stick with the torn, rubber handle-cover propped up in the corner.

Q sighed and nodded. Chass had been extremely caring throughout his recovery, and she deserved only his gratitude. But it was hard to dredge up any positive feelings to show her. Yes, he was getting out of the rehab center. But his life was changed, probably forever, by Red's bullet and her betrayal. She had claimed she wasn't aiming at him, that she was trying to hit Bacon. But how could he trust a damn thing she said after all her scheming, stealing, and backstabbing?

Yeah, he was getting out, but he'd still be an outpatient for weeks to come. He wondered if he'd ever completely regain his strength and his ability to walk.

"I'm sorry," he said to Chass. "It's very nice. Really, I—I appreciate it, and—well, you know—you being here for me through all this."

Chass smiled and bent down to give him a kiss on the cheek. "You got a stretch of road ahead of you, Q, but you're on the road. That's the important thing. And we're just going to keep going forward."

Q had his mother, and he had other people who cared about him, but Chass was something special. He looked at her standing in front of him in a business suit that would have made any courtroom opponent stutter. Her work clothes were always the height of professionalism without hiding a bit of her femininity. She was the sort of woman Red could never be. Chass didn't give him the spark that Red did. She was safe, predictable, reliable. Every man's dream, well, almost every man's dream.

No, he thought. *That bitch doesn't even deserve to be in my thoughts. She wanted me dead, now she's dead to me.*

"Mr. Carter," said a voice from the doorway.

Q turned to see a man pushing a wheelchair and a big, friendly smile into the room. His name tag read DOUGLAS. He was mid-twenties and gym-built.

Q furrowed his brow. "Yes?"

"They tell me you're good to go. I'll be your chauffeur."

Q marveled at the fact that some dudes could be so buffed out, but still look soft as a baby. He was some out-in-the-country nigga—never been in the game. "Uh-uh," Q said. "I've been practicing with a cane for some time now. Besides, I just got this brand new one from my friend here." He held up the cane and nodded to Chass. "I'll use this."

"I understand," said the man, even as he positioned the chair next to the bed for easy transfer.

That's what the hospital and rehab types called it—*transfer.* Around day three or four in the hospital bed, after they'd taken the catheter out, they'd *transferred* him from the bed to a wheelchair. Then they'd *transferred* him from the wheelchair to the toilet. Then they'd *transferred* him from the toilet to the chair again, and then back into the bed. That process had been repeated several times a day. He was done being transferred.

"You can just wheel that piece of shit off into the corner. Told you, I got my cane."

The man's smile didn't fade. "Well, as I was saying, the chair is policy. Insurance. Just until we get you through the front door. You know."

Q was about to stand up in the muthafucka's face, but Chass put a hand on his shoulder and laughed softly.

"Q, they aren't taking any chances while you've got a lawyer literally right by your side. You trip and fall with me as a witness, we're going to sue the foundation right out from under this place."

Douglas forced a laugh. "That's a wise lady friend you have there."

Q looked at Douglas, then at Chass.

Chass smirked and shook her head. "Tell you what. How about if we compromise? You get in the wheelchair, and I'll wheel you out myself." She turned to Douglas. "That all right?"

He shifted from one foot to the other for a moment. "Mmm . . . Well, see . . . Uh . . . Hmm . . . Oh, why not? You need some help transferring him into the chair?"

Q stood up. "No," he said. "I just told you I can walk with a cane. If I can do that, I can sure as hell stand up off the bed and sit in the chair."

Douglas held up his hands in surrender and stepped back. "True that," he said, trying to sound ghetto.

Q steadied himself with the cane in his right hand. With his left, he lifted the gym bag off the foot of the bed into which he'd packed his toiletries, his prescriptions, and the few things Chass and his mother had brought him during his stay. He'd thrown away the bloodstained clothes and shoes he'd been wearing the day his was shot by . . .

Don't go there again, he thought. He sighed and lowered himself into the chair, setting the bag on his lap.

"Good job," said Douglas.

Q glared at him.

"Thanks," said Chass. "We've got it from here."

"Okay, then," said the man. He turned and led the way out of the room. Then he waved as Chass and Q passed him in the hall. "Take care of yourself, Mr. Carter. Best of luck to you. To both of you."

Q shook his head. He turned and spoke over his shoulder to

Chass. "I swear to God I'm about to stand up out this chair and . . ."

Chass leaned close as she continued to push the chair. "Q, he's just doing his job."

"I know he is. I just . . . I know. I'm sorry. I'm sorry to be in such a mood."

Chass stepped around the chair and pressed the button for the elevator. Then she stood behind him again and put a hand on his shoulder. "I know. We're going to make it through this."

CHAPTER EIGHT

*K*era sat on the bunk in her cell and listened to the sounds of the movie playing in the common area below her. She had no desire to socialize with any of those criminals. Besides, the movie was something with Will Smith. Something positive and uplifting. She had no interest in that kind of bullshit. Life affirming—that's what they called it. They wanted you to believe that even with all its struggles and hardships, life was good. Who made that shit up? Life worked out just fine for some people, but not so good for others.

Red. There was somebody who seemed to make life work out for her ass. Kera wondered what that conniving bitch would have done if she'd gotten in trouble the way Kera did.

She'd never been as evil as Red. She was happy to just have a nice little income from her teller job, augmented with what she was due as a tax from Red. So why was it that a scandalous, greedy bitch like Red was always doing just fine, while Kera, with her perfectly reasonable expectations, was in this fucked up shit?

Kera had given her life to God, and he had let this happen to her. She didn't understand that, but she felt there must be a reason. Maybe God knew that some people weren't made for this world. Maybe this was his not-so-subtle way of leading her home. Seemed to Kera that the only people who really got by were the ones who weren't worried about lying and cheating and stealing from others. People like Red only fooled themselves into thinking that life was good by ignoring all the evil they had to do to get by in it.

What *would* Red have done if their roles had been reversed? Red was always good at reading people. The first hint she caught that anybody was on to her, she'd probably have made one last big score and then gone on the run. She'd have taken off across the country—headed out west or some shit.

Fuck no, she thought. *Red would never go on the run like that. Too rough out there on the road. She like the finer things in life. She'd find herself some nice place to lay up.*

Kera slid off the bunk and poked her head out between the cell bars, looking up and down the tier to make sure nobody was lingering too close. This was a tough place to find a few minutes of genuine privacy, but a few minutes was all she needed. She pulled the sheet off her mattress and gathered up the rags she'd laid out flat on the bed to hide them. She'd gotten herself a cleaning gig, which hadn't been too hard to do. Most of the bitches in this place wanted something cushy, like the library gig, or they wanted to work where they could get their hands on something valuable, like the kitchen where they could steal extra food for themselves, or to sell to other inmates. Nobody wanted to scrub shower stalls and empty garbage cans.

Kera didn't mind. Prison was prison. It couldn't get any

worse. What did it matter if you slung food or scrubbed the floor? Besides, it gave her a chance to collect old cleaning rags. Those were more valuable to her than gold now.

Kera rolled each rag tightly along its length, then began tying the ends together. Once she'd roped together eight rags or so, she tied a loop in one end.

She pulled the letter she'd previously written out of the pocket of her jumpsuit and read it one more time.

My Dear Mekel Jr.,

I'm sorry I have to say good-bye to you this way. It's not fair, is it? Not everything in life is fair, but I hope you will find enough good things out there to keep you moving forward, even after your own mother was taken from you unjustly by those who stabbed her in the back. Many things that are rightfully mine have been taken from me. The world is full of players who take things they don't deserve. I too played my game, but only to get my due. If anyone says otherwise, you will know that person is lying to you. Many people will lie to you in this world, and you have to watch out for them. You will hear many lies about me, no doubt. This letter may be your only chance to hear the truth, which is that I loved you unconditionally and did everything to build a happy home for us. But we were both cheated out of that, right? In this harsh world, those who are truly deserving are often betrayed and left with nothing. I hope and pray to God that you get through life being blessed more than you are cheated. I pray that you have more good days than you can ever imagine. I pray that you will always love me.

Your loving mother—Kera

As she folded the paper and tucked it back into her pocket, she was surprised to find that she wasn't crying. She caught a glimpse of herself in the tiny mirror over the washbasin at the far end of the cell and saw the emptiness in her eyes. There was no need for any *good-bye cruel world* bullshit. She was already gone, had been since the first cut against her wrist.

She poked her head out onto the tier again and assured herself that nobody was around. She stood on the lower crosspiece of the bars and tied the makeshift rope around the highest crosspiece. In the common area one level down, the other inhabitants of this hell laughed and carried on, as if they hadn't yet figured out how hopeless their lives were. As she slipped her head through the loop in the rope, she felt sorry for them.

CHAPTER NINE

*T*erry sat at the kitchen table and slowly stirred milk into her coffee as the early morning light streamed in through the window. Mekel lay on the couch reading the paper. They had talked a great deal during the days that followed Mekel Jr.'s removal from the home by Rhonda Davenport and her team from Child Protective Services. Mekel had gone on and on about how he wanted to track Red down and kill her. Terry had cried and lamented the loss of the baby boy she'd come to think of as her own. Mekel had done his best to comfort her. But recently there hadn't been much conversation in the house. It was as if they'd said all they had to say on the subject, and there was no other topic worth discussing.

Soon, they'd have to get ready and head down to the courthouse for a custody hearing. Maybe that would resolve some of the problems in their lives, one way or another. Terry wondered if she had the strength she was going to need for the hearing and raised the coffee cup to her lips. The phone screamed in the silent room, and Terry's hand jerked, spilling coffee down the front of Mekel's Detroit Tigers T-shirt that she wore around the house. She heard the newspaper rustle in the other room as Mekel stirred. "I'll get it, baby," she said. She stepped to the kitchen counter and grabbed the phone out of its base. "Hello?"

"Terry, this is Chass Reed. How are you holding up?"

Terry smiled as she settled back down in her chair at the table. Chass was the angel by way of public defender. They shared a common nuisance in Red, but that didn't seem to matter. Chass somehow managed to keep turning up in her life, and she'd shown up again to take on their child custody case because, according to Chass, she admired the way Terry had gotten her life together. Terry also felt that Chass had something against Red and saw the custody case as a chance to right one of that bitch's many wrongs. She was almost like a godsend. "Hey, Chass. Yeah, I'm—well, I'm—I guess as good as can be expected."

"I know this has been difficult, but I admire the strength you've shown."

Strength? Terry wondered if Chass saw something in her that she herself didn't see. She felt as if recent events with the child abduction, and almost losing Mekel to his baby mother had drained her of all energy. She thought about all that had happened. She'd made some mistakes—she couldn't deny that. Confused and misguided as she had been, she had wanted a baby of her own and had tried to take Mekel Jr. from Kera, who was still with Mekel at the time. And after all the mess that she'd caused, Mekel had forgiven her and welcomed her into his and his son's lives. He'd seen how much she loved the child, even though the baby had been damaged by Kera's drinking and drugging during her pregnancy.

Things had seemed to be going well; well, Red's false allegations of child abuse had ruined everything. Child Protective Services had come into their home and taken MJ by force. It was a nightmare. Red was good at creating nightmares for others as she lived out her dreams.

"You ready for the hearing?" asked Chass.

"Yeah. We're getting off to a bit of a slow start this morning, but we'll be there on time."

"Actually, I was hoping you could speed it up a little and get here a half hour early or so."

Terry looked up to see that Mekel was standing in the door-way, trying to pick up as much as he could about the call. "Uh, I guess we could," she said into the phone. "Why?"

"A couple of things have come up that I need to talk to both of you about, face-to-face, before we go into the hearing. Don't panic. We just need to make sure we got it together."

Terry assured Chass they'd get there quickly. After she hung up, she passed the news on to Mekel, and the two of them raced around the house to get ready and out the door a little earlier than they'd planned.

Chass greeted them just inside the courthouse, and, after going through the security check, she led them into a small, va-cant meeting room and asked them to have a seat at the table there. Chass sat across from them, but she didn't bother to open her briefcase and take out any legal papers—or even a pad to write on—as she usually did. Instead, she folded her hands and rested them on the table.

Mekel saw that as a bad sign. He'd been in the game and was pretty successful at it, which wasn't possible unless you could read people and situations. His old instincts never left him, but lately they seemed closer to the surface. He wondered if he'd ever truly shake the streets. "So is this, like, a good news/bad news thing?" he asked. "Or is it all bad news?"

Chass gave him a tired smile. "It's . . . difficult news."

"All right then," said Mekel, calm and deadpan, as he would have been in his hustling days when faced with a dangerous situation. It was ingrained in him.

"First," said Chass, "I'm sorry to tell you this, but I thought you should know that Kera has taken her own life."

"What?" said Terry. She sat forward in her chair, looked over at Mekel, then turned back to Chass. "Damn! Well, you know we didn't exactly have no love for that—for her. But still . . . That's a muthafucka." Her eyes grew wide. "I mean . . . My bad."

Chass smiled gently. "Terry, I come from the same place as you. And I'm an attorney. I've heard worse language than that, believe me."

"Uh, oh yeah. Okay. I was just, you know, surprised at Kera is all."

Mekel shook his head. "She was a troubled girl." He was *not* surprised. Kera was weak, and prison was no place for the weak. In fact, he'd wondered how long she would make it.

"I know there was no love lost between you," said Chass. "But I thought you should know. She left a note. They'll be mailing it to your home if you request it."

"Yeah, I'll think about it," said Mekel. "She was the boy's biological mother and all. As bad a job as she did of being that, still the note is something we should have."

Terry put a hand on Mekel's and squeezed.

"But really, we here about the boy," said Mekel. "So let's get to that. You said the news was—what did you say? Difficult, right?"

"Do you know anything about where Red is?"

"Red?" Mekel shook his head. "Naw. Like I said, we here about the boy. I ain't even trying to think about that bitch."

"I understand," said Chass. "The only reason I ask is that certain other parties have expressed an interest in your case, and they seem particularly interested in your claim that Red was the anonymous caller who alleged you were abusing the child."

"My *claim*? Ain't no *claim* about it. I mean, excuse me, Ms. Reed, I don't mean to get all blunt about it, but Red the muthafuckin' bitch put us in this mess. No doubt." He raised his hand and brought his index finger down on the table with a thud to emphasize each of Red's attributes as he listed them. "She a lying, thieving, backstabbing, cold-blooded, selfish, heartless, scandalous bitch. They want to say I *claim* she dimed us? Let 'em think what they think. I know what I know. Every damn thing they said about us a muthafuckin' lie, and I know can't nobody lie on a nigga better than Red."

Terry wrapped her hands around his upper arm and leaned in close. "She only trying to help us, baby."

Mekel held up his hands. "I know, I know." Then he turned back to Chass. "I ain't trying to mess with you, Ms. Reed. I know you doing your best to help us. I'm just saying what need to be said. And who these other parties suddenly so interested in Mekel Jr.?"

Chass sat back in her chair and cocked her head. "Federal."

"What?" said Mekel. "Why the feds up in a child custody—?"

"No," said Chass. "That's just it. They're not interested in Mekel Jr. I think they're asking about Red because they're interested in her, specifically. It's a tough read, and they're playing their cards close to the vest, but that's the way it looks."

"Shit," said Mekel, smiling. "'Bout time some federal shit came down on that bitch."

"Well, like I said, I don't know for sure. But there are definitely feds in the mix, and they're gearing up for something. So, no ideas as to her whereabouts? Because, honestly, you did at one time make some statements about tracking her down."

Mekel shook his head slowly. "Yeah, I made some statements. And if she was in the room with me right now? I might have to do something. But really, since all this shit happened to my family, I'm just trying to make it one day to the next. I ain't got time to go on no all-out hunt for that bitch. The feds want her they can have her trifling ass."

"Fair enough," said Chass.

"But I'm guessing that brings us to the real reason we here. If I can put Red in, that's going to be good for Mekel Junior. Right?"

"Nobody's put any deals on the table. But I'm not going to lie to you—a little cooperation may go a long way in this case. You've both done a great job of getting your lives together, but you both have some weight in your pasts, too. Child Protective Services . . . You have to understand, they're required to justify everything they do on paper. Meeting you, getting to know you face-to-face—that doesn't come across on paper too well. Mekel, your past criminal involvements, and Terry, your previous attempt to kidnap the child and your emotional state at that time . . . that's all well documented, and this case has placed it all under a microscope. I mean, we're going to do what we can. We're not giving up. It's a process. But you do see what I'm saying."

Mekel let out a sigh and slumped in his chair. "Yeah, I see, counselor. We can't prove we a couple of saints today, but they can prove we was a couple of evil niggas back in the day."

"That's one way to put it," said Chass. "But like I said . . ."

Mekel waved his hand in front of him. "Naw, you ain't gotta say no more." He turned to Terry. "Motown ain't been too kind to us. But my people's in Tennessee. Let's see how this hearing go, and then maybe we got some talking to do. I'm tired of this shit. The street's been calling my name lately. I don't want to slip back into that life."

The hearing did not go well. Just as Chass had warned, Terry came across as anything but a fit mother. And they talked about Mekel like he was Tony Montana's little brother. And of course they brought up the fact that MJ was a special needs child with multiple development issues. If he had been "normal," that would be one thing, but two shady characters trying to take care of a baby with special needs? After listening to it all, even Mekel wasn't convinced that MJ wouldn't be better off in another home.

By the time Terry and Mekel pulled back into their driveway, they'd all but decided to give up. Taking care of MJ *was* a heavy burden. And Detroit was no picnic. After all they'd accomplished—all their struggles separately and together—to be swallowed up by all this was unthinkable. Tennessee would be much easier on them; Mekel was sure.

True, life had been difficult, but it was Red who had really broken them. Mekel prayed in his heart that the feds caught up with her and gave her what she deserved.

CHAPTER TEN

*T*erry stepped out of Divas salon and into the bright sun. She hadn't felt this good about herself in a long time. Since unfairly losing Mekel Jr. to Child Protective Services, she had been emotional unstable and lacked confidence in herself. Though she still mourned the fact that MJ had been taken from her and Mekel, she was beginning to make peace with the idea that the child might be better off with a family who could take care of his special needs.

As she turned to make her way to her car, she saw Foxy coming toward her, a big smile on her face, her arms spread wide for an embrace.

Terry stood on her tiptoes and threw her arms around the woman. Foxy was tall, even without the high heels she always wore. Hormones had done a lot to make the post-op diva's face more feminine, but for a change in stature she had resorted to the dictionary and gone from *tall* to *Amazonian.*

"I can't believe it!" Foxy squealed. "Terry, you looking good, girl."

Foxy stepped back and looked her up and down. "Somebody been taking good care of you."

Terry bowed her head and smiled, partly embarrassed by the compliment, partly thinking about the hard times she and Mekel had been through in recent days. "So, how you been, Foxy?"

Foxy did a turn on the sidewalk as if she were a supermodel on the runway. Then she spread her hands. "This is how I've been, baby."

"I can see that." Terry tilted her head toward the door to Divas. "You on your way in?"

"I certainly am. I must stay fine so all these other Motown bitches don't forget their place."

"Ain't no bitches getting over on you, girl. Who you going to?"

"My girl Ciara."

Terry touched the ends of her soft curls with the palm of her hand. "That's who just did mine."

"I can see her handiwork from here," said Foxy, putting her hands on her hips. "She a artist, girl." Foxy suddenly straightened up. "Oh, hey! You friends with Red, ain't you?"

"Red?" said Terry. *I ain't friends with that ho*, she thought, then remembered that Foxy had all the 411 in Motown. You could learn a ton of shit listening to her talk for ten minutes. Terry figured she might be able to pick up something juicy—and maybe even useful—about Red. "Yeah, I know Red. But she ain't around no more."

"Honey, she in Arizona."

"Arizona? What the fuck she doing out there?"

"She had to go. You know she shot a man."

"She did?"

"More than one."

"Foxy, where you hear all this?"

Foxy threw her head back. "Honey, you know ain't a word gets spoke in the Motor City don't find its way to my lovely ear sooner or later."

"So, you saying the cops is looking for her?"

"Cops, feds, and others."

"What others?"

"Well, you know Red has engaged in some scandalous behavior from time to time. They some niggas from these very streets would love to put they act right on her."

"So who you hear all this from?"

Foxy turned up her nose.

"Damn, girl," said Terry laughing. "I'm just trying to figure out how a fine lady like you operate, that's all."

Foxy pretended to blush. "I'll give you a hint, girlfriend. I operate best in bed. Beyond that, it's hard for me to remember which man told me what."

Terry swatted her playfully on the arm. "Girl, you so bad."

"Uh-huh," said Foxy. "But I'm so good at it."

"But if you know Red in Arizona, that mean somebody else know too, huh? And if somebody else know . . ."

"Let's just say girlfriend might be headed back this way. Maybe in bracelets, maybe not."

Foxy took a step toward Divas. Terry knew that talking with her on the street was just a warm up for her big audience inside.

"All right, you be good, Foxy."

"You stay in touch, baby. You know if you want the 411 you ain't gonna find it no place else."

Terry turned back toward her car. If there was a possibility that Red would be back in town, she wanted to get down to Tennessee as quickly as possible. She hated to think what might happen if Mekel crossed paths with her.

CHAPTER ELEVEN

*R*ed sat in the Barrio Café sipping coffee and watching the entrance. She'd picked a table near the front, but far enough away from the window. She was sure Catfish hadn't trailed her here and wouldn't be wandering around Phoenix looking in restaurant windows for her, but she had also been sure that no one would be able to find her in Scottsdale's Saguaro Estates—yet somehow that lowlife nigga Catfish had come knocking on her door. She was going to pay attention now, watch her back, look both ways before stepping out on the sidewalk, and never sit with her back to any doors or windows. She hoped she wouldn't have to live like this for the rest of her life. It had only been a couple of days, and it was already wearing on her. Life on the run was fucked up.

She'd used the gas station perv Fred Lindenburg's cash card again on the second day she had it, and then on the third, scoring $200 each time, but she didn't want to keep using it. There was no telling how long he'd stay scared of her, or if he was more scared of his wife than Red. But one thing was for certain, sooner or later, he'd sure as hell have to explain the loss of the card to her. In total, the money she'd scored from Mac Daddy Fred had been enough for cab fare to Phoenix, a few halfway decent restaurant meals, a couple nights in a Marriot Residence Inn, and some additional clothes, including the peach Lilly Pulitzer capris and matching long-sleeved pullover she wore now.

She listened to the people around her chatter about the lives these people lived. They were so different from both the street life she had known and the professional life she wanted to know. She felt alone, which wasn't new for her, but at least in Detroit she'd always had people she could either depend on or manipulate, people to fall back on. And now she was in the desert. No doubt her own doing, but it scared her to be on the tightrope without a safety net below her. So when a black 7-Series with white interior pulled up outside the front window, she straightened her back and craned her neck. Sure enough, Quisha slid out of the car and looked around as if she had just landed on Mars. As Quisha walked through the door of the Barrio Café, Red bowed her head and said a little prayer of thanks. She hadn't prayed in a long time, but with the way things were looking, she might need to do so more frequently now.

Red stood up, smiling from ear to ear, and walked toward Quisha, meeting her halfway. "How you doin', girl?" she asked.

Quisha did a little dance and threw her arms around Red. "Long trip, but I'm fine."

Red looked over her shoulder out the window. "Bitch, I know you didn't drive all the way out here."

"Please," said Quisha, rolling her eyes. "That's a rental. Not nearly as nice as my whip."

"Hmm," said Red, glancing out again. "Looks a lot like yours."

"Yeah, 760, but the interior's plain like baby food, and the stereo got no bottom at all. I don't know how y'all niggas out here roll, but that car ain't shit."

"Yeah, things are a little bit different out here, mos def."

Quisha took a step back and looked Red up and down. "You lookin' better than I thought you was going to. How you holding up?"

Red took a deep breath, not knowing exactly where to begin. Then she shook her head. "Come on. I got us a table. We got some talking to do."

"Yeah," said Quisha, following Red to the table. "Matter of fact, we do."

Red looked over her shoulder and furrowed her brow.

Before they got into a heavy conversation, they ordered and waited for the waitress to bring their food: a Caesar salad and iced tea for Quisha. Two taquitos and a Diet Coke for Red.

"You tell Trap where you were going?" asked Red once the waitress left.

Trap was Quisha's man and a hustler of some standing on the streets of Detroit. He had formed a friendship and potential business relationship with Bacon shortly before Red put Bacon inside. Trap and Bacon hadn't known each other long, so their friendship was not that deep, but Trap was bound to be trippin' over Bacon's fall and Red didn't want any connection to him.

"Fuck no, girl," said Quisha. "I told him I was visiting my auntie in Florida." She drew her right hand slowly down the lovely copper skin of her left forearm. "That way, if I happen to get burned by the Arizona sun, I can explain it."

Red laughed. "Well, we'll get you some sunscreen, just in case." She used her straw to stir the ice in her Diet Coke. "So, tell me what you know."

"Okay," said Quisha. "So, girlfriend needs the 411, where do I go?"

"Divas," said Red.

"I called ahead and asked when Foxy was coming in. She always got the good shit, but you already know all that."

"Plus, I see you just got your hair done. Looks nice." Complimented Red.

Quisha smiled. "Thank you, baby." Then her smile faded as she remembered the news she had to deliver. "There's been some heavy shit going down."

"Yeah? Like what?"

Quisha shook her head. "I know you said some shit about your stepfather Jerome. Well, you ain't never got to worry about him no more. He's gone. Couple niggas walked into his crib, cut him in half with a shotgun."

Red bowed her head. She waited for a minute to let the feeling of it wash over her. But there was nothing. She hated Jerome for what he'd done to her, taking her innocence at such a young age, and making her own mother his accomplice. She had wanted to feel some sense of joy at this death. Or at least closure, victory, satisfaction, some shit, but she just plain didn't feel anything. She realized then that the scars he had put on her were something she'd have to wear for the rest of her life. His death didn't erase anything.

"What about my mother?" asked Red.

"Nuh-uh. Supposedly she wasn't home at the time."

Her mom was alive without Jerome, in a way that was fitting. Her mother had forced her to be part of Jerome's life because she was too weak to leave him. Now she was going to have to see if she was strong enough to make a life without him, just as she should have done so many years ago. Red rolled the idea over in her mind, but still it didn't really make her feel any different.

"My mom?" Red raised her head. "Really?"

"According to Foxy. I don't know who she's hearing it from,

and, uh, you know she ain't gonna mention no names behind this shit. I mean, she ain't trying to snitch. Right?"

Red looked up and saw that Quisha was eyeing her. She froze with her fork halfway to her mouth. "What?"

"You tell me. What Foxy's hearin' is that somebody went after your peoples 'cause you're the one put Bacon in."

Red dropped the fork with a loud clatter. "Who's sayin' that shit?"

"Girl, relax," said Quisha, smiling. "If you had a plan to move Bacon aside and enjoy his riches like a good wifey, that ain't such a bad idea. I mean, I know you know how to get yours. But suddenly you drop off the face of the map and end up in this godforsaken place. I mean, what the fuck you thinkin'?" She sipped iced tea through her straw.

"It's complicated."

"It ain't that complicated. Anyway, there's more."

"So, go on."

"Your girl, Kera."

"That bitch supposed to be inside. Don't tell me her lawyer got her out?"

"Nope. She's gone, too. Hanged herself. And I know there was no love lost between the two of you. But I'm just saying."

"Damn. Well, it's too bad she had to go out like that, but . . ."

"Yeah, I know," said Quisha. "And then your girl Terry and her man Mekel? Somebody dropped a dime on them, too. Shit, come to think of it, somebody been fucking with all your old enemies."

Red looked up again and saw the smirk on Quisha's face. She wasn't sorry for having fucked with anybody who had fucked with her, but the shit about Terry and Mekel might have seemed a little over the line to Quisha. She didn't know them like Red did. And Red needed a friend right now more than she needed a confessional.

"Terry's one of them bitches I was telling you about. The one who shot up my crib. That bitch deserves to be fucked with, but I didn't do shit to her except kick her out of my life."

"Chill, girlfriend. I told you I got your back. But I'ma tell you, I know your shit is all fucked up out here now, but if you're thinking about running back to Motown, you got some enemies back there."

I've always had enemies, thought Red. *But in the past I've always been able to play them better than they could play me.* "I ain't trying to go back to that bitch. I got to move forward, not back."

Quisha looked around at all the middle-class white folks in the restaurant: a bald dude whose pot belly stretched out his golf shirt; a woman with a bad bleach job and an *I heart Phoenix* T-shirt. Teenagers with dyed black hair, black eye makeup, and pale white skin. "Honey," she said, "this ain't forward."

Red laughed. "Hey, there are some fine brothers out this way. I'm talking about lawyers and doctors." She leaned over the table. "Surgeons. Men who know about the intricacies of the female body. Shit, Bacon couldn't tell the difference between my pussy and Foxy's."

Quisha screamed with laughter, then remembered she was in a restaurant and clapped her hand over her mouth. When she finally got herself under control she took her hand way from her face and whispered, "That's nasty."

"You ain't lyin'. Anyway, I'ma stay out this way for a while. Not around here, though. Catfish done fucked this place up for me. But somewhere in the West or Southwest."

"Maybe Montana," said Quisha. "Get you one of them cowboys."

Red rolled her eyes. "Girl, I just told you I had enough of that *Brokeback Mountain* shit with Bacon."

Both women laughed again.

"It sucks though," said Red. "I was just getting the feel of how things work here." She shook her head. "I still can't figure out how Catfish knew where the fuck I was."

Quisha had just taken a bite of her salad and held up a finger while she chewed.

"What?" said Red.

Quisha dug around in her purse for a moment. "A couple days ago I said I wasn't no good at this cloak-and-dagger shit. But then I decided to do a little snooping around in your old crib. It's still on the market."

"You went to my house?"

"I told the Realtor I was in the market for some major up-scale shit. I pulled up in my 7-Series, dressed like I dress, doing like I do. She didn't have no doubts."

"You're not saying . . . No, that's not possible. He tracked me through the records I had on file for the sale of the house? Couldn't be. I had all that shit triple blinded."

"Not what I'm saying." Finally Quisha pulled something out of her purse and handed it to Red.

Red held it on her upturned palm—a black, circular object about the size of a dime but as thick as three of them, with a one-inch wire sticking out one side. "What the fuck is this?"

"Good thing you decided to sell the place furnished. The side table by the couch? The one with the reproduction Tiffany lamp? That was stuck to the underside."

Red's face soured. "You fucking with me? This some kind of joke?"

"Took it to a friend of mine. That there is the latest in high-tech, lowdown, eavesdropping."

Red jumped and flung the thing off her hand and onto the table as if it were a living bug. "Somebody been listening to my shit?"

"Well, it didn't crawl up there by itself."

"Muthafucka!" Her jaw dropped as she looked from the bug

to Quisha, then lowered her voice to a whisper. "Is it still . . . ? Can they hear . . . ?"

Quisha sipped her tea, then shook her head. "My boy says it's dead. 'Sides, it only transmits a couple miles."

"And you think Catfish . . . ? I don't think I talked about where I was moving to on the phone. I might have even mentioned the address for the cable service." She shook her head again. "But Catfish? That nigga stupid as they come. How'd he get all teched up and shit?"

"Well, I didn't dust the damn thing for fingerprints, girl. I don't know who put it there. But Catfish is the only one who's come looking for you. I mean if the cops did it, they wouldn't have told Catfish where to find you."

"Naw, but Catfish was still inside when I left Detroit. He couldn't have done it."

"Maybe he had one of his boys on the outside do it."

It was possible. He had reached out to kill her so-called friend Sasha from inside. Planting a bug wouldn't have been a big thing after that. Red picked up the thing again. She held it between her thumb and forefinger and turned it this way and that. "That bottom feedin' muthfucka!"

"Yeah, well, I got you some other goodies, too. A big suitcase full of clothes, plus a carry-on bag for all the carryin' on you do. And then the other."

Red looked around to make sure nobody was listening. "How much of the other?"

"Four grand. Some of it in twenties, the rest fifties. That was about all I could put my hand to on short notice without Trap gettin' all up in my shit."

"You didn't leave it out in the car, did you?"

"Why? This a rough neighborhood?" She laughed.

Red liked Quisha's sense of humor. She was a good friend. She wished she could hang with her, but she knew that wouldn't work. Quisha had no reason to go on the run, and she was plenty comfortable in Motown playing wifey to Trap. She had everything under control back there.

Red thought about how nice it would be to have that kind of life: but not with somebody like Trap. She wanted to live not as a wifey, but as a wife—Qs wife. That was the one person she regretted fucking with, and fuckin' him up had been an accident. She wished she had asked Quisha to look in on Q or pick up some info on how he was doing, but Quisha didn't know him.

"I'm just messing with you, girl. I got a big manila envelope for you in my Coach bag, but I don't want to hand it to you here. We probably already look like a couple of drug dealers to these folks."

Red smiled and shook her head. "Quisha, you done good, girl. Love you lots. And like I said, this is all going to come back around for you down the line. I'ma make that promise to you."

CHAPTER TWELVE

*D*etective Thomas cracked open a cold can of Budweiser and propped his feet up on his coffee table to watch the evening news. Despite all the posturing done by Marquez Nuñez, he was actually enjoying administrative leave with the possibility of pay pending the filing of any charges against him. The fact that Raven Gomez had disappeared was good in that it undercut the department's case against him, and it prevented the state from bringing actual rape charges in a criminal court.

Still, as he sipped his beer and listened to the same old, same old in the world of politics and business, he couldn't help wishing he could get his hands on her again. He owed her some payback for the trouble he was in, and his suspicions about her involvement in Zeke's death were stronger than ever now. The two might go hand in hand. Hauling her ass in for murder would be satisfying, but he couldn't help fantasizing about other forms of retribution as well.

The phone rang just as he was finishing his first of what

promised to be several beers that evening. Leaning forward, he grabbed the phone off the coffee table and punched "talk." "Yeah, hello."

"Detective Thomas?" said the caller. The voice was vaguely familiar, but he couldn't place it.

"This is. Who's calling?"

"We didn't actually get a chance to meet today, but I attended your hearing. Special Agent Marcus Holt, FBI."

Thomas scowled and sat up. "Yeah, I remember. What can I do for you?"

"I wonder if you'd mind meeting me at my office."

"Naw, that's something you're going to have to set up through my attorney. As you no doubt observed today, he's better at this talking bullshit than I am. And any interrogations you want to conduct—"

"This won't be an interrogation. We're not interested in you."

"I wondered what you were doing at that hearing. Who are you interested in?"

"I'll give you one guess."

Thomas took the last swig of his beer and smirked. "Raven Gomez?"

"She seems to be on a lot of people's minds these days, huh?"

"What do you want to know about her?"

"You rape her?"

"Hell no, I didn't rape that bitch." Thomas slammed the empty beer can down on the table. "How many fuckin' times I gotta say it? And if that ain't an interrogation, I don't know what the fuck is!"

"Relax, Detective Thomas. I just wanted to hear it from you. Fact is, I believe you."

"Really?" said Thomas, doubting the man's sincerity.

"Really."

"And why's that?"

"Let's just say her name has come up in a number of situations. It's beginning to look to the Bureau as if she might be . . ."

"A scandalous bitch?"

Holt laughed. "I was going to say fundamentally dishonest."

"Yeah, I've noticed you feds always have a funny way of saying shit."

There was a silence for a moment. "Yes, well, be that as it may, Detective, we're inclined to think Ms. Gomez is a rather accomplished con artist."

"Well, I don't know where she is, so that's pretty much that. Thanks for the call." He started to get up off the couch and head to the fridge for another cold one.

"Would you *like* to know where she is?" asked Holt.

Thomas froze and sunk back into the couch. "Would I like to know where she is? No, not really."

"Oh, come on, Detective. After all the shit she's put you through? And I've looked at your notes, too. She's a suspect in the Zeke Morrison killing. You don't want to see if you can nail her for that?"

"I don't really give a fuck. I just want her to stay the fuck out of my life. In case you haven't noticed, that pack of wolves in IA would cut my professional dick off if they could get her to testify against me, so, truthfully? I hope I never see the bitch again." He pushed himself up to his feet and carried the phone with him into the kitchen.

"I've got to tell you, I saw the tape of the event for which you're under investigation."

Event? thought Thomas as he grabbed another can of beer out of the fridge. *Why the fuck can't you starch collar muthafuckas talk like human beings?* "So?" he said, settling back on the couch.

"So there's not a jury in the country that could say beyond a reasonable doubt that what they saw on that video was rape."

"Well, Special Agent," said Thomas, putting a sarcastic emphasis on the title, "For your information, Internal Affairs hearings in the Detroit Police Department aren't held to the same standards as criminal juries. They're not unbiased, they're not impartial, and they aren't especially merciful, especially if there's a muthafucka in the case that has a personal grudge against the officer charged. And I got one of those. Fella by the name of Marquez Nuñez? You might have noticed him. Sawed-off runt with a big head?" He cracked the beer and took a sip.

"On the other hand, Detective, a commendation from the Bureau might not be a bad thing to have in your jacket, and a personal statement from me at your hearing could easily sway things in your favor."

Thomas fidgeted in his seat. "Why you telling me this? I said I don't know where she is. I don't know shit about her. What is it you think I can do for you?"

"I need somebody I can work with on this. Somebody who's motivated to see that Ms. Gomez is brought down. And it occurs to me that some of your colleagues might be more interested in protecting her just to—what was the phrase you used? Cut your professional dick off?"

"You want me to work with you? Work with you how?"

"Like I said, I want you to come down to my office. I'd like you here when I make a phone call. I think you'll be very interested in what the party on the other end of the line has to say."

"What party?"

"Come down and you'll see."

Thomas rubbed his whole face with his hand. "All right, but not too early in the morning."

"Morning?" said Holt. "No, no, Detective. Tonight. Right now. Be here in half an hour. I'll text you the address and office door number."

"Half a—" Thomas looked at his watch and then at the perspiring can of beer. "If I come down there and you got Mickey Mouse on the other end of the line, I'ma be pissed."

Holt chuckled. "I don't think you'll be disappointed."

After he hung up, Thomas took a couple of swigs of beer, not wanting to waste the newly-opened can. Then he pulled on a pair of white Reeboks, grabbed his keys, and headed out.

As he made his way through traffic, he thought about who the person on the other end of Agent Holt's line could be. The whole thing seemed off. Why was Holt being so secretive? It wasn't like the feds to be coy. He didn't rule out the possibility that it was a set up. He didn't really have anything to worry about, though, because he hadn't done anything wrong, but he made up his mind that he wouldn't say shit about anything but the weather in case Holt's office was wired. There was no telling how somebody might twist his words in a court of law or an IA hearing.

After twenty minutes of driving, he pushed his way through the doors of the FBI's Detroit field office and found Holt with his feet propped up on a desk, paging through a file. There was no one else around and most of the lights were off.

"Y'all don't work nights, huh?" asked Thomas.

Holt swung his feet off the desk and stood. "We work twenty-four hours a day, Detective. Come on back this way. I think you're going to like this phone call."

Thomas followed the agent deeper into the recesses of the suite and into a cramped, nondescript office with a small desk stacked with files. Holt went around to the desk chair, so Thomas sat across from him in a cheap straight-backed chair made of steel and black vinyl.

"I thought you feds were supposed to have all the money in the law enforcement game," said Thomas. "From the looks of this office, you aren't getting much of it."

"I've only been with the Bureau four years, but I intend to

move up." Holt smirked. He definitely had something up his sleeve.

Thomas waited for several seconds while Holt rocked in his desk chair and played with a stray paper clip. "So?" he finally said. "You gonna make a phone call, or what?"

"Not make a call," said Holt. "We're going to be getting a call in a minute here. It'll be worth the wait."

Thomas slumped in the chair and thought about the beer he'd left behind.

A few minutes later the phone rang. Holt pushed the speaker button. "Special Agent Marcus Holt," he said.

"Yeah, my nigga," said the voice on the other end. "This Catfish."

Catfish? thought Thomas. Catfish was supposed to be locked up. But when a person received a call from someone inside, the call started with a recorded message stating that it was coming from a Department of Corrections facility. There had been no recorded message.

"Catfish," said Holt. "I have you on speaker. Detective Thomas of the Detroit Police Department is in the room with me. You know him."

"Yeah, the cop that put the new charge on me for that shit about Sasha." Catfish laughed. "Guess that bitch Red didn't do too good for you on that one, Detective. Sorry."

Raven had told Thomas that Catfish was responsible for the death of a friend of hers named Sasha. She'd visited Catfish in prison while wearing a wire and had gotten him to talk about the killing. Based on that recording, Thomas had charged him with the murder. But instead of years being added to the man's sentence, here he was, laughing about the charge.

"Where are you, Catfish?" said Thomas.

"What, right now? Right now I'm in my room, but I'm fixin' to go chill by the pool soon as I finish talking to you niggas."

"What pool?"

"The pool here at La Quinta in Phoenix. Holt, you ain't told your boy nothin' about this shit? Oh, yeah, Detective. I'm free as a muthafucka."

Holt rocked forward in his chair and put his forearms on the desk. "First of all, you didn't tell me you were going to Phoenix. Second, your freedom is contingent upon your cooperation, Catfish. I'm not sure you have time to be *chillin'* by the pool."

"Why you trippin', G-man?"

"Would someone mind telling me what the fuck is going on here?" said Thomas.

"I'll tell you this," said Catfish. "First thing you need to do is stop trying to put charges on a nigga using bogus evidence."

Holt crossed his arms over his chest and looked at Thomas. "That recording Raven gave you didn't stand up."

"Why not?"

"The quality just wasn't good enough. It couldn't be determined that the other voice was Catfish."

"That's bullshit," said Thomas.

"Damn straight," said Catfish. "And Red the one shovelin' it. You know what I think? I think she staged that tape with some nigga on the outside. Then she came to see me and claimed she made the tape then. She a scandalous bitch. I'm telling you. She always be fuckin' with niggas. Ain't that right, Detective Thomas?"

"So, what are you doing in Phoenix?" asked Holt. "You didn't clear that with me. Keep on and I'm gonna have to put an ankle bracelet on your ass."

"I'm just—what is it y'all say? Goin' where the evidence leads me."

"You're saying Raven Gomez is in Phoenix?"

"Scottsdale. 'Bout thirty minutes from Phoenix. I got her address and everything."

Holt fidgeted in his chair. "And how did you get all that? *We* couldn't track her."

"I got skills."

Thomas pursed his lips. From what he knew about Catfish, he didn't have much upstairs. Still, he had to have something if he'd found Red.

"What's the address?" asked Holt.

"Naw, man. I give you the address, who's to say you won't think I outlived my usefulness? 'Sides, I got to verify when she be home. You know Red like to get around."

"There's still the black tar. If you don't deliver on that, you *will* have outlived your usefulness."

"You ain't got to worry about me, boss. You and me gonna be dealing in Red, black tar, green cash, all the muthafuckin' colors of the rainbow."

"Call me back tomorrow, same time," said Holt. "And in the meantime, don't lay a hand on Raven."

"Yeah, we cool," said Catfish. "I'll holla at you tomorrow."

Catfish hung up the phone and walked into the bathroom to check himself in the mirror. His face was busted up pretty good, but he'd been in worse fights. He held up his hand and looked at his taped fingers. They were still throbbing. He was surprised at how fast Red was with that champagne bottle. He should have known better than to drop his guard around that bitch, even for a second. But he'd pay her back. "Naw, G-man," he said into the mirror. "I ain't gonna lay a finger on Ms. Red."

Detective Thomas stood up and paced in the small area in front of Holt's desk. "You sprung that hustler from prison?"

"We expedited his parole."

"Expe . . . He reached out to have a woman murdered. He was running a criminal enterprise from inside prison. He should be in a Supermax behind that shit. And you expedited his parole?"

Holt held up his hands to calm the detective. "In return for his promise of cooperation with a couple of things."

"Cooperation? He's off the leash. You didn't even give him a simple ass ankle monitor. Hell, you didn't even know where he was until just now."

"He called in, didn't he?"

"Called in? Have you got any idea . . . He didn't want to tell where Raven is because he already killed her. She's buried in the desert right now. That's my guess."

"Relax. He wants to help us on this black tar heroin thing. He and Bacon used to be partners. Didn't end well. He wants to give us Bacon's connect as payback. He helps us put it all together, I put together a joint FBI-DEA task force, and suddenly I've got a bigger office and much more cred with the bosses."

"So what the fuck do you need me for?" asked Thomas. "You got the whole Federal Bureau of Investigation behind your ass."

"Not yet I don't. Truth is, I cut a few corners putting the deal together for Catfish. I'm not exactly employee of the month around here. I'm kind of on my own. But if I can impress the bosses, I can get back in their good graces. You know how that is, right, Detective? Being out of favor with the bosses?"

"You gotta be kidding me. Now I'm teamed with a rogue FBI agent and a murdering, drug dealing street thug who's out wandering around the country instead of sitting in prison where he should be." Thomas shook his head and chuckled. "My life just keeps getting better and better."

"So, for the time being, we can't let anybody know our plans," Holt insisted. "Just be cool at the hearing, I'll stand up for you. And everything will work out just fine."

CHAPTER THIRTEEN

*D*eputy Commissioner Conrad interlaced his fingers and rested his hands on the table in the IA hearing room. He brought the meeting to order and stated for the record the names of all those present: Detectives Lynn, Robinson, and Nuñez; Detective Thomas and attorney Shaw; and FBI Special Agent Marcus Holt. "Now, Agent Holt," said the Deputy Commissioner, turned to Agent Holt "it's been two days. Are we any closer to producing Raven Gomez?"

"Not as close as we'd hoped, Deputy Commissioner. You'll have to forgive me for being overly optimistic."

Conrad scowled at the agent. "I don't have to forgive you for anything. You've wasted a good deal of this inquiry's time. Do you have anything to present here?"

Marquez Nuñez waved Red's sworn statement in the air. "We have—"

"Detective Nuñez," said Conrad. "There's no question before you. I was addressing Special Agent Holt."

Nuñez lowered his hand, crestfallen.

The Deputy Commissioner turned to Holt again. "Sir?"

"Yes, I would like to say that I've developed a confidential informant in connection with our investigation into matters that pertain to this inquiry." Holt nodded toward Thomas. "The detective here is familiar with our informant and is acting as something of a liaison, facilitating the Bureau's communication with him."

"I'm sure the Detroit Police Department could find any number of detectives far more suited to help you in this matter," said Nuñez.

Conrad turned to him slowly. "Detective, you are aware of the fact that I outrank you."

Nuñez stiffened. "Yes, sir."

"And that I'm in the middle of questioning the agent?"

"Yes, sir."

"I wonder if you'd be good enough to refrain from interrupting me."

"Yes, sir."

Detective Thomas gritted his teeth, trying to keep from smiling.

"Now, Special Agent Holt," said Conrad. "You're working with Detective Thomas?"

"That's correct. I'd also like to say that after examining the evidence, I have serious doubts about the validity of the rape charge."

"That's the Bureau's opinion?"

Thomas knew this was the tricky moment for Holt. He had to make his opinion sound official without saying anything on the record that could bite him on the ass with the Bureau if his plan turned to shit.

Holt didn't miss a beat. "If you're asking for the Director's position, I don't believe he's following the case personally. My office is rendering this opinion."

My office, thought Thomas. *As in the rinky-dink, piece-of-shit closet where you have your desk.*

Conrad thought about it for a moment, then turned to Detective Robinson.

"As to the conduct unbecoming, aside from the complainant's statement, is there any corroborating testimony to be offered?"

"No, sir," said Robinson.

Conrad turned to Nuñez. "Okay, I understand you have plenty of physical evidence supporting the fact that sexual intercourse took place, but do you have evidence of force? Do you have him striking her on the video?"

"No, sir," said Nuñez. "But we do have bruising."

"I've seen the rape kit photos. You have minor bruising caused by two people having intense physical contact. That's not necessarily rape."

Nuñez held up the sworn statement again. "Well, we have—"

"Nope," said Conrad. "You have a complainant who's in the wind. She left behind a sworn statement, but she's deprived Detective Thomas of his right to face his accuser. I'm not trying to minimize the rape accusation, but I wish we had more than the statement."

Conrad turned to Roylon Shaw. "Counselor, you said you had something for us."

"Thank you, Deputy Commissioner. First of all, I've seen the video, as all of you have. My client asserts, and the tape clearly shows, that he was seduced by Ms. Gomez."

Everyone on the panel laughed. Nuñez spoke up. "No doubt the detective believes he's so good looking that women are compelled to seduce him."

"Jealous she didn't go after you?" asked Thomas. "She likes men who are—uh—*bigger* than you."

Shaw put a hand on his shoulder. "Calm down," he whispered.

"Stow the personal shit, detectives," said Conrad. "Both of you." He looked at Shaw again. "The video doesn't show seduction. It's ambiguous at best and could easily be interpreted the other way. Anything else?"

Shaw held up a file folder. "These are copies of Detective Thomas's notes on his investigation into the murder of Ezekiel Morrison. They show that Ms. Gomez also made unsubstantiated claims of rape against him. This may suggest a pattern of making these kinds of allegations. And the notes include forensic evidence that strongly suggests Ms. Gomez herself poisoned Mr. Morrison. Knowing that Detective Thomas was on the trail of such evidence, she may have sought to discredit him by charging him with rape."

"So she seduced him, and charged him with rape, to discredit him?" asked Conrad.

Shaw remained stone-faced. "It almost worked, didn't it?"

"We'll look at the notes," said Conrad, extending his hand for them.

Shaw rose, crossed the few feet between them, and handed him the file folder.

Conrad nodded. "All right, counselor, you and your client may wait in the seating area at the end of the hall while we deliberate. We'll call you when we're ready."

Thomas and Shaw strolled down the corridor towards the sunlight streaming in through the big window. Thomas shook his head. "They say when it all comes to an end, you find yourself walking towards a bright light, right?"

Shaw laughed. "Don't be so fuckin' morbid, my man. I think we have a good chance to make it go away. And if it does go against you, there's always an appeal."

"Oh, good. So I'ma have to go through this shit again."

They reached the seating area, and Thomas dropped into a big, upholstered chair.

"Don't fret," said Shaw. "Just relax here. I got to go take a piss. And at my age, that could take a while. But they'll be more than a few minutes anyway."

"Yeah, I'll just sit here and count my blessings."

Shaw rounded a corner down a side corridor to the restrooms, and Thomas was left alone to consider all that had happened over the last few days. The fed's statement during the hearing couldn't hurt. And if they did buy the idea that Red was guilty of murder, and then he helped bring her back, any lingering doubts about him would evaporate.

"You've looked better, Detective," said a woman's voice.

She stood with the light in the window behind her, and in the glare he couldn't focus on her face. For a moment he almost believed it was Raven Gomez from the glimpse of her rear end. He put his hand up to shield his eyes from the glare and the woman took a couple of steps forward. "Chass Reed," he said.

"You were expecting someone else?"

"I was—no, I—I don't know what I was thinking. How are you, Ms. Reed?"

"Fine, under the circumstances." She sat in a chair across from him.

"What brings you to headquarters this morning?"

She patted her briefcase. "A lawyer's work is never done."

"No rest for the wicked, huh?" he said with a laugh. "I'm just joking."

Chass laughed, too. "I know you are. Lawyers can have a sense of humor too, you know."

Detective Thomas turned serious, remembering how things had been going in Chass's world. "How's Q?"

"Well, you haven't been coming around to hassle him lately. That's a plus."

He shrugged. "I get aggressive when I'm working. But then again, so do you."

She nodded slowly. "True. But sometimes I wonder if I'm aggressive enough."

"Oh? In what way?"

"Red," she said, and she thought for a minute. "I just wish . . ."

"You wish what?"

"I could never actually do it, mind you, but sometimes I fantasize about it being just her and me and a nine millimeter in a dark alley." She held up a hand. "Just a fantasy."

"I think you and I have some very similar fantasies."

She chuckled. "You too, huh?"

"Actually, I think there are a number of us in that club."

"Maybe I should meet some more of our fellow members. Like I said, I could never do it myself, but I think I might be able to look the other way if somebody else wanted to step up." She looked at Thomas and raised her eyebrows, then cocked her head.

CHAPTER FOURTEEN

*D*etective Thomas adjusted his chair at the little table in the IA hearing room where the opposing sides had reconvened. He sat there waiting to hear if Internal Affairs intended to pursue departmental charges against him and refer his case to the state attorney for criminal prosecution. As he considered all that Red had put him through, Chass Reed's words rung in his ears. *I think I might be able to look the other way if somebody else wanted to step up.*

"Our pint-sized friend doesn't look too happy," Shaw whispered to him.

Thomas looked across at Nuñez, who looked like he'd just bitten into a shit sandwich.

Shaw patted him on the back. "My guess is that's good news for us."

"Detective Thomas," said Deputy Commissioner Conrad. "A number of things went into our deliberations today, including a more extensive discussion with Special Agent Holt about what role you might play in his investigation. We would love to have had Raven Gomez here to back up her charges against you. As it is, we've come to believe that she herself should be answering to the evidence that your investigation has turned up as to her possible involvement in the death of Ezekiel Morrison."

Roylon Shaw put an arm across Thomas's back and gave him a little shake as they received confirmation that the hearing had gone their way.

"Also," Conrad added, "If things develop as we think they might, she should also answer to charges of making false allegations against a DPD detective, something we don't take lightly. Therefore, your administrative leave is to end, effective immediately, and you are hereby detailed to the FBI's investigations into Ms. Gomez's whereabouts. You're to act as liaison between the FBI and this department, and copy us on all developments in the case. Is that understood?"

"Yes, sir," said Thomas.

"Now, I believe Detective Nuñez has a couple of items that belong to you." Conrad turned to Nuñez and waited.

Nuñez stood and walked around the end of the table and across the room. He handed Thomas his service weapon and shield. He leaned down close to Thomas and whispered, "This is a long way from over."

"Oh, you damn right it ain't," said Thomas.

Detective Thomas met Agent Marcus Holt later that afternoon in a park, away from inquisitive ears.

Holt took a sip from his Starbucks cup as he sat on a bench with Thomas. "I get the feeling you don't entirely trust Catfish."

"That'd be a safe bet."

"I don't either. He wants something from us, but I'm not sure what. My guess is he thinks he may need us if he gets jammed up. He may also be asking for more operating funds, vehicles, whatever he can get."

"More?" said Thomas.

"I gave him two grand to work with off the bat. I figured it wouldn't get him too far, but it would be something he could use to pay any informants he developed, do a bit of traveling. Makes me very nervous, though, that he's so close to the Mexican border."

"I heard that. You should be keeping that nigga on a much shorter leash." He took a sip of his own coffee and watched a couple of fine ladies walking their dogs past the fountain.

"But I suspect Red really is in the Phoenix area," said Holt.

"You trust him that much, huh?"

"No, but if he didn't think she was there, he might very well have crossed over into Mexico already. He has something against Red."

"Who doesn't?" said Thomas.

Holt laughed. "I get that feeling. Anyway, Catfish is motivated to find her. So, guess where you're going."

"Who, me?"

"I can't move a field operation to Phoenix, but my DPD attaché, on the other hand . . ."

"Is that what I am? Your attaché?"

Holt smiled. "Believe it or not, that's what you've been since I came up with this idea. It's just that nobody else knew it until today. We need to get down there—and by we, I mean you—before he actually does get his hands on her. Once he does that, his reasons for staying in touch with us just might dry up."

"What's his angle on the black tar?"

"He says he wants to help us get Bacon's connect, but if he gives us the slip, he may just end up making that connect for himself."

Thomas nodded and thought for a minute. Then a smile

crept across his face. "So, you gave your nigga Catfish two grand of walking around money. How much you giving me?"

Holt scoffed. "You get a salary from the DPD."

"Bullshit. You expect me to pay travel and hotel expenses out of my own pocket?"

"I start requisitioning two grand every other day this shit's going to be over before it starts."

"Well, you get a salary from the FBI. I'm sure it's a lot bigger than my salary."

Holt laughed and shook his head. "I'll requisition the money." Then he pointed at Thomas. "You have to keep receipts, though."

Thomas sat back, sipped his coffee, and watched the ladies. "Yeah," he said. "I'll keep the receipts."

"And remember, you're going to have to keep Catfish in check, not kill him. Your primary goal is to find Red. She's the real reason you're going out there."

"Trust me," said Thomas. "I ain't gonna forget about Red."

CHAPTER FIFTEEN

Q sat on the couch in his mother's house, holding the remote in his hand and flipping through the channels. Occasionally, he would stop on ESPN to catch up on sports scores, trades, injuries, all that. Mostly he just kept his thumb moving on the channel-up button. TV had become a big part of his life. In the hospital all he could do was watch TV. In the rehab center, when he wasn't suffering through painful routines with the physical therapists, (or the *physical terrorists,* as he'd come to call them) he was watching TV, flipping the channels between soap operas, game shows, reality shows, news talk shows. He watched Obama haters, Palin haters, and any and all brands of arrogant mutha-fuckas who were addicted to the sound of their own voices. He couldn't stand it anymore. If there was a game on, that would relax him somewhat, but he wasn't a man to sit on the sidelines of life. He'd always been a player, not a spectator.

Now all he could do was veg out on his mom's couch, since his mom and Chass felt he needed someone around to watch out for him at all times. And since Chass's schedule was so crazy, they'd decided he should stay at his mom's so she could wait on him hand and foot. It made him sick. He loved his mom and was grateful for her help, but he was a baller. He hadn't needed a woman to take care of him since he was eleven years old. Just then, his mom and Chass were out shopping for him. He felt he should have been out shopping for them instead. He should have been buying his mom nice things, and maybe taking Chass out to dinner at a fine restaurant.

He thought about Chass and how his feelings for her had changed. He'd always considered her a friend and a fine lady, but his experience with Red and her friends in the game had made him see Chass in a new light. And the attention she'd been paying him surprised him. He'd always thought he was too rough for her, but it didn't seem like she felt that way.

Q punched the "off" button on the remote and tossed it aside on the couch. His life was bullshit and he was tired of it. With his left hand on the arm of the couch and his right on his cane, he pushed himself up onto his feet. He was determined to do something useful instead of sitting around like an invalid.

Chass and his mom had pulled a box of his old stuff out of the hall closet and had been going through it, reminiscing together. They'd left it on a chair for him to sort through, in case he wanted to throw some of it away. Now he made his way down the hall to put it away. He'd sort through the box later. For now, he just wanted to prove to them that he was still worth a damn. He'd put the box back up on the closet shelf. He anticipated that it might be difficult, so he preferred to do it while they weren't around. Then, when they looked in the closet and saw the box back in its right spot, there'd be no denying how it got there. He'd play it off like it was no big deal.

After opening the closet door, he stood his cane up in the corner. Then he folded the flaps of the box back into place and lifted it off the chair. It was heavier than he thought it should be. *What the fuck?* he thought. All it contained were a couple of high school baseball trophies, a few postcards from friends, some birthday cards from his mom that he'd saved, and a shoe box full of old photographs. Had he gotten that weak? He thought about all the sports he'd played throughout his life, all the shit he'd handled on the streets, the niggas he'd run with over the years and the way they'd looked up to him. There was no way that box was gonna get the better of him.

Determined not to be beaten by Red's bullet, he raised the box until it was level with his head and tried to push it up onto the shelf. A sharp pain tore through his side. He swayed and then leaned against the door frame of the closet, trembling and breathing hard. *One more push,* he thought. *Then I can rest up before they get home.* But as he put all his strength into the effort he began to get dizzy. He fell out of the doorway and slammed against the opposite wall in the hallway, then fell across the hall table, breaking it. The contents of the box went everywhere.

He grabbed for his side, below his ribcage. The pain tore through him almost as vividly as when Red shot him. And when he pulled his hand away and looked at it, there was blood, just like that day. Not as much this time, but the wound had opened up.

The front door opened. Chass and his mom came in chattering away.

"I'll give you that recipe, Chass. It's not complicated at all and it's one of Q's favorites."

"I don't know," said Chass. "You're a better cook than I am. I have a feeling you make everything seem easy."

Q tried to sit up before they saw him. He knew they were on their way to the kitchen. If he could get to his feet and make it into the bathroom to get cleaned up, maybe they'd never know. He'd laugh off the spilled box and the broken table. *Just clumsy,* he'd tell them. But as he tightened his stomach muscles to pull himself up, the pain was so sharp that he let out an involuntary yell.

Chass turned and looked up the hall. "Oh, my God!" she yelled. "Q!"

His mother saw him too and screamed. They both ran to his side.

"I'm okay," he said. "I'm okay." But he knew he wasn't fooling anyone. He was bathed in sweat and clutching a bloody wound.

Chass knelt on one side of him, his mother on the other. "What the hell happened?" asked Chass.

Q still wanted to find a way to play it off casually, but as he tried to say something reassuring a wave of nausea overtook him and he rolled onto his side, throwing up the tomato soup he'd had for lunch.

"Oh, God," screamed Mrs. Carter. "He's bleeding internally."

Chass ran to her purse, grabbed her cell phone, and punched 911.

Q shook his head, trying to reassure his mom that he had no internal bleeding.

"It's okay, Mrs. Carter," said Chass, as she waited for the 911 dispatcher to pick up. "I fixed him some tomato soup before we went out to shop. But he is hurt."

"Oh, no," said his mom. She rocked on her knees, hovering over him. "Hang on, son. Please hang on."

The operator answered, and Chass took a deep breath and tried to speak clearly and distinctly into the phone, but she heard her voice tremble as she began. "Yes, we need a medical response. We have a man who's bleeding."

She gave the address, then listened for a moment. "What? Uh, gunshot wound."

No, thought Q. He wanted to ask her for the phone so he could explain the situation, but he couldn't talk at all.

"No," said Chass. "I mean, he didn't just get shot. He was shot a while ago . . . No, not earlier today. Weeks ago . . . No, he *did* get treatment. He—just—just roll the response, please. He's bleeding."

Mrs. Carter rode in the ambulance with Q. Chass followed in her car. The ER doctor was able to stabilize Q, who then began answering questions. Unless it was about his pain or perceptions, he let Chass answer. Soon the doctor began talking directly to her.

"So, he was shot, had surgery, was in rehab. Was there major organ damage?"

"No, nothing that wasn't repaired."

"And how long ago was he released from rehab?" asked the doctor.

"Just a few days."

"So, what happened? Why the sudden reversal in the recovery?"

Chass looked at Q, but he turned his head away. "His mom and I went out to do some shopping. I think he just fell as he was walking down the hall to the bathroom."

The doctor raised his eyebrows. "Just fell? Gosh, that seems like a major injury for a simple fall. Did he fall down the stairs maybe?"

"No, no," said Chass. "Just in the middle of the hall."

The doctor turned to him. "Mr. Carter, are you sure there wasn't someone in the house with you? Did you get in a fight with someone?"

Yeah, muthafucka, thought Q. *I got in a fight with myself. And I lost.* "I was alone."

"Well," said the doctor, shaking his head in bewilderment. "I guess—hmm. I mean, the only thing I can tell you, Ms. Reed, is that I wouldn't leave him alone again. I think he needs more or less constant supervision if his condition is this delicate."

"Goddamn it!" yelled Q. "I don't need constant supervision. All right? I was trying to put a box up on a shelf. And it was a little heavy. I mean—it wasn't that heavy, but—I was trying—look, I just picked it up and was lifting it and I opened up the wound. I shifted some stuff around inside and I tore the wound open, and . . ."

The doctor nodded. "I can see that. If you were trying to lift a heavy box."

"No! It wasn't heavy, it was just—shit, I . . ."

"All right," said the doctor. "It's okay."

"Q," said Chass, "You didn't need to put that box back. I could have done it."

"I don't need you to do shit for me. You heard? You treat me like I'm a fuckin' weak ass muthafucka who can't do shit for himself. I can do what I need to do. So maybe y'all could just leave me the fuck alone and stop acting like I . . ."

Chass let some edge creep into her voice. "Q, I'm trying to do what has to be done for you to get better. And you're not being very cooperative. And at the moment you're not being very appreciative of all your mother and I are doing for you." She bowed her head and shook it. "As a matter of fact, you know what? I *will* give you some time for yourself." Then she turned and walked out of the exam room.

"Well," said the doctor with a weak smile. "We'll need to keep you overnight, but you'll be fine. For now, just liquids, I think. I'll send somebody in with a couple of juice boxes."

After the doctor left, Q could hear bits and pieces of the conversation between his mom and Chass. They must have been sitting somewhere near the exam room.

"Why did this have to happen to him?" he heard his mom ask. "He was doing so well."

"I know, Mrs. Carter. He'll come through this. He's a strong man."

Bullshit, thought Q. *I ain't no strong man anymore.*

"What was all that yelling about?" That was his mom again.

"I think he's just frustrated right now. And I guess I got a little frustrated with him too. Maybe we all need a good night's rest."

Q looked up at the ceiling tiles. He was going to need more than a good night's rest to get over the shit he was going through. But he was thankful he had somebody like Chass in his corner. Even after he yelled at her, she was out in the hall comforting his mom. She was such a different woman from Red. He wished he and that bitch had never met. And if he ever saw her again, she was going to wish the same thing.

CHAPTER SIXTEEN

*T*homas sat in the detective's squad room of the Phoenix Police Department taking in the hustle and bustle. It wasn't Detroit, but he knew Phoenix had its own distinct policing problems including immigration issues, drug trafficking from Mexico, and gang violence both in Phoenix and across the boarder. These were hardworking detectives juggling multiple cases who probably had to deal with the same administrative bullshit Detroit cops had to deal with.

He sat beside the desk of Detective Morales, waiting for him to wrap up his call. "Okay," Morales said into the phone in a slight Mexican accent. "I just want to talk to him, but if he doesn't come in to see me, that means I have to find him. And that means I have to hassle all his friends, all his family, everybody he knows. And if any of them are into any shit . . . If they're moving weed, if they're moving coke, if they got green card issues . . . *Me entiendes?* So, tell him to come see me. I don't want to have to go that way with it. All right?"

He hung up the phone with more force than he needed to. "Fuckin' cholo asshole." Then he turned to Thomas and let out a sigh. "So, Detroit, huh? I hear they have snow there."

"Sometimes," said Thomas with a smile.

Morales shook his head. "Not for me. So, what courtesy can I extend the Detroit Police Department and its star detective today? I mean I guess that's what you are, right? Their star detective? Otherwise how would you rate a vacation to our fair city?"

Star detective, thought Thomas. *Not exactly.* "I appreciate the vote of confidence," he said, reaching into his case and pulling out a file folder. "I just wanted to apprise you of the fact that I'll be here for a day or two. Maybe more." He handed a photo to Morales. "We're looking for this woman. Name of Raven Gomez, aka Red. She may have adopted any number of other aliases."

Morales nodded. "Nice."

"Don't underestimate her," said Thomas. "Don't turn your back on her."

"No, I think I'd prefer to do her from behind."

Thomas laughed. *Cops. Same wherever you go.* "Anyway, she's wanted for murder, attempted murder, and making false allegations against a detective."

"Uh-oh," said Morales. "That last one a friend of yours?"

"My very best." He pointed to his chest.

"Ah, so this is business *and* personal."

"You could say that. We also have a CI on her trail in town from Detroit. Obviously, I can't tell you his name or show you a picture, but he's a bit of a loose cannon. If he fucks us, or if he causes any undue trouble in paradise, I won't hesitate to haul his ass into your jail."

Morales interlaced his fingers behind his head and leaned back. "Well, we're overcrowded as it is, but what the fuck, the more the merrier I always say."

"I'll let you know how things progress." Thomas pushed himself up out of the chair.

"Cool. And if you think your girl might be hooked up with any of the local gang talent, be careful. I don't know how they roll in Detroit, but firepower is no object to some of these fuckers."

"I'll keep that in mind."

"Oh, and, uh, where you staying?"

"La Quinta," said Thomas over his shoulder.

After getting settled in his room, Thomas took the elevator up one floor, found the room he was looking for, and knocked on the door.

Catfish opened it wearing only jeans. His face was bruised, and his scraggly mustache was wet. Thomas glanced down and saw that the man had a drink in his hand. The fingers of that hand were taped. Catfish grinned from ear to ear. "'Sup, my nigga?"

"What you been into?"

"Aw, nothing, man. Got in a little scuffle with some niggas in the joint just before I got out."

"That tape job on your fingers doesn't look professional."

Catfish moved the drink to his left hand and examined the injured one. "Yeah, them Internet degreed doctors don't know shit. I swear half them muthafuckas got they medical degrees off the back of a matchbook. For real."

Thomas pushed past him into the room and looked around. The dresser was strewn with empty mini bottles. "I see you're all settled in."

"Fuck yeah. I *been* settled into this bitch. Hey, they just got the standard shit in the mini bar. No Courvoisier or nothin' like that, but if you want something I'll hook you up. Jack or something."

Thomas shrugged and dropped into the side chair. "Why not. If that's what you're having."

Catfish scratched his nipple. "Naw, man, I'm drinking J&B, but I about polished that shit off."

"Jack's fine."

Catfish plunged a clear plastic cup into the ice bucket, then spun the cap off the Jack Daniels mini, sending it skittering across the dresser top. "They got some nice rooms up in this muthafucka. Big screens, nice big bed, little fridge." He handed Thomas the drink. "Shit is on, my nigga."

Thomas took the drink and poured half of it down his throat. He'd need it to deal with this asshole.

"And the shower. You take a shower yet in your room?"

"No, Catfish. I just checked in."

"Aw, you gotta check it out. Big muthafuckin' showerhead, make you feel like you in a waterfall. You gonna love it."

"Tomorrow morning, I'm sure."

Catfish sat on the edge of the bed. "You know, ya'll niggas didn't need to send nobody out here to babysit me. I got this."

"That's very reassuring, but you don't have the power to arrest her. I'm the one with the badge."

Catfish laughed, then saluted. "Yes, sir, officer. Put the bracelets on that bitch." He moved up to the head of the bed and leaned back against the ample bank of pillows. "Probably be easier to shoot her ass, though. I mean, if you really want to take her back to Detroit, cargo section cheaper than coach, right?"

"Let's hope it doesn't come to that."

Catfish looked out across the room and mumbled. "You hope what you want to hope."

"So, you have an address for us to check out?"

"Yeah."

"How'd you track her, anyway?"

"Aw, you know, I'm a confidential informant, so I can't tell you that shit."

Thomas scoffed. "The fact that you're a CI just means we're not going to reveal your identity. You don't keep secrets from us."

"They's stuff you just don't talk about. You know, like when ya'll beat a nigga down to get a confession, and then you say he got hurt resisting arrest? Or when you put an illegal wiretap on somebody? Like that."

"Anyway, let's pay her a visit."

Catfish finished his drink and rattled the ice in the plastic cup. "Yeah, we could check out that address. I don't know if she's still laying her head there, though."

"I thought you had her current address."

"It's fresh, yeah. But she a slippery bitch. Always bobbin' and weavin'. She a tough bitch to lay a glove on."

"Be that as it may . . ." Thomas threw back the rest of his drink and stood. "Let's go."

Catfish struggled to his feet, obviously drunk. Thomas watched as he pulled on a Tommy Hilfiger shirt and buttoned it up, then sat back down to put on his shoes. Finally, the man stood and made his way to the door. He stopped at the dresser and opened a drawer. Inside was a nine millimeter.

Thomas stepped up before Catfish could reach for it. "Uh-uh. You won't need that."

Catfish shook his head. "Why you trippin'? Muthafucka's registered, my nigga."

"You got a carry permit in the state of Arizona?"

"Do you?"

"I'm a detective with the DPD. My carry permit's good everywhere."

"I don't roll without the nine," said Catfish rolling his big bug eyes. "'Sides, you might could use some backup. You don't know Red like I do. She will do any nigga don't go heavy on her. You feel me, partner?"

"Oh, I feel you. But first, you ain't my partner. And second, if we go into her place and both of you are both waving guns around, I won't know which one of you to drop."

"Aw, that's some cold shit, right there."

"And third, you're drunk. I don't need to get shot by some fucked up gangsta who can't see straight."

"I'm your CI, nigga. We supposed to be together on this shit."

Thomas grabbed him by the upper arm and escorted him through the doorway and out into the hall. "You seem to be having a lot of trouble understanding just what a CI is. You get in the passenger seat. I'll drive where you tell me to drive. Other than directions, you keep your mouth shut. The only reason you're coming on this ride is because I don't want you in that room alone where you can call her, or call somebody else you hooked up with out here. Because, honestly, I don't trust your muthafuckin' ass."

"Goddamn," said Catfish, stumbling down the hall, still in Thomas's grip. "Why popo always got to be down on a nigga? We supposed to be helping each other."

Thomas punched the button for the elevator. "Help me by shutting the fuck up."

Catfish guided Thomas to Saguaro Estates as the sun sat low on the desert. They pulled up to the guardhouse at the gated entrance and Thomas rolled down the window.

A man in uniform stepped out. "Good afternoon, sir. And who are we visiting today?"

Thomas showed the man his badge and gave him the address. "Do you know if she's in?"

"I haven't seen her coming or going for a few days. She should be home unless she's out of town on business."

"Okay, thanks," said Thomas.

Catfish leaned across him. "Yeah, thank—thank you. That's, uh, very kind, sir. Mr."

Thomas rolled up the window and stepped on the gas.

"See," said Catfish. "We on the same page. You act like I don't know how to talk to folks."

Thomas rolled into the neighborhood past MacMansions that he figured must have gone for a million or two, maybe more. He remembered the feelings he'd had for Red, the thoughts and fantasies about a possible future with her. For a moment he allowed himself to believe he could have had a life like this. Then he thought about what a lying ho she was and how she'd fucked up his life and his career. He pulled up a couple of houses away from the address Catfish gave him. From there they could see Red's driveway and the Benz parked in it.

"That her ride?" asked Thomas.

Catfish shrugged. "I suppose. Kind of whip she push, anyway."

"I really don't want to leave you in my rental. If I bring you along, you think you can manage not to fall down?"

"Shit, nigga, you talkin' to a big baller. I know how to hold my liquor."

Thomas rolled his eyes. "Problem is, right now you're holding almost everything out of your mini bar."

"Don't worry, boss man. I got your back."

"All right, come on." He popped the door and started toward the house, while Catfish ambled behind.

Thomas wasn't going to knock on the door. He'd look in the windows first, try to see where she was in the house, then see if he could find an unlocked door or window. When he looked through the sheer curtains of the front window, he found he could see all the way through to the back of the house. Red was nowhere in sight, but he saw something else he wanted to see.

"Let's go around back," he said to Catfish. "She left the big sliding glass door open."

"Oh, really," said Catfish, pretending to be surprised.

As they made their way through the gate in her back yard, Thomas drew his weapon. There was a towel on the pool deck, and an ice bucket full of water, not ice. Thomas edged his way up to the open glass door and looked inside. There was no movement, no TV playing, no stereo.

He turned back to Catfish. "Stay here. I'm going to check out the inside."

"Whatever," said Catfish. "I'ma chill by the pool."

"No. Stay up close to the house. I don't want her to see you if she looks out a window."

"Yeah, sure thing."

Thomas stepped into the house, gun ready, not quite sure what he'd do when he found her. If she had a weapon, if she went for it, there'd be no question about it. She'd get what she had coming to her. But Red wasn't a shooter. She was a poisoner, a manipulator who turned people against each other, and a con artist who would set a nigga up in a heartbeat. But if she did happen to have a gun, that'd work out just fine.

He looked into several rooms and was about to head up the stairs when he noticed another door down a short hall. He slowly worked his way around the corner and found himself in some kind of office or library. And it was completely fucked up. The little desk was turned over, and papers were everywhere. There was blood on the desk and on the papers, and there was an empty champagne bottle on the floor. There was blood on that, too.

Suddenly, Thomas got it. All of Catfish's bullshit about not knowing if Red was still living in the house. All his dragging his heels about coming over here. He spun around, half expecting Catfish to be right behind him with a knife, or an ax, or whatever else he might have been able to find around the house. Instead, he heard cabinet doors opening and closing in the kitchen.

Thomas walked into the kitchen, gun still on the level, and found Catfish helping himself.

"Check this out." He held up a bottle. "Courvoisier! Bitch knew how to live the life." He opened the bottle and took a snifter from the rack hanging under the upper cabinet.

"Knew? You bury her in the desert?" asked Thomas, pointing the gun directly at him now.

Catfish scrunched up his face. "Bury her? What the fuck you talking about?" He poured the golden liquid and swirled it around in the snifter.

"I saw all the blood back there, gangsta. Now I know why your face and hand are all fucked-up. She fought back, huh?"

Catfish laughed and took a gulp of the cognac. "I'ma tell you something. And since I'm your confidential informant, this gonna be just between us 'cause I don't want this shit hitting the streets back in Motown." He swallowed the rest of what was in the glass and set it down. "All that blood you seen in there? That's mines." He shook his head mournfully. "Nasty bitch got the jump on me. She surely did. She had me 'fore I knew what the fuck was happenin'."

Thomas began to relax his gun arm a bit. "You fuckin' with me?"

"I ain't fucking with you, Detective," said Catfish as he poured himself another cognac. "I had my nine with me that day. Like I always do, by the way. And I chased her out the back of the house, but I couldn't get no shot off. She done fucked up my hand." He held up the taped fingers.

"What, you couldn't run her down?" Thomas smirked.

"She a muthafuckin' jackrabbit. Tore off into that desert. I ain't never been in no desert before, but I know they got rattlesnakes all back in there. Figured they'd do my work for me. But I paid a couple Mexican kids to go back in there and find her for me the next day. Nothin'."

The gun now hung at the end of Thomas's limp arm. "So she's alive? That's what you're swearing to me."

"Last time I saw that bitch, her fine booty was jigglin' off into the desert."

"And we have no idea where she is," sighed Thomas. "Right back to fuckin' square one."

CHAPTER SEVENTEEN

*T*he doctor had said he was only keeping Q overnight, but still, he hated waking up in a hospital bed again. He'd spent too fuckin' much time in beds and hospitals and rehabs, getting poked and checked and monitored and told what he could do and what he couldn't do, always encouraged in that sweet, condescending tone of voice they all used. The doctors, the nurses, the aides, the physical terrorists. All talked the same. Everything about being back in a hospital bed again, consistently listening to the beeps of the monitors with an IV taped to the back of his hand were relentless reminders.

On top of all that, the pain was worse now than it had been since the week after surgery. He now had to hide pain, throbbing when he relaxed, sharp when he moved or breathed in too deeply. He hadn't been able to sleep all night, and he'd told the nurses repeatedly that he needed something to kill the pain. They'd notified the doctor on duty, but they kept telling Q the doctor was too busy to write a prescription for anything.

In excruciating pain, he sat in bed and stabbed with a plastic fork at the cold scrambled eggs on the tray in front of him, unable to eat a bite.

"Oops," said the cheery blonde nurse as she breezed into the room. "Not eating, I see. Is the pain still bad, Mr. Carter?"

Q fidgeted and tried to find a more comfortable position, but moving just a little bit hurt like a muthafucka. He gritted his teeth. "The pain is—yes, bad."

"Well, your doctor should be by to see you in a few hours. I'll let him know that—"

"A few hours?" yelled Q. "I was only supposed to stay here overnight. Now you tellin' me I got to stay here and wait a few *hours* for a doctor to come and see me. You got doctors runnin' all over the place up in this bitch. Grab one of them and tell him to write me a script for the pain and sign me the fuck out."

"I know you're hurt," said the nurse in that sweet, pitying voice again. "But it's more complicated than that. I'll try to get someone to see you as quickly as possible. I promise."

Q sighed in frustration, the sharp pain tearing through him as he did.

The nurse turned and walked out of the room.

An hour went by and a different nurse came in to take his vitals. When she moved his arm to put the blood pressure cuff on, he thought he was going to pass out from the pain.

"What about my pain meds?" he asked.

She had the stethoscope in her ears and held the cool disc on his arm so she could hear his heartbeats. "Wait. I have to listen to this. Give me a sec, hun."

He sat there and waited, then endured the pain as she yanked the cuff off his arm.

"Okay, your temp and BP look good." She turned to walk out of the room.

"Wait," said Q. "I asked about the pain meds."

The nurse looked at his chart. "Mm, I don't see any pain script. I can give you a Tylenol."

"I don't have a prescription. I'm asking for a doctor to *write* me a prescription."

"Your doctor should be in soon," she said with a smile. "Okay?"

Q managed to sit up. "Wait a fuckin' minute. Now I'm about to get up out this bed and tear this whole fucking building down if you can't get me something for the pain. Just taking my blood pressure right now about killed me. So you go out there and find a doctor who can either write me a script or explain to a jury why I been laying here in pain for the past eighteen hours. You heard me?"

The nurse looked truly terrified, but Q didn't know if she was afraid of him or his lawyer. Either was fine with him.

Five minutes later, a doctor, yet another that he hadn't seen before, walked into the room and casually picked up his chart. "Mr. Carter?" he said, while he was still reading. "Are you experiencing some pain?"

"Experiencing it? Yeah, that's a good word. I'm experiencing it."

Still reading the chart, the doctor mumbled out a review of the case. "Gunshot wound some weeks ago, reinjury yesterday while at home, and we've had you on Tylenol." He finally looked at Q. "On a scale of one to ten, ten being the worst pain you've ever felt, where are we this morning?"

"Ten and a half."

The doctor raised his eyebrows. "Ten being the worst pain you've ever experienced in your life."

"I said, ten and a half!"

"Okay. Let's get you some pain meds."

He walked out of the room and two minutes later a nurse came in and handed Q a tiny plastic cup containing one large pill. She poured him a cup of water from the bedside pitcher. "Down the hatch, Mr. Carter."

Q gratefully swallowed the pill and all the water.

"Okay, you should begin to get some relief from the pain within ten minutes or so, and you'll get the full effect within half an hour. We'll send you home with a script."

"Thank you," he said.

The nurse started to walk out.

"Nurse?" said Q.

She turned back. "Yes?"

"What was that?"

"Oxycodone. Highest dosage."

Oxycodone, thought Q. *That shit's supposed to be as strong as heroin. I guess the muthafuckas are finally taking me seriously.*

Chass picked him up after the hospital released him and drove him back to his mom's place. The pain had drifted away. The drug was doing exactly what he had hoped it would do. For the pain, at least. His mood was still dark. He didn't say a word to Chass during the ride, although he did consider apologizing to her for the day before, but when he got to the house, he went right to bed and climbed in.

Then he remembered the prescription the doctor had written him and fished it out of his pocket. The writing was as illegible as always with doctors, but on the line at the top that indicated the number of refills, nothing was circled. *What the fuck does that mean?* thought Q. *He doesn't want me to get any refills?*

He called for Chass and, dutifully, she came right to his side.

He held out the slip of paper. "I forgot to stop and fill this. Can you run out and get it?"

"Sure," she said, and held out her hand for it.

"First, I need a blue pen. Can you find one?"

She started to go into the kitchen to look for one, but she saw a pen on the bedside table. "Oh, here's one," she said, and picked it up.

Q took it, but then set it on the table again. "Naw, that one's black. I need blue ink."

"What difference does the color make?" asked Chass, furrowing her brow.

"The prescription's written in blue ink, but the doc forgot to circle the number of refills."

"Oh," said Chass. "Well, I can have him call that into the pharmacy."

Q's temper had flared when he was in pain. Now feeling mellow from the drugs, he didn't snap at Chass, but he was insistent. "Easier if I just fill it in."

"Yeah, but . . ."

"But, what?"

"How do you know how many refills he wants you to have?"

"I don't care how many refills he wants me to have. I'm tired of fuckin' with doctors and hospitals. I'll just get my refills, and not have to deal with none of them muthafuckas."

Chass didn't like the idea, but she felt like Q had been fighting with her and pulling away from her for a while now, even before he fell. At least now he was calm, if not cheerful. She decided to give in to him about the refills and fight whatever fight she needed to later. She left and came back with a blue ink pen and handed it to Q.

Q made a mark on the slip of paper and handed both it and the pen to Chass.

Chass looked at the prescription and saw that he'd circled the maximum number of refills available.

After Chass left to get the prescription, Q relaxed in bed for the first time since he could remember. Not only was there no pain, but there was no discomfort. Not physical anyway. The worries of his life swirled through his head, and he wondered if those would ever go away. He told himself it didn't matter. If his life was going to be fucked up, so be it. He didn't care anymore. He closed his eyes and drifted off.

CHAPTER EIGHTEEN

*G*asping for breath, Red jerked herself out of her nightmare. In the pitch black she was disoriented for a moment. She reached for the night table beside her bed in Saguaro Estates, but it felt strange. As she groped for the switch on the table lamp, she realized that was different too. "What the fuck is going on?" she half screamed, half whispered, fearing that the intruders from her dream would hear her and track the sound of her voice.

When she finally managed to get the light on, she was startled to find that she was not in her bedroom. For a moment, she didn't recognize the place. She was sweating profusely, her heart was racing, and her hands were trembling. She looked across the room to the strange dresser and saw the placard. WELCOME TO THE MARRIOT RESIDENCE INN, PHOENIX.

"Muthafucka," she said, and she stumbled out of bed to pour herself a drink.

She was happy to have awakened from the nightmare, but

she knew it could come true at any moment. In the dream she'd been walking through the desert at night, enjoying the breeze and the stars. She found it odd that she was wandering out there, since that was not her habit. But it was very pleasant, so she continued on.

Then she heard noises behind her. She turned and saw several large coyotes loping toward her. Their eyes glowed and they kept their heads low, as if they could pick up a scent better that way. Then she realized they weren't just looking for *a* scent. They were looking for *her* scent. And as they locked onto it, they picked up their pace.

Red turned and ran as fast as she could, stumbling over cactuses that cut her feet and tore the skin on her legs. As she ran she could hear the breathing of the coyotes. She tried to find a place to hide, but the desert was wide open and flat.

And then she heard the scream. *"Reeeeeed!"* It was stepfather Jerome's voice off to her left. She turned and looked down into a grave in the desert floor. "I loved you," said Jerome from the bottom, a gaping hole in his gut. "You know I always loved you, little girl. Why you do me this way?"

"Reeeed!" yelled another voice from behind her. She turned to see that the coyotes had turned into men. She couldn't see who they were because of the hoods they wore. But she could see that they carried guns.

She turned and started to run again, faster now, panicked.

"Reeeed!" screamed one of the men. "We gonna make this desert run with Red. You can't last forever. We gonna catch you, bitch. We gonna pay you back."

Now, thankfully awake, she opened two minis of Dewar's. She drank the first one straight from the bottle. Then she looked in the mirror above the dresser. The side of her face was red. She was bleeding. Her heart skipped a beat as she groped for another light. When she turned it on, she saw that what she'd thought was blood was just a trick of the nightlight coming from the bathroom.

She felt she was cracking up. She poured the second Dewar's into a cup and dropped in a small fistful of wet ice from the bucket. She leaned against the wall and slid down it until her ass hit the floor. Things were catching up with her. Catfish and her nightmares for one. But she was sure there was more coming. "You been a bad girl, Red," she said aloud. "Don't you know every bad girl gets spanked sooner or later." She gulped the scotch.

Phoenix was blown for her. She knew that. She'd known it since the minute that scraggly-ass Catfish knocked on her door. If his weak ass could find her, he could definitely find a way to send more people after her. So why was she still here? Truth was, she was in uncharted territory. She could run a little scam here and there, but in an effort to cut her old ties, she'd placed herself in unfamiliar surroundings. So it was time to get out of Dodge, but she had no idea where to go. Without a getaway bag or even a simple ID—real or fake—she couldn't hightail it to some foreign country and give the U.S. a royal fuck you, but she had to figure something out, and soon. She had most of the four grand Quisha had brought her, but that wouldn't last long if she had serious running to do. She had to do some scamming so she could stretch that shit.

She finished her drink and got to her feet. The hotel clock glowed red on the bedside table and said it was three thirty. She doubted she could sleep any more that night, but she should try to get some rest at least. Tomorrow was going to be a big day.

CHAPTER NINETEEN

*I*f she was going to make anything work for her, Red knew she couldn't look like no cheap ho. And the middle-class suburbanite routine was out, too. She had to look like class. She could pull that off with the four grand Quisha had brought her, but then she'd have no operating capital. One thing she'd learned dealing with the real estate and publishing businesses was that a bitch had to have operating capital if she was going to make anything happen.

Le Boutique was the place to put her plan into action. They had the high-end shit she deserved and needed, their security was light, and she'd only been in there once before, so the staff wouldn't be likely to recognize her. She entered the store carrying a large Louis Vuitton Damier Ebene handbag and wearing Prada aviators. The items had cost her, but you had to spend money to make money. She knew bitches who wore knockoffs, but to Red that was too tacky. Besides, they might fool the niggas on the fucked up streets of Motown, but the true big ballers would spot that fake shit a mile away.

She was looking for a few upscale dresses she could fit into the handbag, maybe a pair of shoes. A watch would be nice to round things out. Le Boutique was not an authorized Rolex dealer, but she spotted a $4,000 Tag Heuer Monaco that would do for the time being. The problem was that the watches were inside a locked case. She'd need a major distraction to pull that off, and it was a high risk boost even at that. She decided to pass on the watch.

She found a spot between racks of clothes and set her open Vuitton bag on the floor. As she pretended to sort through the dresses, sliding the hangers noisily from left to right, she found a fine Fendi in her size, plucked it off the hanger, and dropped it. Then she went right on browsing, waiting for someone to notice. When no one did, she bent down, stuffed the dress in her bag in one quick motion, then picked up the bag and moved to another rack.

Most of the ladies in the store were white, but there were a few women of color, Mexican *doñas* decked out in Valentino and Cartier. No doubt some of them came by their money legit. But she caught the look in the eyes of a couple and knew she wasn't the only player in the store that afternoon. *Amiguitas*, wifeys, to the Mexican versions of Bacon and Trap.

"I see you like Fendi," said a voice behind her.

Red's first instinct was to run. Instead, she took a breath and forced herself to glance casually over her shoulder, a friendly smile on her face.

The woman was a couple of inches shorter than her and thicker in places, but well proportioned. She seemed to have been born to wear her Marc Jacob dress. Her ebony skin was flawless. Her face was framed in soft curls and her Cupid's bow lips spread into a smile when the two women made eye contact through Red's Pradas.

Red blinked twice "I'm sorry?"

"Oh, don't be sorry, my dear," said the woman in what sounded like a slight, affected European accent. "Fendi is to die for."

"Oh, yes, I was browsing the Fendi," said Red turning around completely.

The woman raised an eyebrow and smirked. "Mm-hmm."

So, let the other shoe drop, bitch, thought Red. *I get it. You saw me. So if you're security, bust me. If not, laugh it off and walk the fuck away.*

The woman extended a perfectly manicured hand. "I'm Meme."

Red took it, tentatively. "Meme. Do you, uh, work here?"

Meme put her fingertips to her lips and snickered. "No, indeed. And further, I believe you and I are sisters. And I don't just mean in color. I didn't catch your name."

What name should she give? Raven Gomez? Lisa Lennox? Hillary Clinton? She pulled the sunglasses down a bit and looked over the top of the frames into Meme's eyes. "I'm Red."

"Pleased to make your acquaintance, my dear."

"Are you from around here, Meme?"

Meme picked up a teal green Chanel scarf, held it up to her shoulder, and glanced in the mirror. "I'm from all over, but lately I've called Las Vegas my home."

"Sin City?"

Meme tossed the scarf aside and gave her a wicked, sideways glance. "If that's the first thing that comes to your mind, then we truly are sisters."

Red immediately saw the possibilities of hooking up with a woman like this, and especially one who lived in Vegas. She felt she was halfway into the passenger seat of Meme's ride as it was.

"Your moves are good my dear. A little raw, perhaps, but practice makes perfect."

"And you've had practice?"

"Let's just say my skill set is broad and extremely well developed."

"I'm intrigued," said Red, running her hand through a display of cashmere sweaters. "Shoplifting, and . . . ?"

"Mm, financial activities—checks, credit cards. An occasional burglary, if the jewels in question are properly cut. And the sort of things that only a woman such as you or I would be able to accomplish."

"Oh?"

Meme held up her left pinky. "Let's just say I've had a number of men wrapped around this little finger." Then the right. "And this little finger. Often at the same time."

Red smiled. "Can I buy you lunch?"

"Oh, how kind of you to ask. But first . . ." She glanced around the store. "Was there anything else you wanted to, uh, *shop* for?"

Red liked the way this woman thought and conducted herself. She was open and unapologetic about her needs and what she had to do to satisfy them. She outclassed all the other women Red had known: Terry, Kera, Sasha—she even outclassed that lawyer bitch, Chass Reed. "I did need a couple more dresses," said Red. "And . . ." She hesitated, then looked towards the jewelry case.

"And?" said Meme.

"I had my eye on a Tag Heuer."

"Which?"

"The Monaco."

"Oh, I like your taste, dear."

"But I was thinking it might be a bit too ambitious."

"Nonsense, darling." Meme looked around the store. "Let's

do the clothes shopping first, then I'll help you with the time-piece."

Red felt intoxicated as she let the pro help her pick up several additional items. She observed every move Meme made, memorizing them for future reference. And she had impeccable taste. Only the best names went into the bag, most of them Italian: Gucci, Versace, Armani. Still, the longer they lingered in the store, the more Red's heart pounded. She wondered if they were pushing their luck. Meme, on the other hand, was cool as a martini.

"Maybe we should call it a day," said Red.

"Don't be silly," said Meme, angling toward the jewelry. "How can we call it a day when we don't even know what time it is? For that, we'll need another accessory, true?"

She put her back to the jewelry display so that Red could see it looking past her. Then she put both hands on Red's shoulders. "Do you see the man behind the counter? Not the fat one. The gay gentleman?"

Red noticed the thirtyish blond with the upturned chin and the austere look in his eye. "Yes."

"Keep those marvelous sunglasses of yours on at all times. Ask that fellow to show you two watches side by side. The one you want and any other."

"All right," said Red.

"When things start to happen, make sure he's not looking at you. Don't worry about the fat one. He'll be otherwise occupied. When the blond gentleman turns away in panic, casually collect the watch into your bag, and walk out."

"In panic?" said Red. She put her hands on her hips. "Is there a muthafuckin' gun involved in this plan?"

Meme lifted an eyebrow. "That would be just too gauche. As I said, walk out of the store and meet me at Benedetto's where, yes, you may buy me lunch."

"Are you sure about this?" asked Red. "Right now I mostly need to stay free."

"I have one hundred percent confidence in my plan."

Red nodded and strolled past Meme to the jewelry counter. As she approached, she saw the heavyset man liven up to wait on her. She made a direct route to the blond. "Excuse me," she said, looking right at him. "Can you help me?"

He looked a bit annoyed, but in a store like Le Boutique, the customer is always right. "Yes, ma'am, what can I do for you?"

She asked to see the Tag Heuer she wanted and a lesser model in the same line. As she asked about the features of each, she saw Meme behind her, approaching fast.

"Oh, my dear God," Meme screamed at the top of her lungs, but sounding no less elegant than she had moments earlier. She pointed to a back corner of the store. "There's a rat, with—it's—I think it's foaming at the mouth."

A wave of gasps and barely restrained screams moved through the store as customers began moving toward the exit.

"Oh, God," said Meme. "It's hideous. Its teeth are—Oh, no, I can't stay here." She hurried toward the exit waving her hands. "I can't stay here. I'm sorry."

The blond salesman clasped his terror stricken cheeks with his hands. "Oh, dear!" he said. "Oh, no!" He began to look around him as if for a place to hide. But there was none.

The fat salesman came around the end of the counter. "It's all right, Jonathan," he said. "I'll take care of it."

"Oh, dear," said Jonathan. "Oh, dear me."

"Don't freak out," said the other salesman, now deeper in the store.

Red casually turned from the counter, her new watch in her hand. She dropped it into the bag and joined the rest of the customers in their hasty exit.

Just before she reached the door, out of the corner of her eye she spotted a display of money clips. One was in the form of a bloodred poker chip. She came to a stuttering stop in front of it. If ever there was a sign, this was it. She picked it up, dropped it in her bag, and continued out the door.

CHAPTER TWENTY

*B*acon knew there was little his lawyer could do for him, even as the man sat next to him in court, shuffling his papers like he was going to work some kind of miracle. Bacon hadn't been in the van that was transporting the black tar heroin when it was pulled over, but he and Blue had been in a Mustang escorting the truck on the run to New York. Bacon had a sweet connect from his nigga, Juan, in Mexico. That should have been a relationship that would have kept filling his pockets full for years to come. But some snitch had fingered both the truck and the Mustang, so the cops had pulled them both over. Not only did the feds know the truck was carrying black tar, the muthafuckas went right for the side panels the shit was stashed behind.

At first, Bacon had been in tears as the agents put the bracelets on him. Not because he was afraid of going inside. Shit, he'd done his share of time. But he'd been thinking about all that he'd built with Red. She was his wifey, and he loved her. Now he had to lose all that. But Blue opened his eyes to the fact that Red was the bitch that snitched on 'em. That, plus the kinds of questions the feds asked, made him realize he'd been done by the very muthafuckin' bitch he cared so much for and had given so much to. She was always a scandalous ho, stabbin' niggas in the back, pullin' all kinds of hustles to get what she wanted. And he'd had to put some act-right on her himself from time to time. But she was a dime, and they had a good thing going. He didn't understand why she had to fuck it all up. He had been hoping to see her in court when she testified so that he could eyeball her and let her know what was coming. But they told him she was in the wind. The Raven had done flown. Wasn't that a bitch?

Although distracted for the moment, he reminded himself that there was plenty of business to take care of as the next witness was called.

Black was looking somber as he took the stand, but he held his head up. Bacon knew he wasn't the kind of nigga to shrink from confrontation. But this was a fucked up move. No doubt the feds had done a deal with him over some charge or other in exchange for his testimony against Bacon. And now there he was, being all disloyal to a nigga.

Black wouldn't be nowhere if it wasn't for him. Bacon had made moves on the street that Black couldn't even have thought of. Bacon had even introduced him to Trap, a baller he'd meet through Red's girlfriend Quisha. He and Trap were all set to do some business together right before the bust.

The prosecutor had Black describe everything he knew about the deal and the transportation. After he finished was the defense's turn.

Bacon's lawyer started with the usual pleasantries. *How you doin'?* and shit. Bacon never understood that bullshit. Why lawyers always did that? Why not just be straight with a nigga. *I'm about to try to fuck you up hard as I can.* Just fuckin' say it. Everybody knew what was coming anyway.

After a few questions leading up to the serious shit, Bacon's lawyer got heavy. "Others in this courtroom have testified that the defendant was not in the truck carrying the heroin. Are you aware of that?"

Black smiled. "A nigga who smart enough to run things ain't stupid enough to be in the car with the dope."

"Maybe he was just unlucky enough to be on the road close to the truck at the time the truck was pulled over. Isn't that possible?"

"Naw, it ain't like that. Everybody know Bacon got the connect. He bring the H. in, package it up, put it on the road. He like a kingpin and shit."

"Your honor," said the attorney. "I'd like the last statement stricken from the record."

"So ordered," said the judge.

Kingpin was a serious word. It meant far more than *drug dealer* in legal terms. It meant somebody who was the head of an ongoing criminal enterprise. As Bacon sat there listing to his running buddy, he couldn't believe his ears. Black wasn't just being disloyal for the sake of cutting a deal. He was sending Bacon a message. *You gone, muthafucka,* Black was saying. *And I'ma do all I can to make sure you stay gone.*

Also, he'd mentioned Bacon's connect, but didn't say anything more about him. That made Bacon think maybe Black had business plans of his own with Juan.

But after ruling on the objection, the judge seemed to have other things on his mind. He straightened up in his chair and pointed to something behind Bacon. "Hey, what was that?" he said. And he was pissed.

A murmur went through the courtroom.

The judge turned to a bailiff. "What was that? See what that was."

A bailiff stormed past the defense table. Bacon turned around to watch what was going on.

The bailiff towered over a nigga in the seats. "Was that a cell phone camera? Did you just take a picture?"

"Naw," said the man. "I was just looking at a text message."

"In the first place, cell phones are not allowed in court. But I'm going to check and see what pictures you have on there."

The man held the phone away from the bailiff. "You ain't touching my phone, nigga."

"Oh, yes, I think I will take it." He made a grab for it past the man's body.

Two other bailiffs rushed forward from the back of the courtroom.

Another spectator stood up. "Get the fuck off him, muthafucka." He took a swing at the first bailiff, who backed away to regroup.

A fourth bailiff ducked his head out of the courtroom and waved in extra security from the corridor.

Now an actual brawl erupted in the seats, as the bailiffs tried to confiscate the phone. The guy who'd taken the picture obviously didn't want to part with it, and his friends were backing him up.

Bacon turned to his lawyer. "What's this world comin' to," he said with a smile.

"Clear this court," yelled the judge.

The deputy sheriff who was escorting Black grabbed him out of the witness stand and began to hustle him out of the room. By the time they reached the defense table, the path was jammed. They had to stop and wait for a clearing.

Bacon looked up at the deputy's name tag. *Seger*, it said. Then he looked at Black. "Hey, snitch nigga," he said. "What's on your mind?"

"Nigga, you let that scandalous ho Red play you like a bitch. All 'cause she the first thing you fucked with a pussy since before you went inside. And I ain't even considering Foxy, 'cause you know that shit ain't real. You deserve to get played."

Bacon would have stood up right then if Seger hadn't already had a hand on his holstered gun. "You think I can't reach out to you from in there?"

Black sneered. "Nigga, reach behind you with some Vaseline."

Then the crowd opened up and Black was pulled away. Bacon looked over his shoulder and watched him go, already counting the names of the niggas he was going to put on him.

He turned to his lawyer while the pushing and shoving was still going on. "If they going to recess this shit, I got to get to a phone."

His attorney shook his head. "New court order just came down this morning. No talking on the phone."

Bacon recoiled. "What the fuck? They ain't buying that kingpin bullshit, is they?"

"You heard the judge strike that statement from the record. It's not about that. They just want to protect Black."

Bacon looked over his shoulder once again and caught sight of Black just as he was going through the door. *Yeah,* he thought. *That nigga need protectin'.*

CHAPTER TWENTY-ONE

*B*lack sat in the unmarked van and gazed out the tinted windows at the bleak Detroit cityscape. "You coulda just stopped at McDonald's or something, man. 'Stead of just sittin' in this van waitin'."

"Relax," said Deputy Seger. "He'll be here. We'll go to the drive-thru as soon as we're done."

"Don't know why we got to do all this clandestine bullshit anyway. Everybody already saw me go into court. What difference does it make now?"

Seger shrugged. "I'm just the fuckin' driver."

"They get that nigga with the camera?" asked Black.

"Yeah, they got him. I don't even think that was about you, though."

"Oh, no? What it was about then?"

"Just the typical fun shit that happens in court."

Black wasn't sure about that. Detroit niggas was serious when it came to snitches. But Black didn't consider himself a snitch. If Bacon had taken care of business and not let his wifey get into his shit, everything would have been cool. Red was the one who put him in. If a nigga was gonna let his wifey play him like that, he needed to be someplace where they were gonna give him three meals a day, 'cause he didn't have what it took to make his own bread.

He heard the back door of the van open and looked back to see Special Agent Marcus Holt climb in.

"What's up?" he said. "Listen, I was just tellin' Deputy here that I'ma need y'all to hook me up with some muthafuckin' food before too much longer. This shit takin' all day."

"You're not even finished with your testimony yet," said Holt. "We'll get you some food before we take you back to court."

Then Holt nodded to Brickell and the deputy popped the driver's door and stepped out of the van.

After that, Holt didn't waste any time. "So, Bacon introduced you to Trap."

Black waited for more, then shrugged. "Yeah? So?"

"Word we hear is that Trap is moving on Bacon's connect. We want in."

Muthafucka, thought Black. *I shoulda known all kinda niggas would be trying to make that connect with Bacon out the way. That shit should be mine.* "And?"

"And we want you to hook up with Trap, stick close to him, be his new best friend."

If Black helped the FBI and the DEA bust the niggas Bacon was doing business with in Mexico, he'd be left with nothing. That was the best black tar he knew of, and, at the moment, it was just wide open. But if he could make some moves that put Trap in for something major before the po-po got into the shit in Mexico, he might still be able to make it work. He hated doing that to Trap because, unlike Bacon, that nigga kept it tight. But if the feds was already onto him anyway, Black couldn't save him.

"All right," said Black. "I might could hook you up with that."

Holt shook his head. "Not *might, could,* Black. You take us to Mexico, or the deal's off."

Black twisted completely around in his seat. "Naw, nigga, this here deal was I help you with Bacon, you keep me out of prison."

"Deals are sometimes more fluid than we would want them to be."

"Say what?"

"Things change."

"Fuck no, muthafucka. That deal is set."

"What's the problem?" asked Holt. "Stick with Trap. He'll give us everything we want. We'll all go home happy."

"Naw, then fuck it. You can just put me in. I ain't goin' back to court today. I ain't helping you with Trap. None of it."

"What the fuck are you getting so worked up about?"

"Man, I don't even know who he knows in Mexico. You feel me? I can't make no guarantees he even gonna trust me enough to take me down there. Now you talkin' about if I don't get you all the way to the connect, I don't get nothing from you? That's bullshit."

"All right, all right," said Holt. "Just get us in with Trap and follow it as far as it goes. If all we get is Trap, your deal's still good."

Black turned around to face the front of the van before Holt could see him smile. This was going to work out just right. Trap would be out of the way, and the black tar would be all his. "All right," he said. "Now get me some food, 'fore I fall out."

After finishing his testimony, Black headed to his crib to clean up and change into some clothes more suited to partying.

Trap liked to hang out at Bar Eleven, so he knew right where to find him, but he didn't want to get there too early. He chilled until about ten thirty, then headed over there and found the party in full swing.

Trap was near the bar with his girl Quisha and a couple of other ladies. He strolled over there with a big grin on his face, genuinely happy to see Trap, but also eager to put his plan to work.

Trap waved him over when he saw him. "I'm buying a round, nigga. Get in on this shit."

Black bumped shoulder with him. "What we drinking?"

"Grey Goose."

"Sound good. I can go for some vodka."

As Trap leaned over the bar to speak with the bartender, Black leaned in and kissed Quisha on the cheek. "Hey, girl. What's up?"

"Just chillin'," she said with her usual, charming smile. "You know how I do."

"Yeah," said Black. "Hey, you was tight with Red for a while there, huh?"

"Yeah, we hung out."

"You ain't heard from her or nothin'?"

Quisha looked at him and blinked. "No, not a word."

"All right. Just wondering if she's around or anything."

Trap motioned everybody forward to collect their shots and make a toast. "To the players," he said, raising his glass.

Everybody threw their shots back and slapped their glasses on the bar.

"So, what we celebratin'?" asked Black.

Trap shrugged. "You know. Business been good."

Black knew better. Bacon had promised to bring Trap into the black tar he'd been getting from Mexico, and now Trap would have to make that happen on his own. Black nodded. "Nigga, you look like you set. I ain't lying."

"Well, you know, I'm going good, but I'm always lookin' for new opportunities."

"I feel you. A nigga got to stay on his toes."

"For real," said Black. "And I mean stay looking forward, and watch his back. I'm still trippin' about what happened to Bacon."

Trap shook his head. "That nigga going inside for a long time. Too bad too, 'cause him and me was just gettin' into doing some business together."

"Yeah, and Bacon knew how to party, too."

"No doubt," said Trap. "We talked about going out to Vegas together. Have some fun, maybe put together some business, too."

"Man, I ain't been to Vegas in a while. I miss some of the fun times I done had out that way."

Trap patted him in the chest with the back of his hand. "Maybe you and me could tear it up out there. Bacon told me you a good man to have around. Matter of fact, since one of my boys fell through on some personal shit, maybe we could head out there this week unless you got something else going on."

"I tell you what," said Black. "I need to take care of a couple things tomorrow. After that, I'm ready to party." *Damn*, thought Black, *I didn't even have to talk my way into this shit. Easy as good pussy.*

Quisha had been hanging close while Black and Trap talked. At her first opportunity, she slipped outside and flipped open her cell phone. She went into *received calls* and scrolled down until she found the number she wanted. Red had mentioned that she was going to be on the move somewhere out West. She had to make sure it wasn't Vegas. She hit the call button and waited. It was almost midnight in Detroit, but would be three hours earlier in Phoenix. She just hoped her girl hadn't yet ditched the phone she'd been using.

"Hello?" said a man's voice on the other end of the line.

"Who dis?" said Quisha.

"Huh? This is Fred Lindenburg. Who the hell is this?"

"Aw, muthafucka!" said Quisha.

"Excuse me?"

"Go back to bed, Fred."

She flipped the phone shut and shook her head. No doubt Fred had reported the phone stolen and gotten his old number on his replacement phone. Anyway, she now had no way to contact Red. Girlfriend was on her own.

The next day Black met with Agent Holt to let him know about the trip to Vegas. At first Holt wanted to set up a schedule for Black to call in every day. Black told him to fuck himself. He'd call in when he could.

He and Trap stepped off the plane in Vegas ready to play and also ready to find new business opportunities. They stepped up to the luxury rental car desk, and Trap laid down his driver license. The guy behind the counter looked like a young Donny Osmond, but with short hair. "Yeah, I holla'd at y'all yesterday and asked for a Lexus. But really, lemme push a Escalade."

The boy looked at him, bewildered, hesitant. "Push a . . . Well, all our cars come with gas already in them."

Black bent over laughing. Trap shook his head at the rental agent. "Boy, you dumb as . . . All right, how 'bout this." He switched to his white voice. "Sir, may I please drive one of your Cadillac Escalades?"

The kid turned beat red and nodded like a bobble-head doll. "Absolutely. I believe we have one available. Just let me . . ." He tapped his keyboard for a minute, then assured Trap that the car would be brought around within minutes.

Leaving the airport, they headed right into the heart of Vegas. They'd each made reservations at the Bellagio and wanted to get checked in right away so they could check out the action. Trap had brought along a few CDs and slid some Fabolous into the stereo. "You Be Killin Em" flowed like a soundtrack as they rolled down the Strip and took in the sights.

"Did you bring anything with you?" asked Trap. He put his thumb and forefinger to his lips.

"Naw," said Black. "With all the extra security they got going, I didn't want to take no chances. Figured we'd get something here."

"For real," said Trap. "With all that full body scan bullshit they be busting niggas for just carrying a eighth. That shit is fucked up."

"No doubt. But you know they always got good shit in this party town."

In Vegas, with so many service industry workers, earning tips by providing the 411 to out-of-towners, not to mention hos all over the streets, in the bars, and in the casinos, Trap and Black both knew it was easy to find anything a man could want. When they checked into the Bellagio, the bellboy hooked them up with a nigga who sold them an ounce of blow and an eighth of weed.

They decided since they were staying at the Bellagio, they'd check out the action at some other hotels and casinos and work their way back as the afternoon and evening wore on. They took the coke with them.

As Trap drove, Black flipped through several cards that guys had handed him on the sidewalk on the way to the car. "See, this how you know you in a party town, nigga. When the mutha-fuckin' hos got bubble gum cards just like baseball players." He turned one toward Trap—a blonde with pointy tits and a tribal tattoo on her upper arm. "Check this bitch out. Jasmine. You think Jasmine really look like that?"

"Nigga, I seen that bitch all over the Internet. You know that ain't real. Call up, they say, 'Jasmine out sick.'"

"Yeah," said Black. "They be like, 'We hook you up with Melissa. They sistas anyway.'"

At a stop light, Trap snorted some more blow. When the light turned green, he laid on the gas. "This shit is good. See, this the kind of shit we could move in Motown. We gonna have to find out more about this here."

"Yeah, we should shop around, though. We might find somethin' even better. Or a better price."

Trap nodded as he muscled the Escalade through traffic. "We gonna check it all out. Chop me up some more of that shit."

Black opened the glove box again and took out the mirror he was using to chop out lines. "Nigga, would you slow this bitch down so I can do this without spilling half the shit?"

But Trap didn't slow down. Instead, he sped up and whipped the wheel to the right and the left. Powder went everywhere all over the front seat.

"Muthafucka," said Black. "What the—"

"Po-po on our tail, nigga."

"What?" Black looked over his shoulder and saw the blue lights. He began wiping coke off the seat onto the floorboards. "Oh, shit, I got it all over my hands now."

"All right," said Trap. "All right. Just stay cool. They ain't even gonna notice." Trap pulled the car over to the curb right on the strip.

Black couldn't believe it. "Is you crazy, or just too high to think straight? You can't pull the fuck over. This shit all over the place."

Trap was jittery and paranoid. "Muthafucka. We gonna have to make a move here."

"A move?" said Black. "What kind of move? Just drive this bitch."

But instead of driving, Trap rolled down his window for the officer who was standing right outside now.

"Sir, we ran your tag and the car came back as a rental. Are you from out of town?"

"Yeah, officer, we're from Detroit," said Trap. "Just here on vacation. You know."

"I do. We get a lot of visitors from out of town, but you still have to follow the rules of the road. Can I see your license and registration?"

"Oh, was I doing something wrong?"

"Yes, you were using excessive speed and weaving in and out of traffic."

Trap glared at the cop. "Did you have a radar gun on me or something?"

"No. I need to see your license."

"Well, how you know I was speeding if you didn't have no muthafuckin' radar?"

The cop widened his stance and raised his voice a little. "Because I was speeding when I caught up with you. Your license."

Trap began to reach into his back pocket for his wallet.

The cop pointed to Black. "Sir, what's that all over your pants?"

Black looked down and saw that there was coke all over his jeans. "This? This just, uh, baby powder."

"Baby powder? You have a baby onboard?"

His heart started to pound. "No, I use it. Myself. Sometimes. You know, if I get, like, a rash. Sometimes."

"A rash?" said the cop.

"Yes, sir."

"You ever get a rash in your nose?"

"My—Oh, shit!" yelled Black as he saw Trap come out from behind his back with a gun.

Trap brought the nine across his body. But it was like he was moving in slow motion.

The cop drew his weapon before Trap could come completely around. "Drop it," he yelled. And almost before he'd finished, he fired. Three shots.

Trap screamed and jerked way from the gunshots, then fell dead across Black's lap.

Black saw the cop reach for his body mic. He popped the passenger door and bolted into the crowd. People on the sidewalk were running everywhere, screaming in panic. Black kept his head low and zigzagged between them, then took a right at the first intersection.

When he did, he nearly ran right into a familiar face. He wanted to stop. To grab her, to throw her to the sidewalk and beat her. But all that was just a fantasy. The cops would be right behind him. His only chance was to sprint and not look back.

Red's heart skipped a beat when she saw Black come around the corner at a full clip, running right for her, ready to grab her, anger in his eyes. Now that nigga had found her too. But how? Bacon was reaching out for her, no doubt. And she had no doubt what was on his mind. After dodging Catfish and surviving by her wits for the past few days, now she was about to be killed by Bacon.

But as she cringed and threw her hands up, knowing there was no way she could defend herself against him, he ran right past her. And then two cops rounded the corner. And they ran right past her, too.

CHAPTER TWENTY-TWO

I don't believe I ever really did thank you for this," said Q as he moved along the pathway in the park, cane in his right hand, Chass's hand in his left. "Not properly, anyway."

"For what?" Chass asked.

"This—extra appendage of mine."

"The cane?"

"Yeah. I hate to even say the word, but I really am grateful. It was a very thoughtful gift, but I was just so—I guess bitter, at the time. I just wasn't right with my feelings about you."

Chass leaned in close and put her head on his shoulder as they walked. "I understand that, Q. You've been through so much. I couldn't expect you to be all fun and laughs at that time."

"Well, anyway," he said, "now that I'm about ready to stop using it, after all these months, I really felt I should say thank you."

Q had made good progress since leaving the hospital the second time. The pain in his side, which had radiated into his back and down his leg, had been relieved by the Oxycodone. The drug had also taken the edge off his anger. And that had given him time to think clearly for the first time since the shooting. He'd begun to come to grips with what had happened to him and was finding peace.

It didn't hurt that he and Chass had finally begun to talk about their feelings for each other. She'd sat him down not long after his return from the hospital, when he was so despondent, and told him she loved him. At first he wondered if she was saying it just to help snap him out of his depression. After all, how could a classy lady like her be interested in a retread thug like him? But when he looked in her eyes, he saw that she meant it.

He'd finally made the decision to ask her to marry him. He was just waiting for the right moment.

Still, there was something missing between them. There was a politeness, a formal quality to their relationship. He actually felt a little numb around her. But it was a pleasant, unfeeling sort of numb. They had fun together, they laughed, but still, there wasn't the easiness that he'd felt with other women. With— well—with Red.

But that was crazy. Red had been the worst thing in the world for him. Maybe he felt a little stiff around Chass because he just wasn't used to being around a woman who wasn't in the game as deeply as Red had been. Chass loved him, and she was good for him. That was the important thing. Wasn't it? If things hadn't quite clicked with them, they would in time. He'd get used to being settled, instead of always being on his toes around some of the wild bitches he'd been with. Like—Red.

There was no denying Red knew how to have fun. There was an ease about her, and a love of fun that was deep down in her soul. When times were good they laughed like kids together. They had really had something. And he had to believe that meant something to her. She said she didn't mean to pull the trigger on Q. That she'd been trying to hit Bacon. Was that so hard to believe? Q knew the kind of man Bacon was. Most women would probably love to shoot him.

What the fuck is wrong with me? he thought, as he turned and nuzzled his nose into Chass's hair. *How could I be thinking about that scandalous bitch when I've got this great woman right here beside me?*

His heart pounded as he tried to work up the courage to do what he'd planned on. That surprised him. He'd been a big baller on the streets. He'd handled himself in plenty of situations with thugs and popo. So why was this so hard? *It shouldn't be,* he thought. *Just go for it.*

He cleared his throat. "So, anyway. I wanted to, uh, thank you for your gift. You know. And give you a little gift in return."

"Oh?" said Chass. "What kind of gift?"

Q stopped and let go of Chass's hand. "Uh, well, let's see if I can find it now." He moved his cane to his left hand and reached into his right pocket for the ring box.

Chass took hold of his left arm to steady him. "What is it?"

Q continued to dig around among the items in his pocket. "You'll see in just a second. I got it right here."

As Q got a hold of the ring box and tried to pull it from his pocket, something else came out with it and fell to the ground.

"Oh, I'll get it," said Chass. Without seeing the ring box, she bent down to pick up the item on the ground. Then she stood up, slowly, looking at the pill bottle in her hand, reading the prescription with a furrowed brow.

She looked up at him. "Q? Oxycodone? You're still taking this?"

"You know I been using that."

She took a step back from him and looked at the label again. "I know you *were* using it, but you said you were tapering off."

Q shoved the ring box back into his pocket. "I am tapering off, Chass."

She shook her head. "This prescription is the same dosage, same number of times a day, as the last refill. And you just got it five days ago, and it's already half gone." She looked up at him, angry now. "You've been taking more than you're supposed to."

Q tried to laugh it off. "Girl, you are trippin' on this way too much. I'm tapering off, but some days I need it more than others. I'm just using it till the pain goes away."

"Well, how do you know if the pain is better or worse if you're always high on this stuff?"

"I know because I get pain in the morning when I haven't had one all night. As soon as that stops, *I'll* stop. Besides, I'm not using it to get high."

"I think you are," said Chass. "Q, sometimes I notice you're itchy and fidgety. That's when you're coming down off this stuff, isn't it?" She rattled the bottle in his face. "About the time you feel a little twinge of pain, you're twitching. You're jonesin', baby."

Q reached out and grabbed her wrist with one hand, then he dropped the cane and used his other hand to pry the pill bottle away from her. "Girl, that is not true. How can you stand there and tell me how *I* feel? How much pain *I'm* in? What kind of medication *I* need to be on?" He bent down to try to recover his cane and almost fell over.

Chass reached out to steady him. "Q, you're not yourself around me. You're—I don't know, it's like you're numbed out. I sometimes feel like I can't reach you. Like there's some invisible wall between us. You're standing on the other side of that wall, and you're smiling, and being very nice and sweet, but it's like you're over there and I'm over here."

"Oh, that's how you feel about it, huh? That's how you really feel about me?" He took a step back from her.

"Q, I care about you very much. I'm just trying to get you to see that there's more going on with this Oxy than you realize."

"Let me see if I remember this," said Q, scoffing. "Were you the one who got shot, or was that me?"

"Q!"

"No, no, that's all right. Maybe I'm remembering it wrong. But I just think that if a nigga gets shot, it might affect his personality a little bit."

"Q, I do understand that. I do."

Q stopped and stared at her for a moment. *I do.* He had wanted to hear her say those words. But not like this. "You know what, baby. I'm getting through this shit day by day." He rattled the pill bottle, then stuffed it back in his pocket on top of the ring box. "And that's just how this here shit is." He never got to the gift, and Chass didn't ask.

CHAPTER TWENTY-THREE

*W*hen Red got back to her room at the Mirage, she threw her shit together in three minutes flat and got the fuck out. She had no idea how Black had gotten onto her, but if he knew she was in Vegas, maybe he knew what hotel she was staying at. But she didn't see how that was possible. She hadn't been using any credit cards. She hadn't been getting any money wired to her. No checks. Nothing. The only thing she could figure was that some nigga recognized her on the street and dropped a dime on her fine black Puerto Rican ass. First order of business after finding new digs would be to change her look.

Even though the sun was going down, she wore the oversized Prada sunglasses when she stepped out to the curb to get a cab. That, plus the big Burberry cap she tucked her hair up under would have to do for a disguise for the time being. Even so, she had the driver drop her a block from the Flamingo, then she walked back.

She got the most inexpensive room they had. She wasn't

going to deprive herself of a fine hotel, but she still wasn't as flush as she wanted to be. She'd learned a lot from Meme and was still working with her, learning the shoplifting moves and other endeavors. They made a good team, and they had fun together. But she doubted even Meme would have stayed cool with that nigga Black bearing down on her, looking all wild and shit.

She liked the Caribbean vibe the Flamingo had going on. This would be the perfect place to stay. But she wouldn't be spending much time here. She'd have to get out and start making money. Real money. And to do that, she'd need Meme's help.

After settling into her room, she went to a pay phone a block away and called her. It felt paranoid, even to Red, but she wasn't taking chances, considering the close calls she'd had recently.

"Hey, girlfriend," she said when Meme answered the phone.

"Oh, Raven," said Meme. "I tried to call your room, but they said you'd checked out. I was worried sick."

"I had to change hotels."

"Rats at the Mirage?"

It had been a running joke with them ever since they pulled their scam for the Tag Heuer watch in Phoenix. If they didn't like a place, they would simply say it had rats. And they would laugh, remembering the panic they'd caused at Le Boutique, the terror-stricken face of the gay salesman, and the butch salesman's brave march to the back of the store to confront the beast.

But Red wasn't laughing now. "Something like that," she said. "I'll explain all about it when I see you. Can you come to the Flamingo?"

"Can I? I love the Flamingo. I'll be there in twenty minutes."

Red gave her the room number, then hurried back to get some ice and search the mini bar before she arrived.

"You'll be moving up to something more extravagant in no time," said Meme, minutes later, as she sipped a Cuba Libre and surveyed the room.

"And I need you to teach me all you can to help me make that happen, Miss Meme. I think I'm ready for the next step."

The next step was something Red and Meme had talked about. Meme made no apologies for her money-making exploits, one of which was what Red would have called straight hookin'. Meme called it escorting, and a great way to make lots of money with the right Johns.

Meme gave her a wicked smile. "For dimes like you and me, it's not a step, it's a walk in the clouds, and you, with your reddish glow and your fine features, can easily make two grand a night, with time left over to enjoy your earnings."

"That's what you keep saying, and I'm ready for you to show me how to pick the right men. But first, I have a problem."

Meme sat on the edge of the bed next to Red and clasped her hand. "Tell Meme all about it."

Red wasn't sure how much to say. She trusted her new friend, but she didn't want to scare her off with stories about niggas from Motown swooping in from all directions trying to off a bitch. She decided to tone it down a bit. "I have an old boyfriend who's in town, and I don't want him to spot me. I need to change my appearance some. I mean—not some—a lot."

"Is the gentleman actually looking for you?"

Gentleman? thought Red. *Ain't nothin' gentlemanly about Black, or none of them niggas he runs with.* "I think so."

"Oh, this will be a wonderful challenge. To hide you—but not your beauty—so completely than your old boyfriend himself won't recognize you." Meme squirmed with delight.

She stood and took Red's hand and tugged her over to the mirror. "Of course, the hair," she said. "We'll start with that. Something with volume."

"Something with volume?" asked Red.

"Absolutely. We want all eyes riveted to you when you enter a room." She sat Red down and stood behind her. She began playing with her hair, moving it into different shapes. "It's a shame to tamper with the natural red cast of your hair, but I'm afraid we must. We could go blond. That would be striking on you. But I'm thinking black. Shimmering onyx black with loads of big curls. We'll let them spill over your forehead and flow down your cheeks. It will actually change the shape of your face."

"Really?" said Red. "Curls?"

"Of course." Meme used her hands like an orchestra conductor and a sculptor rolled into one, creating the vision in the mirror. "And black eye shadow so that you'll smolder from deep within that lioness mane."

Red nodded and smiled. "I can see that."

"And a subtle shade of pink lipstick. We don't want it to clash with the dark image we're creating, but we want it to be a faint illumination to tease men and make them want to see you in a greater light. And how do they cast that greater light on you, dear?"

Red giggled. Meme's words and ideas were intoxicating. She was beginning to feel like an Egyptian goddess. "Uh . . . I—"

"With cash," said Meme. "They illuminate you with cash. Hundred dollar bills. Many of them."

"I could shine in that light, girlfriend."

"Yes, you will. And you'll need earrings."

"Earrings? You really think different earrings are going to change my appearance?"

"I do. Big feather earrings. Red, I think, since we don't want to lose your essence." Again, Meme worked with her hands to show Red what she meant. "They'll be full and long and at a glance will appear as red highlights peeking out in your hair. They'll fill this space on the sides of your throat, making your neck seem thinner and longer."

Meme suddenly straightened up, almost like she'd been shocked.

"What's wrong?" Red asked.

"Did I say two grand a night?"

Red furrowed her brow. "Uh, yeah, I think you did."

"That's not what I see in the mirror of my imagination. That was a conservative estimate." Red believed her and hoped desperately that she was right. She thought to herself that not only was she trusting Meme with the success of her new look, but also her life.

CHAPTER TWENTY-FOUR

*A*s Red strolled into the casino at the Bellagio, she caught a glimpse of herself in a mirror. She had to do a double take. She still couldn't believe the lady in the mirror was her. The makeover had turned out almost exactly as Meme had envisioned and described it the previous night. As for the transformation into an upscale escort, that had been no problem.

"You've been dealing with men to get what you want all your life," Meme had said over the room service brunch in her suite. "This is the same thing, except that you can be much more up-front about your needs."

Meme schooled her on the finer points of selecting a John. She taught her how to spot a real Rolex, size up a bankroll, and tell when a man was bluffing. "The more money a man loses at the tables, the better. If he drops a few hundred, he may just be a weekend player; a few thousand, a gambling addict working his way through a second mortgage. But if he's throwing away tens of thousands, he's a whale. He's looking for ways to express his power, and you can provide him with such."

Red took a sip of her mimosa and shook her head. "Yeah, but I don't know if I really want to get with some fat, old mutha-fucka."

"You'll find men you enjoy being with, and those you'll be re-pulsed by. In the case of the latter, you may want to adjust your approach."

"Adjust? And how do I . . . ?"

"It's almost as if men want us to take their money," said Meme, as she stirred real cream into her coffee. "They package it all up neatly in a leather case they keep in their back pockets. Like a gift. Of course the decision is up to you, but if you go into a room with a man you find unattractive, and you ask him to wash himself before you begin, it's a relatively easy thing to take that gift and depart, leaving him with his dick hanging out."

Red thought about Fred Lindenburg and the way she'd walked out on him at the gas station in Scottsdale. Meme's ap-proach was more elegant, but accomplished the same thing. Red would have no problem with such a move.

And now, as she wandered—reborn—through the casino, she spotted a whale almost immediately at the blackjack table. He was wearing Bruno Magli shoes, an Armani blazer, and a Patek Philippe Calatrava watch. All of it genuine.

"Winner, winner, chicken dinner," said the dealer as he paid the man on a natural.

"Ooo," said Red squeezing in next to him. "You're a man to get close to."

He turned to her and smiled. He was in his late fifties with a pudgy face, hair plugs, and several tall stacks of chips. "I can do no wrong."

"Well, you have to do some wrong, once in a while. Other-wise, where's the fun in life?"

Black stood at the craps table in the Bellagio doing what he did. This was a game he'd been playing in the alleys of Detroit since he was six years old. He could work the odds in his head as fast as any Vegas old timer. But money wasn't what he was after at the moment. He just wanted something that would take his mind off the shit he'd been through since arriving in Vegas.

He'd barley escaped a shootout with the police, just missed his chance to pay back Red for all the scandalous shit she'd been throwing down, and was now trying to figure out a way to tell Agent Holt that Trap wasn't going to stand trial, much less lead the feds anywhere near the source of the Mexican black tar. If Holt was the hard ass Black thought he was, he'd call off their deal on a technicality, namely that Trap was dead.

He backed off from the craps table after he'd won a couple grand. Some of the ladies wanted him to stay, and if things had gone right, he'd have hit one of them for sure. This was supposed to be a business trip in more ways than one, but he thought about how much fun he'd be having right now if that nigga Trap hadn't gotten himself shot down.

Black wandered over to the blackjack tables. There was a fine-looking bitch at one of them. That was something he really could have hit. But she was working a fat, old, white dude. He couldn't blame her. Bitch had to get paid, too. She had an exotic look like he'd never seen, but there was something familiar about her.

He circled back around and came behind her.

"Well, you have to do some wrong, once in a while," she was saying. "Otherwise, where's the fun in life?"

Oh, my God, thought Black as he recognized the voice. *Can a nigga be that lucky?* He stood there for a moment, within arm's reach of the bitch, and he just wanted to reach out, grab her by her new 'do, drag her out to the sidewalk and beat her bitch ass down. But he'd never get away with that shit in this crowd. In a casino, especially a classy joint like the Bellagio, just about every other person on the floor was security, and cameras watched every square inch of the place.

He'd have to wait and watch, follow her, and find his opening. The only question was, what would he do about the John? He could put him down easy enough, but was it worth the hassle? Maybe he could wait out the transaction, catch Red when she left. But there was always a chance he might miss her if he didn't keep his eye on her the whole time. He wasn't going to let that happen again. Not when he'd been within arm's length of the bitch twice in twenty-four hours and couldn't do shit about it either time. No, it was worth the hassle to take care of the John. *Muthafucka just in the wrong place at the wrong time,* he thought. *Life just be that way sometimes.*

Black stepped over to another blackjack table and angled himself so that he could pretend to watch the action on it while keeping an eye on Red in the background. Bitch had game. No doubt. The dude she was working was in heaven. Like Black's uncle always used to say, *cards fallin' right, ladies' pussy tight.* It wouldn't be long before he'd had enough of one and turned his full attention to the other.

An old dude at the table he was standing by made a big play, made twenty on five cards, and the table went crazy. Black saw Red look over her shoulder, and he ducked his head, hoping she wouldn't notice him.

Red was rubbing her first official John just right and knew she had the muthafucka just where she wanted him. And then the table behind her went into full party mode over something. She looked back to see what all the fuss was. She caught a glimpse of a nigga ducking his head just as she turned. She could have sworn he'd been scoping her the second before. She squinted and looked a little closer. She could only see the top of his head as he bent down to look at his shoes or some shit. There was something about the way he held himself, even in that position. And then he looked up again. Right at her.

Her heart skipped a beat. How could this shit be happening? She had transformed herself completely with Meme's help. So how was it that Black was standing right there in the mutha-fuckin' Bellagio casino, fifteen yards away, looking her square in the eye. That shit was not real. Black turned away again for a moment, but then he gave up trying to hide. The nigga knew she'd spotted him, and she knew he was on her ass.

For a moment she froze, without a single, muthafuckin' idea what to do. If Catfish and his runnin' buddies had bugged her house in Detroit, that explained how he got on her. But now in Vegas? How? Unless she was *wearing* a muthafuckin' bug. She thought about somebody fucking with her clothes. But everything was new since she ran to get away from Catfish. Did she having something stuck to her? Was that even possible? Something she swallowed? Did somebody slip some kind of tracking device into her drink at some point? But even if that was possible, who would have done it?

Her John continued to play on, not noticing how distracted she was. And she suddenly didn't give a fuck about him. Instead she began to scan the room for any other Detroit niggas who might be around. It suddenly felt like they were hunting her in packs, just like the coyotes in her nightmare. She didn't see any other familiar faces, but every time her eyes came back around to Black, he was still there, just staring at her, not even pretending to be sly about it.

Red slid away from the blackjack table and took a few steps to her right. Black moved that way, too. Not in a hurry. Like he didn't have a care in the world. He was just checking out the carpet. Then she moved to her left. Muthafucka did the same. She didn't think he'd try anything right in the middle of the casino, but you could never tell. Some niggas was just crazy. Catfish might have just blasted her right there. Bacon probably would have walked up to her and told her to leave with him—and as serious as that muthafucka was, she might have had to do it. Q? What would Q have done when he was back in the game? That nigga had his moments. He'd been known to slap a bitch around from time to time if she was acting up on him. And he wasn't afraid to go toe to toe with whoever else might be around to try to interfere. But Q was a smart nigga, too. He wouldn't cause a scene in the Bellagio.

So which kind was Black? He was street smart. But she wouldn't call him sophisticated. She had no idea what was in his mind at that moment.

She stepped backwards away from him, and he stepped toward her. So this dance could go on all night. She was going to have to make some kind of move. *What the fuck!* she thought. *When in doubt, run!*

She turned away from Black and took off into the crowd. She was afraid to look over her shoulder. She just kept going, dodging tables and drunks and parties, going for the front door. As she turned down the path between the slot machines, there was Black, waiting for her. *Muthafuckin' mind reader,* she thought.

She turned and started in the other direction. She faded to the right, then cut left toward the elevators. She had nowhere to go upstairs, but she was sure she could find a set of back stairs, or a service elevator, or a fire escape, or some shit that would get her down to the street where she could find some running room. She looked back long enough to see that Black had fallen for the move. He'd gone to his right, the long way around the slots. She reached the elevators and hit the button. She looked back again and saw Black coming. He wasn't running at a full sprint. He had to play it cool. Like he was hurrying to make a convention seminar. Not like he was running to kill some bitch. Nigga was gangsta, but not stupid enough to run full sprint after a made-up bitch. Security would jump his ass quick, but then they might try to question her.

Red jabbed at the elevator button over and over. "Come on, come on, come on, come on!" she said out loud.

The doors opened, she stepped on, and she jabbed at the button for the twentieth floor so hard she almost broke her finger. "Close, muthafucka," she said. "Close."

She could see Black put on a bit of a sprint. Then the doors started to close. They were moving much slower than Black. She pressed herself against the back of the elevator and closed her eyes. The doors closed with a ding. She felt the elevator start to move. And then she heard someone breathing hard, standing right in front of her. She swallowed hard. Then she opened her eyes.

"Wow!" said the pink-faced man in the Tommy Bahama shirt. "I barely made this one." He laughed.

"Oh," said Red, a big smile spreading across her face. "Yeah, you gotta be quick."

"Riiiiight," he said as he punched the twenty-third floor. "So, any luck this evening?"

Red shrugged. "Uh, yeah. Some."

CHAPTER TWENTY-FIVE

*C*hass pulled into the driveway of her mom's house in suburban Detroit. It always felt good coming home, even though this was not the home she'd grown up in. It was still her mom's house and contained a lot of the furniture and artwork that had always been around. And, most important, it was where her mother lived. She'd helped her mom buy this place after she'd gotten established in the law. It wasn't extravagant, but it was a nice house in a good neighborhood where her mom could go outside at night without worrying she was going to get shot by warring drug slingers or mugged by addicts.

As she walked up the path to the front door, she wondered about the possibilities of having her own home some day. She knew she was an attractive, desirable woman, and she'd had plenty of opportunities with men, but many of them found her too high powered. And then there was Q. He had her head spinning in a million different directions.

Her mom made them both tea with honey, and they sat on

the couch together and talked. Chass remembered with fondness all the hours she'd spent on that same couch as a kid, watching cartoons, and having talks with her mom about all the issues of life. Mom had always been someone she could talk to, so when she was troubled by Q's behavior, there was no question where she would go for counsel.

"I just wonder if I have a future with him," she said.

Her mother chuckled. "You've wondered if you have a future with any man."

"Well, I don't want to have a future with *just* any man. I'm not going to settle."

"The problem is that you don't *have* a future. You have to *make* a future." She put her hand on Chass's knee. "Question is, are you ready to do that?"

"Yes, of course. You don't think I want a family? A good man?"

"And you're not sure Q is that."

Chass tilted her head. "He comes from a pretty rough background."

"I remember him from around the neighborhood. He was no saint. That's true. But you say he's grown out of that."

"He's grown out of some things, and into others. I'm just not sure he has control of his emotions, his feelings. I'm afraid this medication they have him on is running away with him."

"Chass, you're not going to sit there and tell me you think it's easy to get shot. That you just pick up and go on with your life afterwards. There's some adjusting to do."

"Mom, I know that," said Chass as she leaned back and rubbed her eyes.

"You say he's a strong man, right?"

"Yes."

"Then he'll make his adjustments. But, now, look at me."

Chass sat up straight and turned to her mother.

"You do realize that you'll have to make some adjustments, too. It can't be all him, changing to suit your needs and wants. You ask a man to do that, you'll be waiting till judgment day and beyond. You have to bend into the shapes of each other's lives. Just because you have a law degree and you stand toe to toe with those big boys in the courtroom doesn't mean you can't compromise when it comes to love. I raised you to be powerful and strong, and you've done that, but it never hurts to at least pretend to be weak for a man."

Chass looked into her tea, shook her head, and smiled. "Oh, Mom, you cut through all my nonsense, don't you?"

"That what moms are for, dear. You'll find out one day when you have your own kids. One day soon, I hope."

"Yes, mother," said Chass, laughing. "I get the hint. Not too subtle."

As she drove home to get ready for dinner with Q, she thought about her mom's advice, wise as always. But there were things her mom didn't know about. She'd never told her mom much about Red. She didn't need to fill her mom's head with stories about that bitch.

Bitch or not, Red had something that Q had found very attractive. At one time, anyway. And she couldn't help wondering if he still felt anything positive for Red. He talked like he couldn't stand her, and for good reason. It wasn't every ex-lover who shot her man down. Still, there had been times when Q had mentioned her, even when he'd spoken angrily about her, that she could see something going on behind his eyes. There was a lot of history between them. Like he could still remember a time when there was something special between them, maybe more special than what she experienced with him now. Like maybe a time they got caught out in the rain. She lost her shoe, and when they got to cover, he ran back out to get it for her and slipped and fell on his ass. They laughed about it as they kissed each other's wet faces. Some romantic bullshit like that.

The point was that he had loved a woman like Raven Gomez at one time. *Raven Gomez!* Chass was nothing like Red. Never wanted to be, never would be. So what did Q see in her? Stability? Booooring! Success? Maybe. Ambition? She had plenty of that, but it kept her focused on her work more than most men wanted their women to be.

Q had loved Red. And he loved Chass. Or did he? He felt something for her. She was sure of that. But was it love? And is that what *she* felt for *him*? Could she even be happy with him not knowing if he fully loved her? She knew that he respected her, no doubt about it, and that he cared for her. Respect will keep a man from slapping her senseless, but only love will make him content to spend the rest of his life by her side.

By the time he pulled out her chair for her at Allegretti's, she still hadn't sorted it out. But Q was in a better mood than she'd seen him in for some time. A little nervous, which was unlike him, but playful and happy.

"Now I know I've been laid up for a while," he said as he settled into his own chair across from Chass. "But I do have money tucked away, so I don't want you pulling any of that lady lawyer stuff and trying to pick up the check."

"I will grant you the pleasure—the privilege . . ." she said playfully.

"Ah," said Q with a smile.

". . . of taking me to dinner."

"All right. It *will* be my pleasure. *And* privilege."

When Chass opened the menu and glanced at the prices, she saw why Q was making an issue of it. This was a very high-end restaurant and the fact that he'd been laid up meant it could have been a strain on his wallet. But she did know he had some money tucked away, and if he was in the mood to spend some of it, far be it for her to object.

Q had never really mentioned the argument they'd had about his use of Oxycodone, but he'd been treating her very nicely ever since. She felt he was making an apology in his own way. But the drug use still bothered her, and she'd been looking for a non-threatening way to discuss it with him. She realized that in their previous discussion she'd come across as accusatory rather than empathetic, but that was only because she'd been surprised by how much he'd been taking. The truth was, she was scared for him.

Maybe tonight, while he was in a good mood, she could just float the topic and see if he was receptive to talking about it.

When the waiter came and Q ordered a bottle of Pinot Grigio, Chass cringed a bit. *Should he be mixing wine with his meds?* she wondered. But she had to remind herself that, as her mom had said, he was a big boy and was making his own adjustments.

The menu was in Italian, and they laughed at each other's attempts to pronounce their orders. Q finally gave up completely on his. "I guess that means veal parmigiana, right?"

"Yes, sir," said the waiter, smiling.

"Okay then, however you pronounce it, that's what I'm gonna have."

"Very good, sir," said the waiter.

Q was very much at ease. When he asked where Chass had gone earlier, she told him she'd seen her mother. That brought up comparisons of their moms and ultimately led to swapping stories about their childhoods. Not their teenage years, but the lives they'd lived before there were any thoughts of hustlin', or making money, or growing up. Lives lived before they knew how hard life was going to get. They laughed and joked and quoted lines from old TV shows and tripped on their childhood clothing styles.

Before Chass knew it, the meal was over, and she figured the mood was too good to spoil with talk of anything remotely serious like prescription meds. That's when Q broadsided her.

"I did," she was saying. "I had the *Fat Albert and the Cosby Kids* lunchbox. I remember it had the—"

And then Q reached out and placed a black ring box on the table and held it in place.

"What's that?" asked Chass. She realized how stupid it sounded even as she said it.

Q reached forward with his other hand and lifted the lid on the box. The ring inside bore a large center diamond with a slightly smaller diamond on each side.

She sat transfixed by the sight of it until she realized Q was staring at her. She looked up and held his gaze.

He took a deep breath. "Now, you have to know that if it wasn't for this cane nonsense, I'd be down on one knee right now, but maybe it's actually better this way because I'll know you can take me with my faults."

Chass swallowed hard.

"Anyway, the words are the same if I'm sitting or kneeling."

"Words?" she said.

"Chass Reed, will you marry me?"

"Oh, my God, Q," she said and her eyes glistened. "Yes. Yes, I will Quentin Carter."

$\mathcal{A}$ month later Red didn't even know if it was safe to go back to her room at the Flamingo. All of Motown seemed to be moving on her. How the fuck were they tracking her? And how far did they have her narrowed down? Vegas, the Strip, the Flamingo, her room number?

Not her room number. Not as of the time she left Black's ass at the Bellagio casino at any rate. If Black or any other nigga had known that much, he'd have kicked in her door and taken her down already. But how did Black know she'd be in the Bellagio that night? Maybe he'd just been checking all the joints up and down the Strip and just gotten lucky. There was another alternative, but Red didn't even want to think about that.

The only person she knew in Vegas—the only one who could have dimed her—was Meme. But that just couldn't be. Meme had taught her so much and helped her get what she needed to survive. If Meme wanted to betray her, she could have done it days ago. Besides, why would she? Money? Could Black and his runnin' partners have put a bounty out on her? Possibly. After all, Meme was a straight player.

She thought about all the bitches she herself had stabbed in the back. But that had been business. If a bitch messed with you, you had to fuck her over. Red hadn't messed with Meme. Then again, what did she know about Meme? Maybe she was Kera's cousin out for payback. *Bitch, you just gettin' too paranoid now,* she thought. *There ain't no muthafuckin' way Kera and Meme came from the same bloodline.* Besides, Meme knew her room number. If she had put Black on her plans for the Bellagio, why not just point him to the room itself?

In the end, it didn't really matter. Bottom line, she couldn't completely trust Meme or anyone else at this point. But she was confident that her room was not blown. Yet. And she had cash stashed up there from the scams she and Meme had put down. Lots of cash.

She decided she had to risk going back to her room to collect it, along with her clothes, but she needed to be careful about it. She wasn't going to hang around. She had a cab driver drop her two blocks past the hotel, then she walked back. She entered through a side door and spent ten minutes surveying the lobby to make sure there were no Detroit niggas creeping around. Then she took the elevator up, got off two floors above her room, and took the stairs back down. She scooped everything into a single suitcase as quickly as she could. The cash she kept in the same Louis Vuitton bag she'd been carrying when she first met Meme. If she got caught out in the open and it turned into a foot chase, she could take the Louis Vuitton with her. The suitcase she'd have to ditch. She wanted the cash as portable as it could be.

When she was ready to go, she sat on the foot of the bed to catch her breath. She looked up and saw herself in the mirror. She shook her head. "The fuck is going on in your life?" she said. Had it come to the point where she couldn't trust anybody? Not even a fast friend like Meme? Was that the price she had to pay for all her back stabbin' and scammin'? She wondered if there would ever again be anybody in her life that she could trust.

Could there be one, solid nigga she could rely on? If it was anybody, it might be Q. He was a lot of things and had put up with a lot of Red's shit. But when he had the chance to put her in for shooting him, he didn't take it. *Q wouldn't come after me like that*, she thought. Then she looked at herself in the mirror again and laughed. It was pathetic. Now she was measuring how much trust she could put in a nigga by whether or not he'd come after her after she shot him. She really was cracking up. She had to get a grip. She had to get someplace where she could clear her muthafuckin' head, plant her feet on the ground, and get some balance. And right now was the time to get there.

She stood up and grabbed the Louis Vuitton and the suitcase. She didn't check her messages or make any calls. And she didn't check out of her room. Nothing to raise any dust. She did, however, slip into a janitor's closet and steal a screwdriver and a pair of pliers.

She wheeled her suitcase across the Strip, hailed a cab, and had the driver drop her near one of the smaller casinos. She found a standard production model Honda Accord in the parking lot. Meme had told her it was one of the most commonly stolen cars on the American road. And she knew that many serious gamblers spent hours at low-end casinos, sometimes settling into serious, all-night poker games. If she rolled out in the Accord, she might just get to her destination before the owner even knew it was missing.

She used the screwdriver and the pliers to crack the steering column and force the ignition. She rolled out of the lot, checking to make sure nobody came screaming out of the casino. And then she was on the road.

It was risky driving a stolen car. Getting pulled over could be a career ender. But she figured once she got out of Vegas, she'd be safer. In fact, traveling the desert at night was as safe as this shit was going to get. And it was a risk she had to take. Somehow she had to shake off the pack of niggas hounding her ass.

Get your muthafuckin' ass to Mexico, bitch. That was her thought. That was her plan. After all, Mexico was the classic hideout. And a bitch who had some brains could find ways to get her life happening down there. No doubt. Whether it was drugs, stealing, tricking, scamming, enterprising, or whatever, she would do what it took. She'd had time with Meme to gather herself, get ID for the hotel check-ins, all the necessary shit. Besides, Mexico was a place Q always wanted to go. She thought maybe she'd feel close to him down there. Maybe she'd find a piece of his soul in some little beach town. Maybe she could reclaim her own.

But to get down there, she had to make a stop elsewhere first. Crossing the border in a stolen car? That *would* be foolish. No, she'd have to lay up somewhere and make some more money so she could buy a car. Or find some sugar daddy who'd give her one. Where could she make money? Where could she find a sugar daddy? The place for Red—the only logical place—was Cali. And not just any place in Cali. It had to be Southern. And even more specifically, it had to be Beverly Hills. There was lots of money there. And it was the home of the ultimate sugar daddy, Hugh Hefner. Even though Hef never seemed to lust after her particular complexion, he put Beverly Hills on the map as the sugar daddy capital of the world.

All these thoughts swirled through Red's mind as she drove on. In the night desert, she lost all sense of time and speed. She constantly had to watch the speedometer. The last thing she wanted to do at this point was get pulled over by some *Electra Glide in Blue* muthafucka. The dark landscape brought back memories of her nightmare. When she looked to either side of the car, she imagined she could see coyotes out there waiting for her, or paralleling the car at a flat out run.

To make matters worse, the muthafucka she stole the car from was a country music fan. His CDs were all twangy noise with no bottom. She flung each disc out the window as she rejected them one by one. No matter. Once she got over the mountains, she picked up some FM out of L.A. West Coast niggas were tight. She rocked to Xzibit, Snoop, even some vintage Tupac. But then she had to watch that speedometer again, 'cause the beat was pushing her foot down.

She drove for what felt like forever. Never having driven to Beverly Hills, she let the music take her there. She thought about every distant memory, the ones she still embraced, like Q, and the memories she wished to God she could forget. The sun may rise in the East, but that night, as she drove west, Red understood where her new day was dawning. Way off in the distance, there was a brightness in the sky. And she knew that under that bright spot was the glittering city of L.A., a city of dreams and possibility. Hopefully the sun would shine with grace on her new future.

CHAPTER TWENTY-SEVEN

*C*hass turned away from her mother and reached into her purse for her ringing phone. She looked at the caller ID and smiled as she flipped it open. "Hi, baby."

"What's up, almost-Mrs.-Carter? Or is it almost-Mrs.-Reed-Carter?"

Chass laughed and took a few steps off toward a quiet corner, away from the excited hum of the bridal store. "Well, just for the business cards. I don't want to confuse my clientele too much."

"All right," he said. "I can see that. So what you up to?"

"I'm with my two helpers—your mom and my mom. I'm trying on gowns. There are some beautiful things here. And how about you? What are you doing?"

"Me? Chillin'. Bored."

"Aww, I'm sorry, baby."

"How 'bout I come down there and meet you? See what you're picking out?"

"What? Are you crazy? Q, you know it's bad luck for a groom to see his bride in her dress before the wedding. Don't jinx us!"

"I've seen you in your birthday suit. What's the difference?"

Chass looked around to make sure no one was listening. Then she lowered her voice. "And you're going to see me in my birthday suit again in a few hours. *If* you're a good boy."

"Oh, well, if I'm good, what's the point of seeing you in your birthday suit?"

"Hush," said Chass, fighting back her laughter. "If you're bad, I'm going to have to file motions on you all night."

"Mmm. I promise I can be a very cooperative witness."

"I'm going to make you raise your right arm. And some other parts too."

"I do solemnly swear I'm going to really get into your opening. Argument, I mean."

Chass put her hand over her mouth and just about doubled over. "Okay, we have to stop now before we get into full blown phone sex right here in the middle of the bridal store. See, I *told* you you were bad."

"So, lock me up and give me my conjugal visit."

Chass looked up and saw Q's mom waving her over and holding up another dress for her to look at—white satin with a medium V cut, lace cuffs. "Oh, okay, Mrs. Carter. I'll be—it's your son on the phone. We were just—uh—making plans for this evening."

Q laughed into the phone.

"I got to go," whispered Chass. Then she flipped the phone shut.

Lying on the couch in his mother's house, Q set his phone on the coffee table, a big smile on his face. But the smile soon faded to a wistful look, then to a frown. The wedding was to be a small one, just a few guests, but one fewer than he would have liked. Zeke and he had promised that they would be best men at each other's weddings. Zeke was his nigga, his brother in a very real sense. The term *best man* had been made to describe Zeke. But now he was dead.

Q stood and walked into the kitchen to grab a Coke, leaving his cane propped against the couch. He still needed it much of the time, but he was happy to be able to walk short distances in the house without it. His injuries were healing, his pain was under control with the help of the Oxycodone, and his life seemed to be in better order than it had been for many years. But he couldn't convince himself that everything was all right.

He'd had a lot of crazy ideas about Zeke's death, but he still didn't know for sure exactly what had happened to him. He hated the idea of losing him, but he'd been able to let it go, in a sense. He was gone. Left up out of this bitch. Live like a thug, die like a thug. One of the great truths of the street.

The nearly new, two-liter bottle of Coke hissed as he turned the cap. He carefully poured the soda over a huge cup of ice, then replaced the cap and headed back to the living room, a slight hitch in his step. He wanted a beer instead of soda, but the one thing he had promised Chass was that he would take it easy on the alcohol if he was going to keep using the pills. He'd always been a man who kept his promises, and now was no time to stop doing that.

Settling back into the couch, he let himself dwell on Zeke a little longer. He smiled as he wondered if Zeke would have approved of Chass, and what he would have said if he didn't. He didn't have any problem letting Q know what he thought of Red and her scandalous ways. Q laughed out loud at the thought of how wound up Zeke got about Red. He was one to tell it like it was. But that didn't mean he was always right.

Zeke didn't know Red the way Q did. The fact was, that girl had been through some shit in her life. It was amazing to him that she could suffer all the damage she had and still be so full of life, so funny, so exciting. There was something to admire in that. He'd seen a lot of people beat down by life. Some of them folded, and some of them rose above.

That was one thing Chass and Red had in common. Chass came from some humble beginnings. And she'd made it all the way to the big time. Just like Red. Well, Red had taken the back staircase to the top floor. But could he blame her? With the way her stepfather had treated her, and the way her mother responded to it, she'd been trained to believe in a backwards golden rule: Do unto other muthafuckas before they muthafuckin' do unto you. As far as her world was concerned, she had it right.

God damn, thought Q. *Bitch could do whatever it took to take care of herself. And she could still give a nigga some good love.*

Two days later, Q did see Chass in her wedding dress. He stood next to her in the courthouse, surrounded by a few of her friends and a couple of his, and both his and Chass's mothers. He had skipped the best man thing. His best man wasn't there. Simple as that.

As he exchanged vows with his bride, he thought about the fact that he really didn't feel any magic. He felt—safe. He was going to have a safe and simple life. After all he'd been through, that didn't seem so bad. It wasn't magic, but it was good. It was fine. He'd be—just—fine.

"Mexico, here we come," said Chass as Q drove them away from the courthouse.

Mexico, thought Q. *That's something magical.* He'd always wanted to go there. With Red. His heart beat a little faster as old feelings mixed with new possibilities.

"Slow down, Q," said Chass. "You don't want to get us killed before the honeymoon even begins."

Q looked down at the speedometer and realized he was pushing it pretty hard. "Damn," he said. "My bad. I didn't realize how fast I was going."

"It's okay. But we've got plenty of time to make our flight. We just need to stop by your mom's place to change and get our bags, and we'll still get to the airport a couple of hours before departure. That's plenty for an international flight."

"Okay, and we also need to make time for a quick stop at the drive-thru."

Chass smirked. "We could have had a reception. Then you wouldn't be so hungry."

"We talked about that. We wouldn't have made this flight. We would've had to wait till tomorrow. Besides, a reception after a courthouse marriage?"

"Q, I'm just teasing you. I want to get on with the honeymoon as bad as you do. And, yes, we can stop at Mickey D's. Just make sure you pop a breath mint afterwards. Oh, and I almost forgot."

"What's that?" said Q.

"I've got a special wedding gift for you."

Q glanced over at her. "I hope so."

She swatted at his arm playfully. "Yeah, I got some of that for you too, but this is different."

"Okay, is it at the house?"

"Mmm, no. It's just something I can tell you about. You won't actually get it till after the honeymoon."

Q smiled. "Oh, okay. Which model of Mercedes did you envision me in?"

"No, no. It's something better than that."

"Bentley?"

"No, this is serious now."

"I'm just clowning. I'm sure it's wonderful if it comes from you. So . . . What is it?"

"Okay, you know I have lots of contacts."

Q furrowed his brow. "Contacts? Okay."

"And, based on my recommendation, you've been offered a job working in an investigative unit at a law firm."

Q turned to her again and stared until he started to swerve into another lane.

"Q, watch the road, please," said Chass.

Q straightened up and regained control of the car. "You mean I'm going to be like a cop?"

"No," said Chass, rolling her eyes. "This firm does defense work. You'll be helping keep people out."

"Yeah, by putting somebody else in."

"Honey, no. Trust me. It doesn't work like that. Not at that level, anyway. It's just looking at the evidence. Finding witnesses who contradict other witnesses. I mean . . . Damn! I thought you'd be pleased. It's legit work. And it's not great money to start, but it can turn into something. It's a new start."

Q drove in silence for several blocks. Chass had a different set of values than he did. Not bad values. Just different. Some of the things she had in her world, he wanted for himself. And other things he wasn't so sure about. But either way, he knew she was just trying to do something good for him. She really did care about his life, his future, his success. "Yeah, uh . . ." he said. "Naw, you're right, baby. I just—like you said, it's all new. This kind of stuff is a different way of seeing the world. But, yeah, that's something that could work out for me. I mean, I know the streets. I know the kind of people'd be in that kind of situation. Needin' help like that. Yeah, I could see that for me."

"For real?" said Chass.

He glanced at her again and smiled. "Yeah. Thank you. I appreciate your help in finding some legit work."

Q could tell she was still hurt, so he tried to lighten the mood. "And, actually, I got a gift for you, too."

CHAPTER TWENTY-EIGHT

*R*ed had reached L.A. well before sunrise. She drove around for a while, checking out the area, and when she found herself somewhere near the heart of the city, she turned down a side street. She had no idea where she was, but it seemed like a quiet, safe neighborhood, a perfect place to catch some sleep. In order to meet her goal of making it to Mexico, she was determined to save as much money as she could, so she didn't bother with a hotel room. She could sleep in the Accord until the sun came up in a few hours, then figure out what her first move in SoCal should be.

In her dreams that night, she was standing on a balcony looking out at the Pacific Ocean. The breeze carried the salt sea scent to her nose and blew back her hair, which was once again its natural reddish tint. A bright sun shone down on the ocean making it sparkle like a sea of diamonds all the way from the waves below her to the horizon far out to the west.

And then a large bird flew close to her. It glowed with a blue

"Oh," said Chass, brightening. "Is it bigger than a bread box?"

He looked down at his lap. "Well, not quite that big. But almost."

Chass laughed. "I think you have a somewhat inflated opinion of yourself."

"I'm *gonna* be inflated. Matter of fact, I think I'm gonna be inflated while we're changing clothes at the house."

"Oh, really? You think we have ninety seconds to spare?"

"Naw, you're right. We're gonna have to skip the foreplay."

light and gave a loud, piercing cry. It was so loud, in fact, that it woke her up. As she came awake in the back of the Accord, she was startled to find the blue lights of a police car strobing through the interior of her makeshift bedroom, its siren whooping as it drifted into position beside her.

Muthafucka, she thought. *The fuck was I thinkin', sleeping in a stolen car?* A million thoughts went through her head. She could bail and run, leaving the suitcase filled with her shoplifted goods behind, but then she'd be right back at square one with nothing. She could bail and try to take the suitcase with her. It had wheels, right? She might be able to outrun a cop pulling a suitcase with wheels. No way. That was a fantasy. She could speak to the officer and try to con him. All she was was a homeless woman who'd found the car parked there and wanted a place to sleep. Bullshit. He'd see through that in a heartbeat. She was fucked.

But when she looked to her left she saw that the cop wasn't stopping. He had slowed, but was moving past her. A guy in a Porsche had pulled to the curb several yards beyond, and the cop pulled in behind him.

Popo had no interest in her. Not for now, anyway. But it was definitely time to leave the comfortable confines of the stolen car and put some distance between it and her. She slung her bag over her shoulder, grabbed the handle of her suitcase, and slid out of the car on the curb side. She patted the top of the car. "You done good, baby," she said. Then she turned and walked in the opposite direction from the cop.

She took a left, then a right without paying much attention to where she was going. She didn't really care. New town, new beginning. It felt like a clean break. And the dream had to be a good omen. A balcony overlooking an ocean full of wealth and endless possibilities. And a horizon to the west. Detroit was behind her. Arizona was behind her. Vegas was behind her. And

Catfish and Black and all those other Detroit niggas? They were behind her, too. In fact, they were in just the right position to kiss her fine, black ass.

And then she began to lift her head up and look around. This was a very nice street with some classy shops. When she got to the next corner, she looked at the street sign. A huge smile spread across her face. *If this ain't a good omen, I don't know what is,* she thought. *Rodeo muthafuckin' Drive.*

Bentleys, Maseratis, and Lamborghinis rolled past shops like Yves St. Laurent, Jimmy Choo, Montblanc Boutique, Bulgari, Prada, Bernini, Louis Vuitton, José Eber Salon, Tiffany & Co. Beverly Hills. It just seemed to go on and on. Like the shimmering ocean in her dream. All the way to the horizon—the end of the earth.

This was where she wanted to be, not Mexico. *One step at a time, bitch,* she thought. She knew she couldn't just make it from scratch in a place like this, but if she got her ass down to Mexico and made some shit happen for her down there, she'd be back. In the meantime, she was going to soak up as much of Beverly Hills as she could.

She wanted to walk into one of the grand hotels in the neighborhood and check into their finest suite, but she was going to stick to her plan of economizing for now, so that she could come back better and stronger in the future. There were lots of people out and about on Rodeo Drive, but asking one of them where to find a cheap room didn't seem like a good idea. She could just imagine some fat, old guy in a Bentley thinking she was hookin' with a question like that. On the other hand, she knew exactly who she *could* talk to. Even in a place like Beverly Hills, there were down to earth folks. Rich people always need common folks to wait on them. Service people. Housekeepers, waiters, bartenders, cooks. They'd give her the straight shit without turning up their noses at her.

On the sidewalk half a block down from the Luxe Hotel, she found a couple of busboys wearing Luxe name tags, taking a smoke break. They were both about eighteen. She knew she was disheveled from sleeping in the car, but she was wearing Fendi and didn't look completely out of place. "Excuse me," she said as she approached the kids. "Do you work at the Luxe?"

One of them looked her up and down, looked at her bags, then pointed up the sidewalk. "The lobby is over there." His name tag said *Francisco.*

"Oh, thank you," she said. "I don't know how I got so turned around. I'm, uh, new in town."

"First time in Beverly Hills?" said the other kid in a thick Mexican accent. He stood and smiled. He was much friendlier than the first guy.

Red giggled and eyed his name tag. "Yes, actually, Roberto. It's a bit overwhelming."

"Don't worry about it," he said. "You want me to walk you over there? I'll show you right where the entrance is."

"Actually, I was thinking of staying here at the Luxe, but I was also wondering if there was someplace more—well— economical in the neighborhood."

He turned to his friend and they began speaking Spanish, not realizing she could understand every word they were saying.

"I think she's a whore," said Francisco.

"Fuck you," said Roberto. "She's not a whore. Look at her clothes."

"She looks kind of fucked up."

"Shut up. She's been traveling. She looks a lot better than you, you ugly fucker. She just wants to find a cheap place to stay."

Francisco shrugged. "Tell her she can stay on my cock."

Red had to suppress a laugh.

"That's your problem," said Roberto, shaking his head. "You

don't know how to treat a lady. That's why you don't have a girl-friend."

"Suck my dick."

Roberto turned to Red and switched to English. "Yeah, we're trying to think of a place near here." He turned back to his friend and switched to Spanish again. "Where does that ugly bitch work?"

"Who?"

"That ugly bitch with the crossed eyes and the glasses. The one Manolito used to fuck?"

"Which one?" said Francisco. "He fucks a lot of ugly whores."

"The girl who works as a housekeeper at that hotel over there." He pointed beyond Rodeo Drive. "What's the name of that hotel?"

Francisco thought about it, then nodded slowly. "Oh, yeah. That ugly bitch who steals the toilet paper from the hotel. Why does she do that, man? She can't even afford toilet paper?"

"No, man, she used to steal all kinds of shit from the last hotel she worked in. She stole stuff from the guests' rooms. But she got busted, so she don't do that no more."

"Fuck," said Francisco. "What kind of shit did she get?"

"Oh, man! Everything. All kind of jewelry, watches, clothes. One time when I was over at her place I bought a necktie. She had a whole bunch of 'em."

"You're full of shit," said Francisco. "You never wore a neck-tie. You can't even *tie* a necktie."

"Fuck you. What's the name of the hotel?"

"Del Flores."

"Right," said Roberto. He turned to Red and spoke to her in English. "There's a place three blocks from here that's nice, but has crazy cheap rooms. I mean, for this neighborhood. Hotel Del Flores." He hitched his thumb over his shoulder at the building behind them. "I mean, it's not as nice as the Luxe, or L'Ermitage, or someplace like that, but it's a cool place. You know, like, what's the word . . . ? Charming."

Red gestured in the direction Roberto pointed. "And it's just three blocks this way?"

"Yeah," he said. "Just go to the corner, take a right on Brighton Way, go three blocks to North Crescent, and take a left. You can't miss it."

CHAPTER TWENTY-NINE

*R*oberto was right. Hotel Del Flores was a cozy place with modestly appointed rooms. It didn't have the glamour of some of its more famous neighbors, but Red didn't care. It fit into her plan perfectly. She was in Beverly Hills, and she was making it all work toward getting down to Mexico.

The next day she dressed in YSL and Gucci, selected her Louis Vuitton bag and Prada sunglasses, and got ready to work. Even dressed as she was, when she looked in the mirror she saw what Francisco the busboy had been talking about. She did look fucked up. Meme's makeover was coming undone. The new 'do was a mess, and her eyes looked tired. She spent several minutes on her hair and managed to make it into something presentable. For a moment she thought about Detroit and Divas hair salon. She smirked at herself in the mirror. What she wouldn't have given to be able to spend an hour there. Not just to get her hair done, but to hear all the shit those bitches were talking about her.

She chuckled and spoke out loud to the image in the mirror.

"Red, Raven, whatever the fuck your name is, you gonna be all right, girl. Fuck Motown. You're on to bigger and better shit now. West Coast style."

She was ready to work. She walked the three blocks back to Rodeo and began browsing the merchandise. Security in some of the stores was a little too heavy for her, even with all the tricks Meme had taught her, but she found enough easy pickings to shoplift and managed to acquire a few very nice pieces.

She took a spin through Cartier just for the fun of it. Their security was far too tight to risk doing anything, but she knew she'd be back this way some day, so she wanted to do a little window shopping for future reference. She spent fifteen minutes daydreaming amid the sparkling diamonds, remembering her dream of a couple nights earlier. Then she figured it was time for lunch. She wanted to treat herself to something decadent, something sweet and rich.

She stepped out onto Rodeo again and turned left. She'd only taken a few steps when she heard a familiar, feminine voice behind her.

"Red? I can't believe my eyes!"

Red turned and saw a glamorous Amazon mincing towards her, dressed to the nines, every hair in place. Her heart skipped a beat. Another ghost of her dead Motown past rose up before her. She looked around quickly to see if she was accompanied by any of the thuggish Detroit niggas both of them knew. But she was alone. Red took a couple of wobbly steps forward, relieved, mouth gaping in astonishment. "Foxy? What the . . . ?"

Foxy strode forward, chin in the air, hands fluttering beside her artificially smiling face. "What are you doing here, girl-friend?" She leaned forward and air-kissed Red.

"I was going to ask you the same thing."

"Darling," said Foxy, "I am in my element. This is exactly where I should be."

Bullshit, you tranny ho, thought Red. *You belong in the gutter.* "You—you moved out here?"

Foxy furrowed her brow. "Mm-mm. Naw, baby. I'm out here on a girls' trip. Just me and some of my best and most loyal girlfriends from the Motor City, you know." She put extra emphasis into the word *loyal.*

Red saw a flash of contempt on her face, poorly hidden by a friendly smile at the end of her sentence. She looked around again, wondering if she might know any of the girls Foxy was traveling with, but she seemed to be alone at the moment. "Is Terry with you?"

"Terry? No, hadn't you heard?"

"Heard what?"

"Oh, she and Mekel got in all kinds of trouble with Child Protective Services. Word I got was that somebody filed a false report of child abuse against them. They had to give up Mekel Junior altogether. Can you imagine?" This time Foxy lowered her head and looked at Red from under her brow, dropping the smile completely.

"Damn," said Red. "Well, you know Terry. She always did like to fuck with a bitch. She must have an enemy who just refused to let her get away with her shit."

Now Foxy was practically sneering. "Do tell. Anyway, them two moved down to Tennessee. Mekel's peeps are down there. He wanted to be around some friendly, supportive folks for a change."

Red's pretense at friendliness was wearing thin, too. "I guess some niggas just can't handle shit."

"Oh, they's still some niggas who know how to take care of business. 'Course Bacon locked up again. He got some unfinished business on the outside. That's for damn sure."

Red tilted her head. "Well, I don't know, Foxy. It's hard to see

Bacon standing up like a man when he doesn't even know a real woman when he sees one. You feel me? *Girl?*"

"Bacon know what he like," said Foxy, putting both hands on her hips. "He can tell a glamorous goddess when he see one. And by the way, as one lady to another, you might want to look at yourself in the mirror. I hear there are some very fine West Coast salons. You might want to make an appointment. Frankly, you don't quite look like the neighborhood." She waved her hands around at the fine shops and richly dressed people passing by on the sidewalks.

Red had had enough of Foxy's bullshit. "I suppose I'm letting myself slip into a more casual mode. I thought I'd let my hair down for my trip to Acapulco. And where are you off to after this? Back to your raggedy ass crib in Motown?"

"Raggedy ass, nothin'," said Foxy wagging her head. "My crib where all the action go down, bitch. You know that. When the other bitches can't do what they men need, my door is always open. Just like it was for Bacon."

"I hope they each left ten dollars on your dresser."

Foxy took a step back and let her arms hang at her side. "Oh, no you didn't. You know I ain't afraid to throw down with your skanky ass."

Red placed her bag beside her. "Nuh-uh. I don't want to have to fuck-up your face. I know how much money you spent on those hormone treatments to get it looking so feminine." Then she squinted and leaned forward to examine her more closely. "Sort of."

An elegantly dressed man with long gray hair stepped out of Cartier. "Excuse me, ladies. Is there a problem here?"

Red smiled at Foxy. "You here that? He thinks you're a lady." But she knew she'd drawn enough attention for now, especially because she had a bag of shoplifted merchandise at her feet. She picked it up. "All right, girl. Let's get together for drinks real soon."

"You better hope I don't see you around, bitch."

Red walked away, glancing over her shoulder to blow Foxy a kiss.

Foxy watched her go, then turned up her nose at the man from Cartier as she strolled past him. As she walked back to her car, Foxy swallowed hard and tried to keep it together. Red knew how to cut a bitch to the bone with her tongue. She'd have to remember to let all the niggas back in Detroit know where she'd seen her.

Foxy climbed into her rented Lexus, alone. There was no girls' trip to paradise. Her business in L.A. had nothing to do with fun and games and glamour. But she'd be damned if she was gonna come all the way out here and not take a stroll down Rodeo Drive, the most fabulous street in the world. The previous day she'd spent some time on the Hollywood Walk of Fame. She'd seen all the stars—Joan Crawford, Carole Lombard, and, of course, Marilyn Monroe. The day before that, she'd taken the tour at Universal.

She'd done everything she could to distract herself from the real reason for her visit. But now the time had come. She couldn't put it off any longer. She entered the address in the car's GPS and pulled out into traffic. She followed the directions the GPS voice gave her. The closer she got to her destination, the faster her heart beat. Finally, the GPS said, "Your destination is thirty yards ahead. Turn right into the driveway."

She looked up at the imposing, grey building and read its sign—UCLA MEDICAL CENTER. Her eyes began to water, but she took a deep breath and held it together.

Inside, she found a ladies' room and checked herself in the mirror. She used a bit of toilet paper to dab at her eyes. What did she have to be afraid of? She lifted her chin. She was the picture of glamour and could give any of these Hollywood starlets a run for their money. She'd become what she wanted to be, the person she had always been inside. Red's words had stung her more than she wanted to admit, but she was determined to be strong now.

When she got off the elevator on the fourth floor, she found her way to the nurses' station. The place was busy. A beautiful, cocoa-skinned young girl was on the phone relaying information from some doctor. Her voice had a charming quality. Foxy wistfully thought the two of them could be friends. They'd go out to a club together and find a couple of men to buy them drinks. They'd laugh and dance and party all night. *'Cause Foxy's all about the fun,* she thought.

Finally the girl hung up, and Foxy leaned in over the counter. "Excuse me, honey, can you tell me what room Edward Morse is in?"

The girl smiled. "Sure," she said, in a Southern California accent. "Are you family?"

"Yes, I'm his—his—his child."

She cocked her head. "Oh, I wasn't aware that he had any daughters. Well, it's 412. To your left and around the corner."

Foxy pointed down the hall toward her left for confirmation. She realized her hand was trembling and pulled it back quickly. She walked down the hall, her high heels clicking on the hard, white floor. She stood in front of room 412 for several long seconds, then she pushed the door open.

Her father lay propped up in bed with IVs in his arms and an oxygen tube under his nose. He looked old and gaunt. His hair was white. The TV was on, but he was staring at the wall off to the side.

Foxy stepped into the room and stood at the foot of his bed. "Hello?" she said.

He turned slowly and looked at her, then squinted. "Hello. Who are you?"

She took a deep breath. "Daddy?"

His eyes grew wide, and his mouth turned down at the corners. "What? Who . . . ?"

"Daddy, it's—it's David."

Her father stared at her for several seconds, then spoke in a low, guttural voice. "Oh, my God! You went and did it. You went and did it, didn't you?"

Foxy put her hand on the blanket covering her father's calf. She felt how wire-thin he'd become. "Daddy, I grew up into who I was supposed to be."

"Oh, hell no," he said. "You were supposed to be my son. You *were* my son." He shook his head. "And now look at you. You're . . ."

"I did look at me, Daddy. I looked at myself in the mirror just before I came in here. I'm a glamorous lady." She jutted her chin and swallowed hard, determined not to let him see any tears. "Can't you see that? Can't you see how lovely I am?"

"No! No, I don't. I see how sick you are, boy."

Foxy stiffened and her voice grew stronger. "Daddy, I am *not* a boy. I am a lady."

"You're sick. You always been sick. That day I caught you playing with that boy Reese? I had to run to the bathroom and puke my muthafuckin' guts out."

"That's your limitation, Daddy."

"I tried to fix you. I paid one hundred dollars for the prettiest ho I could find, and I told her to take care of you."

"Daddy, I couldn't do that. Don't you know?"

"Yeah, I know. She told me. She laughed at you, boy. Afterward. After she came out into the front room. Did you know that? Huh?"

Foxy swallowed again and gritted her teeth for a moment. "I heard her from my bedroom." She remembered how the sound of that laughter had stung her.

"Don't you have any shame at all?" He looked her up and down. "I mean, when you was a teenager, at least you went around in secret. I can't believe you go out in public looking like that."

"This is who I am, Daddy. This is who I've always been on the inside."

"Why are you even here? To make me sicker?"

"Aunt Jean told me about—the . . ."

He nodded vigorously. "Cancer. You can say it. Colon cancer. See, *that* ain't nothin' to be ashamed of. Sometimes God gives you something you don't like, but it's natural. That's the way God wants it. And that's just the way it is. You don't fight God, boy."

"I'm not a—" Foxy shook her head. "Daddy, I just wanted to see you before . . ."

"Well, I don't want to see you. Not like this." He began groping for something on his bed.

Foxy took a step forward. "Can I help you with something?"

"Stay the fuck away from me. I don't want you anywhere near me." Finally he found the call button and pressed it with all his might.

"Daddy, it's still me. It's just the me I was supposed to be."

The lovely nurse Foxy had spoken with before breezed into the room from behind her. "Mr. Morse? What do you need?" She sounded so concerned. So compassionate.

"I need you got get this—this *thing* out of my room," he said, sneering at Foxy.

"I'm sorry?" said the nurse.

"Yeah! You heard me. I want that thing out of here."

She turned to Foxy, a look of sympathy in her eyes. "I'm sorry. I'm going to ask you to leave, ma'am."

"No," he shouted. "That ain't no *ma'am*. That's a boy. Supposed to be anyway. My son. But he had it chopped off. Can you believe that? Can you believe a man would do that to his self?"

"Good-bye, Daddy," said Foxy. "That's all I wanted to say. I just wanted to say good-bye to you."

"Get out!" he screamed.

Foxy stumbled out of the room and slumped against the wall in the hallway. The tears gushed out, but she held a fist to her mouth to keep from making any noise her father might be able to overhear. She felt a hand on her shoulder and looked up to see the nurse, that look of compassion and caring in her eyes.

CHAPTER THIRTY

*H*ow many times I gotta tell you this," Detective Thomas said into his cell phone. It was noon and he was pacing back and forth in an empty spot in the parking lot of La Quinta. "Catfish is gone."

"Maybe he's just out," said Agent Holt, who was still back in Detroit. "He could have hooked up with a girl."

"I looked in his room," said Thomas. "He didn't check out, but all his shit is gone. His suitcase, his clothes, everything."

There was silence on the line.

"Holt?" said Thomas.

"Why did we send you out there in the first place? To keep an eye on Catfish."

"*We?* Is this suddenly an FBI operation? I thought it was your own personal career move."

"I *am* the FBI."

"Army of one, huh? All I know is you put a thug who should have been in prison out on the street to do your work for you, and, *surprise,* he disappeared on your ass. And this is *not* on me. You heard?"

"You think he found Red and went off to take care of business without you?"

Thomas wiped sweat off the back of his neck. Arizona was a hot muthafucka. "I don't know. I honestly think he just got tired of looking for her. Got bored."

"Well, what could he be doing now?" said Holt.

"What?" said Thomas, stopping dead in his tracks. "He's a player. What you think he's doing?"

Holt sighed into the phone. "All right, listen. Things are fluid. We just have to roll with it. There's something else you can do for us."

"I know. I'm still trying to find Red."

"Yeah, but something else, too."

Oh, shit, here it comes, thought Thomas.

"There was a development in Vegas," said Holt.

"Development? What development?"

"Trap pulled a gun on a cop."

"No shit? So don't tell me. He's locked up in Vegas and you want me to go babysit him now."

"Nope. He's dead. That leaves Black floating around on his own, and I don't like that idea."

"A cop shot Trap, and Black got away?"

"Yeah, and he hasn't checked in yet. I imagine he's pretty freaked out about it. Probably thinks we might take back our deal with him, now that Trap is dead."

"Would you?"

Holt laughed into the phone. "Fuck yes. If it's easier that way."

"You're kidding me."

"Hey, the deal was he gives us Trap. Do we have Trap?"

"You have his ass on a slab."

"Yeah, but we don't have the connect. That's what having Trap was all about."

Muthafucka, thought Thomas. *He wouldn't think twice about draggin' my ass through the gutter if he doesn't get what he wants from me.* "So Black is fucked. Why you sending me?"

"He might have a chance to redeem himself. Like I said, situation's fluid. We've got to roll with it. Soon as I track down Black, I'll smooth him out. Make him believe everything is cool with us. Then I'll send him your way to assist with finding Red. And maybe Catfish if you can get a line on him. In the meantime, just do what you can on your own."

Thomas flipped his phone shut and walked toward his car, shaking his head and muttering to himself. "Federal mutha-fucka."

Catfish checked into his new room, #670, at the Royal Palms Resort using cash. He had money of his own, but it was funny as fuck living on the federal dime for a while. That Detroit PD ass-hole got on his nerves, though. Big Dick Thomas. Always trying to tell him what to do, act like he had him figured out. He didn't have nothin' figured out. He was just another dumb Detroit cop.

The room was nice. It was big, with a huge muthafuckin' bathroom and a nice, big-screen TV. It overlooked the pool too, so he could check out all the bitches in they bikinis before he even went down there. He opened a Heineken from the mini fridge and stepped out onto the balcony. In the heat he unbut-toned his shirt and let the breeze blow it back behind him. It felt good. And the view was nice. White, black, brown, all kinda bitches was laying out by the pool. Dimes. A few anyway. There were a couple of fat, middle-aged cows, too. *Damn*, he thought. *Why Oprah don't tell them bitches they can't be hangin' out all over the place like that. Rolls of fat drippin' off the lounge chairs and shit. Go inside and sit by your damn bathtub.*

Red was in the wind. All right. No big thing. He'd keep his

eyes open for the bitch, but he had other business to get on with. After spending so much time in the system, he had to get his shit set up again. And he knew exactly how to do it. His partner Ernie Banks had stayed connected in Detroit while Catfish was in the joint. He knew all about Bacon's business and had a direct line to his connect in Mexico.

That nigga knew all the angles. He even got some wiretap shit into Red's crib in Detroit. He listened to everything she said and reported it to Catfish. He nearly choked on a swig of beer as he remembered the way Red's voice trembled when he called her from her very own front doorstep. She must of thought he was some kind of Sherlock Muthafukin' Holmes. It was crazy luck that she ended up in Arizona. He had to be down there anyway so he could hop over to Mexico. She was a slippery bitch. She had some moves. For real. But he'd get back with her again someday. He held up his two taped fingers and flexed the ones on either side.

His cell phone rang, and he switched his beer to his right hand and reached into his pants pocket. The caller ID said what he wanted it to say. "S'up, nigga?"

"Aw, you know," said Ernie Banks. "Ready to do some business. Where you at?"

"Yeah, I got set up in a new place. Royal Palms Resort. You gonna love it."

He gave Banks directions and twenty minutes later Banks was knocking on the door.

"My nigga," said Catfish when he opened the door. He gave his partner a shoulder bump and brought him inside. "Man, grab yourself a Heiny out the mini fridge. And you got to check out this view." He stepped out onto the balcony again and looked over his shoulder.

Banks followed him, cracking the beer as he came. He looked

out at the view across the city, then down at the pool. "Damn, you set up, huh nigga?"

"You know me. I like to live in style. Especially after bein' inside for so long."

"Yeah, but too bad we ain't gonna get to enjoy it. Shit's going off tomorrow."

"Cool. Lay it out."

Banks looked at the balcony to either side of them. Both were empty, but he stepped back inside, motioning for Catfish to follow. "Close that muthafuckin' door, nigga," he said when Catfish had come in.

Catfish chuckled. "All right. I know you all security conscious and shit."

"Hell yes I am," said Banks, a little irritated at his partner's fun-and-games attitude. "This some serious shit we talking here. You know how many niggas want this connect now that Bacon locked up? Not to mention five-oh."

"Yeah, I know. But this place brand new. Ain't nobody know I'm here."

Banks put his beer down on the dresser. "Nigga, I got to explain this to your muthafuckin' ass after you yourself reached all the way out from inside to put all that stealth shit on Red? You don't know who got ears, who gonna dime us out."

Catfish wagged his head. "Damn, E. You trippin' like a muthafucka." He gestured to the door. "All right. We inside. The door closed. Now chill and lay it out for me."

Banks shook his head slowly then picked up his beer and took another sip. "All right. I got us a pilot. He gonna fly us down to a private airstrip outside of Acapulco tomorrow. Juan's people gonna meet us, take us to him."

Catfish smiled, showing all his buck teeth. "So we cool. We in."

"That's why I'm trying to get you to act professional. After that shit went down on Bacon, Juan a little gun-shy. He wants to meet us. Check us out. So you got to keep it tight down there. You feel me?"

"Cool," said Catfish, nodding.

"But don't fret. I gave the dude our bona fides. He know we the genuine article and can move his black tar in the Midwest and elsewhere."

"Yes, we can," said Catfish, and he raised his beer to toast the future with his partner.

They did go down to the pool after dinner and found a couple of nice bitches. Banks hooked up with a white chick, and Catfish took a Latin lovely back to his room.

She was a dark-skinned Colombian and reminded Catfish of Red in some ways. She wasn't as smart. He could tell that the minute she opened her mouth. She went on and on about the stupidest shit. When he finally got her clothes off and was squeezing on her titties, she still couldn't shut up, jaggin' on about when she was growin' up in Bogotá. *Damn, bitch!* he thought. *Nigga is on your tits, and you still talkin' 'bout how daddy taught you to ride a bike.*

Finally she felt the tape on his fingers roughing up her skin and pulled his hand away to look at it. "Aw, Papi," she said. "What happen to your fingers?"

Catfish shook his head and snickered. "You know what, girl?" he said. "You ain't too good at conversation, but I got something else you can do with your mouth. You probably *real* good at that." He pushed her down on her knees and nudged the head of his cock between her lips.

She looked startled and leaned away, eyes wide.

"What's the matter, girl? Daddy never taught you how to suck dick? Or you just ain't never seen one this big?"

She laughed. "Papi, you're so bad," she said. And then she leaned into him again and took him into her mouth.

The next morning the two men checked out of their rooms and returned their rental cars. They had the pilot, Guillermo, meet them at the rental agency and drive them to the airfield outside of Phoenix.

As they approached the small plane on foot, Catfish slowed up. "That it?" he said.

Guillermo, a little Mexican guy with aviator sunglasses and a San Diego Padres baseball cap, turned and nodded enthusiastically. "Cessna 400."

"Smaller than I thought it would be."

"Not big," said Guillermo. "But it's a turbo prop. We'll make good time."

Catfish grabbed Banks' sleeve and pulled him back a bit, letting Guillermo get several yards ahead of them. "What you think, man? This shit safe?"

Banks laughed. "You scared of flying?"

The truth was, Catfish hated flying. "Naw, man. I just—" He gestured to the plane. "You know—just—it's small."

"It's like a car that goes up in the sky, nigga. Hey, the price was right, that's all I know."

Cars ain't supposed to go up in the sky, thought Catfish.

Once they'd leveled off at cruising altitude, Catfish shook his head. He didn't care how fast they were going to get there, it would be too long. The ordinary turbulence of a commercial flight was magnified by twenty in the small craft. He felt like he was in a beer can somebody had thrown, rather than a plane that would stay up until the pilot brought it in for a controlled landing.

He leaned forward in his seat and tried to get the pilot's attention. "Hey, my man. My man."

Guillermo looked over his shoulder. "Everything okay?"

"Uh, yeah, no problem. But, uh, you got any—like, drink service on this bitch?"

Banks laughed. "Nigga, do you see a flight attendant? This ain't the friendly skies of United. You on your own up here."

Guillermo shrugged. "Sorry, I got nothing onboard except this." He reached into his inside jacket pocket and pulled out a flask. "You want some?"

"What is it?"

"Bourbon. Ten High."

Catfish stretched forward and grabbed the flask full of cheap whiskey like it was the finest cognac known to man. "That'll work." He spun the cap off and guzzled half the contents. Then he turned to Banks and offered it to him.

Banks laughed and put his hand over his mouth. "Damn, nigga. I seen you go toe to toe with all kind of gun-totin' thugs, and you afraid of flying."

"Fuck you, nigga. I ain't afraid of shit. I just want to take the edge off is all." He took another pull on the flask, replaced the cap, then handed it back to Guillermo.

The pilot smiled, took both hands off the yoke, removed the cap, and tossed back a couple of healthy swigs.

Catfish pointed through the windshield at the clear sky. "Hey, hey, hey. Watch the—the—uh . . ."

Guillermo leaned forward, looked right, left, up, down. Then he shrugged and took another swig.

Banks nearly fell out of his seat laughing.

Thankfully on the ground again, Catfish followed Banks to a black Humvee limo waiting near the hangar. Two men in jeans and cowboy boots were leaning against the car.

"These got to be the dudes," said Banks. He turned to Catfish and smiled. "And don't worry, nigga. That Hummer ain't gonna leave the ground."

Catfish scoffed and shook his head. "Yeah, you funny as a muthafucka, ain't you?"

One of the men at the Hummer pushed himself off the car when they got close. "Which one of you is Mr. Banks?"

"That'd be me," said Banks.

"And you must be the catfish," he said, turning.

"Naw, man," said Catfish. "Just Catfish. That's my name."

The Mexican turned to his partner and chuckled. He looked at Catfish again. "That is your name?"

"His street name," said Banks. "Don't worry about it."

The man got very serious. "I do not worry about it. If you are not who you say you are, if you are not what you pretend to be, you will be the ones to worry."

His partner pulled a couple of blindfolds out of his pocket and walked behind Catfish.

"The fuck is that?" asked Catfish, turning toward him.

"Please, Mr. Catfish," said the first man. "This is necessary if you are to meet the person you claim you want to meet. You will not enter the Hummer without this on your eyes."

Banks held up a hand to Catfish. "Chill, nigga."

Catfish shrugged. "Cool, man. Ya'll don't want a nigga to do no sightseeing in your lovely resort town, that's cool with me."

He turned his back to the man and allowed himself to be blindfolded. He was taken by the upper arm and guided into the car. He felt Banks situate himself in the seat next to him. The doors closed.

CHAPTER THIRTY-ONE

*R*ed laid all of her shoplifted shit out on her bed at Hotel Del Flores. Stuff she'd gotten in Phoenix, Vegas, and Beverly Hills. There were numerous items of clothing and accessories by designers like Fendi, Dior, Jimmy Choo, Chanel, Versace, Louis Vuitton, Valentino, Gucci. Dresses, scarves, sandals, purses, bracelets, necklaces, several pairs of sunglasses covered the queen size bed.

Snagging all that nice shit had been surprisingly easy. Now came the hard part. Deciding what she should sell and what she should keep. She would have kept it all if she could. Most of it, anyway. But she needed money to get set up in Mexico and launch the next part of her plan. There was a royal blue Christian Dior party dress. Beautiful, but not quite her personal taste. That one could go. A Prada clutch purse. It was beautiful, and it was red. Hell, no. She wasn't about to part with that. She picked up the Tag Heuer watch she'd scored during her first encounter with Meme . . . she picked it up. Red thought of all the ways

Meme had been a good friend and mentor, but in the end, Red couldn't trust her. Meme never did anything to lose Red's trust.

She tossed the watch onto the bed and walked to the window. She looked down onto the streets of Beverly Hills. This wasn't her town. Yet. But even if it would be hers one day, what was the point? If she had no friends, those streets would be just as mean and fucked up as the ones she left behind in Detroit. There would be nobody like Meme to watch her back because she couldn't turn her back on a bitch for two seconds without worrying if she was gonna get stabbed. Nobody like Q to love because . . .

Q. Q and that bitch Chass. *Hmm,* she thought. *That shit ain't gonna last. That stuck up, tight-ass lawyer ain't got no life in her. She can't hang with my Q.*

She thought about the way Q moved when he walked down the street. The rhythm in his speech. His smile. His body. His . . . She chuckled sadly and shook her head. *Look what you dreamin' 'bout, bitch. That train left the station the moment you pulled a trigger on his ass. You fucked up, Red. You fucked a lot of things up.* She turned back to the merchandise on the bed and took a deep breath. *But this time you gonna get it right, baby.*

She set aside a couple of items she wanted to keep for herself, then she left her room and wandered through the halls looking for someone. She'd seen the girl the previous day. Late teens, homely, with crossed eyes and glasses.

She found her at the end of the hall, taking fresh towels off her maid's cart for one of the rooms.

"Excuse me," said Red as she approached.

The girl turned. Her name tag said *Blanca.* "Yes, ma'am?"

"I wonder if you could come to my room for a moment. It's just down here at the end of the hall."

Blanca nodded and placed the towels back on her cart. She followed Red down to her room.

Red led her inside and closed the door. "Roberto said you might be able to help me with some of these things." She pointed to the bed.

"Roberto?" said Blanca. She stepped toward the bed, obviously interested in the merchandise.

"Yes, the busboy at the Luxe."

"Oh, yes. That boy." She turned to Red. "You want me to hang them up for you?"

Red chuckled. "Roberto said you might be able to help me find a buyer. Someone who deals in fine items like these."

"I'm sorry," said Blanca, stiffening. "I must go now." She headed for the door.

Red grabbed her by the upper arm. "Hang on, now." She switched to Spanish. "I just need to leave town for a while. And I need money to do that."

Blanca cocked her head, surprised that Red could speak Spanish so well. She thought about the accent for a moment. "Dominican? Or Puerto Rican?"

"Costa Rican," Red lied. She knew that when she spoke Spanish her accent was Antillia, not Central American. But she also knew that the Mexican girl might have fewer prejudices against Costa Ricans, and she hoped she could pass.

Blanca let her guard down a bit. "You need to get out of town?"

Red nodded. "Let's just say it's a legal issue."

Blanca looked around the room until she spotted the purse. She pointed to it. "You mind if I look in there?"

"Not at all," said Red. She knew the girl was looking for a badge, a gun, a microphone, whatever might indicate Red was a cop.

After a thorough search she nodded. "I get ten percent."

"Only if you can get me a good deal. I don't play with amateurs."

"I am not an amateur," said Blanca, smiling confidently.

An hour later a man showed up with an empty suitcase, spent forty-five minutes haggling with Red, packed up the merchandise, and left three grand in cash on the bed in its place. Red gladly paid Blanca her $300, waited for the girl to leave, then started calling cruise lines. She booked passage on Norwegian departing the next day.

She'd made out quite well, even while keeping a few choice items of clothing and jewelry. She'd also held onto a simple laptop. That item she'd bought. It had been too big and bulky to shoplift. She needed some way to stay connected to what was going on. At least she could check her friends on Facebook and see what they were saying in their posts. If they were saying anything about her, or about anybody she knew, if they were talking about any nigga leaving town to run an errand, she wanted to know about it. The laptop was a good investment. And the items she kept were helpful to her as well. And she'd still ended up with a nice stack.

That night she cut up a copy of the *Los Angeles Times* until she had about as much of that as she did money. She stuffed it into an envelope and taped it up so it wouldn't be easy to open. She left it out in the open on her dresser. Hopefully, if anybody tried to rip her off in the night, they'd grab the envelope and run without checking to see what they really had.

The guy who'd paid her knew she had the money. Blanca knew. And Blanca might tell Roberto or any number of others. Again, Red was in a position where she just couldn't trust anybody. She could take chances shoplifting shit. She could take chances boosting a car and driving it across the desert. She could take chances doing all kinds of bass ass nonsense. She just couldn't take chances on people.

CHAPTER THIRTY-TWO

Q and Chass landed at Acapulco International early in the evening. It was too dark to see much of the area, but on the cab ride to the hotel, they could see the mountains looming behind the line of hotels along the beach. As they traveled further into the heart of the resort area, Q sat up in the back of the cab. He could feel the energy of the town. People laughed as they spilled out of bars, bringing party music of the places with them through the open doors. The ladies dressed for play and the men carrying attitude that was equal parts laid-back and on top. This was his kind of place. A place he'd always wanted to come. With Red.

He could imagine Red's reaction to being on vacation in Acapulco. She was so alive, so free, and so wild. She would have eaten this place up. She could kick it better than anybody he'd ever known. She'd have turned heads in every club they hit, and she would have loved doing it. The sound of her laughter echoed in his memory as he stared at the city through his own reflection in the window of the cab.

Chass squeezed his hand. "This is so exciting," she said.

He turned to her and forced a smile. "This is what I'm talking about. Place is tight."

She leaned in and gave him a kiss. He kissed her back, then turned to watch the scenery again.

She put her head on his shoulder. "I believe this is a room service night. What do you think?"

"Yeah, room service sounds good," said Q. What he really wanted was to get checked in so he could slip into the bathroom and take a pill. The plane ride, standing around waiting for the luggage, and sitting in the back of the bumpy cab had brought his pain to the surface.

"What about tomorrow?" said Chass.

"First thing I'd like to do is go check out the cliff divers."

"Mm, baby. You don't need to be diving off any cliffs in your condition."

He turned to her and struggled to keep his cool. "I said, *check out* the cliff divers. I didn't say I wanted to jump off myself." He forced a laugh. "Do you think I'm crazy?"

"Not at all," she said, snuggling up to him closer.

Red would have been up for the cliffs, he thought. He could just imagine the two of them watching the divers and daring each other to try it. Teasing each other, laughing. He smiled as he thought about it. Would she have done it? Maybe. She was a crazy lady. Up for almost anything. But cliff diving he wasn't sure about. He had a sudden longing to play that one out. To see which way it would go.

But that would never be. Red was gone and would likely never show her face in Motown again. Besides he was a married man. He allowed himself to fantasize for a moment about going home to find her back in town. Then he thought about what was really waiting for him back in town. A job interviewing crime victims and writing up reports. And for what? Six, seven hundred dollars a week. Shit, he made that in a couple of hours back in the day. He could hit AC, Vegas, Miami at the drop of a hat. The hottest clubs in Detroit were his playground. He could push any kinda whip he wanted. If he walked past an upscale store and saw an Armani suit he wanted, he didn't think twice before rollin' up in there for it.

Chass gently squeezed his hand. She was great. What man wouldn't want to be with a woman like her? She was everything a woman should be: classy, successful, educated, beautiful and caring. She was certainly caring. But he wondered if he was fooling himself, thinking he could leave his world behind for hers to be her husband. She had found him legit work, but the fact was that it was a shit job with a shit wage compared to hers. In a way, he felt like Mr. Chass Reed, rather than the husband of Mrs. Carter.

The cab finally pulled up in front of Las Brisas Hotel. As he got out of the cab and helped get the luggage out of the trunk, he struggled not to show how much pain he was in. Up in the bathroom of their suite, he popped a pill, then found the mini bar and fixed himself a Chivas on the rocks, breaking the promise he'd made to Chass not to drink when he took his meds.

As Chass unzipped her suitcase and started taking a few things out, she noticed the drink in his hand. "You must be feeling pretty good not to need your Oxy. Did you take any at all today?"

"This morning I did. You know I'm always a little sore in the morning."

"I thought I noticed you limping more than usual a little earlier."

He took another sip of the scotch. "Yeah, sitting in the plane so long made me stiffen up a bit, but no pain really."

She smiled and gave him a peck on the lips. "That's great, Q. I'm happy for you. See?"

"See what?"

"This is the start of all kinds of new and good things."

He nodded and smiled as he felt the first wave of the booze and the pill wash over him. He raised his glass. "Can I fix you something?"

She moved to the closet to hang a few things. "What's that, scotch?"

"Yeah."

"Hook me up with a vodka tonic? They have Grey Goose?"

"I think it's Stoli," he said as he leaned down to check the mini bar again. "Yeah."

"Stoli's good," said Chass. "But you know we have to order up champagne with dinner, right?"

He smiled. "I can get behind that. We'll see if they have some Dom, maybe some Cris."

Q fixed her drink and handed it to her. Then he pulled out his laptop, put it on the desk, and opened it up.

"Oh, baby," said Chass. "You're not thinking about getting into a bunch of computer game nonsense right now, are you?"

"No," said Q, hitting the power button. "I just wanted to check my e-mail, maybe let all my Facebook friends know we've arrived."

"Oh, that's a good idea." She took a couple of steps toward the bathroom, then stopped. "Hey!" She suddenly became animated. "Tomorrow we have to take a bunch of pictures and post them to make everybody jealous."

Q laughed. "You bad, girl. But yeah, we'll definitely do that." It was a moment of genuine fun with Chass, but he wondered how much of it was from the meds and booze.

"I'm going to freshen up a bit," said Chass, heading for the bathroom again. "Don't get too engrossed in that because we're going to have to take a look at that room service menu as soon as I get out."

"Hey," said Q, holding up his drink. "Happy honeymoon."

She held up her Stoli and tonic and toasted him back with a smile.

When she'd shut the bathroom door, Q hopped on the Internet and checked his e-mail. There wasn't much there. Something from his mom wishing him a happy honeymoon and warning him not to drink the tap water. He also read messages from a couple of his boys from the old days telling him congrats. There was one from Chass's mom.

He closed that out and opened his Facebook page. In his status box he typed, "In Acapulco with my wife! My *wife*! You heard me?" He signed it with a smiley face. In reality he frowned.

He took another sip of Chivas. He was starting to feel very mellow now. Very deep. Very far away from what he was. He went to the search box and typed in the name *Raven Gomez*. He'd never bothered to cut his friendship link to her but didn't know if she was still even on Facebook. By all accounts she'd dropped off the face of the earth. Probably the Internet too. But when he hit "enter," her profile popped up. He looked at her wall and her info. Nothing had changed. It didn't look like she'd been on in a while.

He heard the shower running and looked over his shoulder at the bathroom. Then he opened Red's photo albums and began browsing through pictures of her. Red at a party. Red in her X6 BMW. Red with some friends in a restaurant in which she had a long string of spaghetti hanging down from her puckered lips. She was crossing her eyes for the camera, acting the fool. He could almost hear the laughter coming from the friends she had around her. One pic was of her in a club. She looked like she was having the time of her life. He recognized the place and smiled as he thought about the good times he'd had with her in that same very club.

He took another big swallow of Chivas, and it was gone. He set the glass down, ice tinkling as it settled. He clicked on "send a message." With the cursor blinking in the box, he sat with his fingers hovering over the keyboard.

Red,

Surprise. Guess where I am?

He deleted the message and started again.

Hey Red,

I've been thinking about you, girl. For real. I mean, I know some shit went down that neither one of us had planned, but I believe you were honest with me about it. You know that you and me . . .

He deleted the message again.

Dear Red,

I miss you. We both have done some crazy shit in our lives. Hell, I might have just done the craziest thing ever. But anyway, I know what happened to us was an accident. I forgive you for all that. I've been thinking about all the shit you've been through in your life and what a survivor you are. You know that means a lot to me. Your toughness and all. But what means even more is your love. We lost something real because we thought it was false. Okay, maybe I'm the one who thought it was false. But I was wrong. And now I'm wondering if there could ever be a way to get it back. I guess what I'm trying to say is that I love you. And I guess I'm asking if you still have any kind of feelings at all for me. I don't even know if you're still checking your page. But if you get this, holla back.

Love,
Q

He put his finger on the touch pad and moved the pointer over the "send" button. He lifted his finger, poised to tap the button. His face was numb. His body felt like it was floating. He raised his finger a little higher, ready to bring it down and send the message. Then he deleted the message, signed off, and closed the laptop.

The fuck you doin', nigga, he thought. *The bitch shot your ass.* He leaned back in his chair and laughed.

"Q?" said Chass, coming up behind him as she dried her hair. "What's so funny?"

Q stood up. "Life is funny, baby. Life is a celebration."

"I like the sound of that," she said.

He danced a few steps. "Look, ma, no cane." He laughed some more.

Chass laughed, too. "How many drinks have you had?"

"Yeah, I guess I've had a few," he lied, hoping she wouldn't notice that there was only one empty in the trash.

"Well, wait for me, now. You don't want to do all your celebrating alone, do you?"

"No," he said. He wrapped his arms around her and squeezed her. "Chass, you're amazing. You're a real woman. You know that?"

"Thank you, my husband. And you're a wonderful man." Chass smiled as Q tilted her head for a kiss.

They kissed passionately. Then he broke away and grabbed the room service menu. "What did you decide on?" he asked. "Cris, or Dom?"

He sat on the edge of the bed, and she crawled up behind him and grabbed him around the neck. "Baby?"

"Yeah," he said, looking at the items on the menu.

"I got some news I've been waiting a few days to tell you."

His eyes landed on the filet mignon and his mouth started to water. "What's that, baby?"

"I'm pregnant."

CHAPTER THIRTY-THREE

*S*till blindfolded, Catfish felt the Hummer slow to a near stop, then go over a bump and up a slight incline. They were going up a driveway. The limo stopped, and he heard an automatic garage door lowering behind them. The sound of the vehicle doors opening and closing echoed in the garage as he and Banks were pulled from the backseat.

"You can take it off now," said one of the men who'd picked them up.

Catfish pulled the blindfold up over his head and looked around. They were inside an eight-car garage deep enough to hold the Hummer limo. Other cars in it included two additional short-body Hummers, a black Porche 911, a white Bentley with gold trim, and an emerald green 1966 Mustang in mint condition.

Catfish nudged Banks and pointed to the Ford. "I'ma tell you right now, that Mustang could definitely make a nigga feel like he airborne. Mm! Shit is tight!"

A strong, deep voice echoed through the garage from the other side. "While you are admiring my cars, perhaps you could tell me why I should not shoot you both right now?"

Catfish turned and saw a big man coming toward them flanked by two bodyguards, one carrying an AK-47, the other an Uzi.

"You must be Juan," said Catfish.

The man looked around at his companions, those who'd met them at the plane, and the ones carrying the heavy firepower. "Now, this is truly amazing. Is it not? A man comes all the way from America to see me, yet he does not know if I am the man he has come to see." Slowly he took a few steps closer to Catfish. "Are you stupid, my friend?"

Catfish took a stance. "Am I stup—"

Banks stepped forward and put a hand on Catfish's shoulder. "I'm Ernie Banks. I'm the one who contacted you. My friend here is . . . See, I'm bringin' him into this. But he reliable. I promise you that."

"Well, Mr. Banks, in answer to your friend's question, yes, I am the man you are looking for. I am Juan. And I assure you both that in my business, I take promises very seriously. So if you are promising me that your man here is reliable, I will hold you responsible for that."

"Yes, sir, I do know that. I run my shit tight up in Detroit. My people, including my man Catfish here, are all proven."

Juan chuckled. "Really? Because I have a very bad feeling about Catfish. I have been told that he has just gotten out of prison in Michigan. Quite a lot earlier than anyone expected him to."

Catfish shrugged. "That's just the way they do up there in the United States. They got parole hearings and shit. A nigga could get his self out if he play his cards right."

Juan nodded. "And is that what you did, Catfish? You played your cards right?"

"Yeah."

"That surprises me. Because you don't seem to be the kind of man to play cards very well. It makes me think that maybe you have made promises to the kind of people I don't like to deal with. Do you know what we mean when we say *las tres letras*? *The three letters?* It means the DEA."

Banks shifted his feet. His heart was beating a little faster. "Look, Juan, my man here got out the joint due to what we call extenuating circumstances. He ain't got nothin' to do with no police, or no drug enforcement shit."

Juan turned to his men. "Do you know what catfish means? *Es un barbo.*" Then he pointed to Catfish's face. "Huh? Doesn't he look like it?"

The men laughed.

"I understand that in the United States many people don't like to eat catfish." He spread his hands. "Here, we eat them all the time."

"Juan," said Banks. "Catfish been my boy in Detroit for many years now. I vouch for him."

"Remove your clothes," said Juan.

Catfish and Banks looked at each other. Then both began undressing. Catfish shook his head. "Yeah, I been strip-searched before."

When they'd gotten completely undressed, Juan directed his men to examine their clothes. When the men had done that they nodded to Juan.

"You are clean for the moment," he said, and he told them to get dressed.

As they did, he turned to the Mustang. "You like this car, Catfish?"

"One of the sweetest cars on the American road," said Catfish, buttoning his shirt.

"The Mexican road, too," he said, raising his eyebrows. "If I decide to do business with you, and our business goes well, I will have it sent up to you in—what is it you call it? Motown?"

"That's right," said Catfish, chuckling. "Motown. Motor town. And that's a very generous gift. That's very kind of you."

"Not yet it's not," said Juan. "Come inside the house."

Catfish and Banks looked at each other, not sure what to expect next. They followed Juan into the house. The armed bodyguards brought up the rear.

They were led down a hall and into a huge room. The entire back of the house was either floor to ceiling windows or sliding glass doors. The room looked out onto an enormous infinity pool, which, in turn, looked out onto the Pacific Ocean.

"Please, have a seat," said Juan, gesturing to the long, white couches arranged in a horseshoe around a coffee table.

He opened one of the sliding glass doors, stepped outside, and spoke to three girls who were lounging by the pool.

Catfish leaned close to Banks. "So, this mean we in?"

"This mean we in the house. More than that, I don't know. But I'm thinking, you know, if he didn't want to meet with us, he wouldn't be meetin' with us."

"Yeah," said Catfish, leaning back in the couch, smug and relaxed.

Juan came back into the house and the three girls from the pool, dressed in bikinis, followed him. "Gentlemen, if you will excuse me for a moment, my hostesses will serve you whatever you would like to drink." He pointed to each one in turn. "This is Claudia, Victoria, and Maria. I have to take care of some business, but I will return in just a few minutes. Please forgive me."

As Juan left the room, Catfish looked the girls up and down and nodded.

"We are not here for that," said Maria. "Would you like something to drink?"

"Yeah," said Banks. *"Cerveza, por favor."*

Victoria and Claudia hurried into the kitchen and brought back two ice cold bottles of Bohemia.

"Oh," said Catfish as he took a bottle from Claudia. "I was expecting Corona. You ain't got that?"

"Neither of them speaks English," said Maria.

"They knew enough to get the beer," said Catfish.

"That's because your friend ordered in Spanish."

"True," said Banks.

"And, no," said Maria. "Your host keeps premium beer in his refrigerator. Bohemia is the finest beer in Mexico."

"Okay," said Catfish. "Well, tell them *gracias.*"

"Again," said Maria. "*Gracias* is Spanish. They understand Spanish but not English. Fortunately for you."

Catfish took a sip of the cold beer. "How you figure. I might like to have a conversation with one of them."

Maria sat on one of the couches facing the men and crossed her legs. "No, you want to have a conversation with me. And you don't want them to understand what we are saying."

"Oh," said Catfish, tittering like a child. He looked at Banks, then back at Maria. "We gonna have a private, romantic conversation?"

"We are going to talk about your relationship with Bacon, a man I came to know very well when he was doing business with Juan. He told me about you, Catfish. And about events mentioned in a book."

Catfish straightened. "What he say about that shit?"

"Things Señor Juan would not like about you."

"The fuck you talkin' about, bitch?"

Maria remained completely calm. She put her finger up to her lips to quiet him. "It's funny that you call me a bitch, because that is how Bacon called you. A bitch and a—what was the other word? Oh, yes. A sneetch. Did I pronounce it right?"

Banks shook his head. "Close enough."

"Man, Bacon got that shit backwards, baby," said Catfish.

"Now we have to guess at which of you was telling lies about the other? Juan has ways of finding out who is lying."

Catfish started to get up. Banks grabbed him and pulled him back down. "Hey, hey," said Banks. "Chill, nigga." Then he turned to Maria. "What you tellin' us this shit for? You wanted to fuck up our business with Juan, you'd have done it already."

Maria frowned. "No, Mr. Banks. I don't not wish to fuck up such good business. I only want a piece of it for myself."

"Damn," said Banks. "Bacon fuckin' with our shit, and he don't even know we here."

Maria smirked. "The world presents us with many difficulties, no?"

"Yeah," said Banks. "But the way Juan acting, we don't even know if this business is gonna work out."

"I can make sure that it does."

"How can you do that?" said Catfish. "Juan so into your pussy he can't say no to you?"

Maria threw back her head and laughed. "My pussy is very tight," she said, wrinkling her nose and opening her legs a little. The bikini was so thin that the men could see her camel toe. "But Juan values me for more than that. I was his liaison with Bacon."

"Meaning what?" said Catfish.

"Meaning I used my pussy to get Bacon to tell me things. That is how I know so much about you. But I can tell Juan that I know differently. I can say that Bacon told me you were very trustworthy. That you would do anything for him. That you went to prison for him. That you would die for him. I can make Juan believe in your loyalty."

"And for all that?" said Catfish. "What you want?"

"Make me an offer."

"Naw," said Banks. "We got to see how this deal work out. We got to see how much the deal worth. How much product he can deliver. How he can deliver it. Where he can deliver it. All that shit. If you can use that tight little pussy of yours to help us with any of that, then we see what you worth. Then we gonna see how many zeros to put on your paycheck."

"And not just zeros," said Maria. "I will need help with immigration to the United States."

Catfish shook his head. "We ain't into—"

"Yeah, yeah, yeah," said Banks. "We hook you up with whatever you need. *If* the deal is right."

"A nice condo in Detroit, or maybe Chicago. Someplace where there are many rich men."

Catfish smiled. "You looking for a rich white man, or a rich black man?"

"That does not matter," said Maria with a shrug. "As long as he does not look like a catfish."

Banks laughed and shook his head. "All right, we got some bargaining points here. Anything else?"

Catfish and Banks burst into laughter. But even as he laughed, Catfish made himself a promise. If he ever found a way to hurt Maria for blackmailing them, he would.

CHAPTER THIRTY-FOUR

*B*lack walked into a sports bar just off the Vegas strip and ordered a Beck's. It was well after midnight, but the place was still going. He took his beer to a table in a dark corner where he could have a bit of privacy and hide in the shadows. As far as he knew, Vegas cops had a BOLO on his ass. He was trying to keep his head down as much as he could, but he was going crazy holing up in his room, so he had to get out. He'd ditched his room at the Bellagio and used cash to check into a cheap, last chance gamblers' dive called Lucky Lou's.

He'd been avoiding Special Agent Holt's call, trying to come up with a way to make things work out for him since he lost Trap to a cop's bullet. He knew Holt would find a way to make him accountable for that shit, but how was he supposed to control every muthfuckin' player in the game? Trap acted the fool, the cop was some kind of quick draw muthafucka, and that was just how it went down. What was Black supposed to do? Step in front of a bullet? Call time out and explain to the cop that he was working for the feds? Make Trap magically grow a brain?

That shit was fucked up, and he was just gonna have to deal with it one way or another. He chugged half the Beck's, then pulled out the burner he'd bought at a convenience store. He dialed the cell number he had for Agent Holt. It rang a few times. Black looked at his watch and realized it was almost three thirty in the morning in Motown.

Finally the man picked up the call. "Special Agent Holt," he said in a groggy voice. "What can I do for you?"

"Holt. This Black."

Holt sighed into the phone. "Black. I didn't recognize the caller ID. You're not using your phone?"

"Hell no, this ain't my phone," said Black. "After that shit with Trap I didn't know how things were with us. And I don't know what kind of shit you got on my phone. I been keeping my head down."

"I noticed. Listen, I heard about Trap. That's too bad. But, you know, I checked into it real good. We know it wasn't your fault."

Black hesitated for a moment. "So, we good, huh?"

"Why wouldn't we be?"

Why wouldn't we be? thought Black. There were all kind of reasons why po-po would turn on a nigga. And now Holt was acting like nothing happened. That didn't feel right. "Yeah, but, so, what we gonna do now?"

"Our man with the Detroit PD is in Phoenix. Detective Thomas. He's down there looking for Red and I know you'd like to find her as much as anybody. I want you to head down there. Hook up with him."

"Head down to Phoenix?"

"Yeah."

Black thought about it. If Holt wanted to burn him, why not

just tell him to come back to Detroit? On the other hand, he was sending him right into the hands of the DPD. That just went against his instincts. But Phoenix was just a stone's throw from Mexico. Trap's connect was down there, which might lead to some valuable action.

"All right, so how do I connect with this dude?"

"Well, you just tell me what number he can call you on."

"Naw, nigga. You tell me what number to call him on."

"How do I know you will?"

"I called your ass, didn't I?"

"Okay, just call him, all right? We need you down there."

The next morning, Black got himself some coffee from a place down the block and took it back to his room at the Lucky Lou's. He would go down to Phoenix and hook up with Thomas, but he still didn't trust everybody involved in this thing. He was determined to bring something to the table.

So, he had one call to make before he contacted Thomas. And this was one he hadn't wanted to make in the middle of the night. If he'd woken her out of her beauty sleep, she'd have been less cooperative.

He sipped his coffee as the phone rang.

"Hello," said a tired voice.

"Foxy, this Black. How you doin', girl?"

Foxy brightened up. "Well, hey Black. You know I'm just fine. How could I be otherwise?"

Black chuckled. "I know you are, Foxy. You da shit, baby."

"I haven't seen you around any of the clubs lately, dear. Where you been keeping your fine self?"

"Oh, you know, takin' care of business."

"Why don't you come around and let *me* take care of your big business?"

"I'm sure nobody could do it good as you."

"That has been said about me so many times, Black. Many

have tried to be me, but none have captured my elegance, my poise, my sensuality."

"Damn," said Black. "Who the bitches in the hood trying to be you?"

"So many aspire."

"I bet Quisha, that girl used to be with Trap."

"Oh, Quisha think she all that, but she know better than to go toe to toe with me!"

"That old girl, Red? She think she all that, too. I bet she wanna be you."

There was silence on the other end of the line.

"Right?" said Black, laughing.

"I suppose," said Foxy, coldly.

"What the 411 on that girl, anyway? She ain't been around."

"Why do you want to know?"

"Naw, just curious, you know."

"Seems like they's a lot of folk curious about Red these days. She ain't nothin'. Last time I saw here she looked rough. Just a tired, old piece of ghetto trash."

"You seen her?" said Black.

"I said, the *last* time I seen her."

"So you ain't got no 411 on Red. Damn, Foxy, I thought you was the—"

"Why all you niggas so interested in Red all the time? I *said*, she ain't nothin'. I'm getting tired of niggas asking me that shit."

"Who else asking about Red?" said Black.

There was a pause. "You know what? This conversation is getting very old. I think I'ma—"

"Hold up, hold up," said Black. "Now, just hold on a minute, Foxy. You know you got it going on. Truth is I got some business to take care of, and I just need a line on Red."

In her kitchen in Detroit, Foxy thought for a moment. Her trip out west hadn't gone like she'd dreamed it would. That encounter with that raggedy-ass Red didn't help matters. But now Black was talking business. Something that involved Red. She knew they was a lot of niggas pissed off at Red, some who even wanted to do her harm. If she could have a hand in that in any way, she would enjoy that. Still, business was business. If Black was getting something out of finding Red, Foxy needed to get paid, too.

"What you need to know about her?"

"Where she at?"

"I might know somethin'."

Black waited for a moment. He was getting tired of Foxy's whinin' and shit. He wished he was in Motown so he could roll over to her crib and smack the shit out of her, the fake ass bitch. But he knew that at a distance he had no choice but to sweet talk her. "Well, that's what I'm saying. Miss Foxy got her ear to the streets. Ain't nobody know what you know."

"Yeah, you can go on and stop that noise," said Foxy. "If you gonna be relying on me for information, you need to pay me what I'm worth."

"All right," said Black. "I can do that. How much you need?"

"It's not just a matter of how much I need. It's how much am I worth. And you said yourself just a moment ago that I am known for my knowledge of what's going down at any given time with any given person."

Black thought about it. How much was Foxy worth? How much would he pay for Red's hide? How much to get out from under the feds and the DPD? "I tell you what. Name the price *you* think is fair, I'll take care of you."

CHAPTER THIRTY-FIVE

*R*ed stood at the rail of the cruise ship alone. In her yellow-and-white-striped Fendi sundress, holding her red Prada clutch purse, she watched the distant coast of California slip by, knowing it would soon turn into the coast of Mexico. She'd seen so many different worlds, made so many different adjustments since leaving Motown. This was just one more. And she had to make it work this time. She was running out of room and out of energy.

"I don't think we're in Detroit anymore, Toto," she said out loud.

"Pardon me," said a man's voice behind her.

She turned and saw a tall, clean-cut black man in his late thirties with a friendly smile. He was wearing a Tommy Bahama shirt, white shorts, and nice sandals, maybe Gucci. "Oh, sorry. I didn't realize there was anyone else around."

He smirked and pointed back the way he'd come. "Well, if I'm intruding I could . . ."

"No, no," said Red. "I'm sorry. I didn't mean it like that." She extended a hand. "I'm Raven."

He shook hands with her. "I'm Robert. Good to meet you, Raven." He turned to the east. "Nice view."

"Yeah. America looks different from here."

"It'll look even more different from where we're going. Have you ever been south of the border?"

Red felt her paranoia begin to kick in. He didn't *look* like the street. But how could she be sure who his friends were. She decided it was best to give away as little as she could. "Nope. I'm a virgin."

Robert laughed. "A woman as, uh, adventurous looking as you, that's hard to believe. Where are you from?"

Where *was* she from? Hell, with all the places she'd been, she could tell the truth and still not be giving anything away. "I'm from New York."

"Oh, so you *are* a long way from home. And Toto, too."

Red blushed. "Ah, you *did* hear that. I'm embarrassed."

"Not at all," said Robert. "One of my favorite movies."

All right, thought Red. *So, maybe he's gay. That doesn't mean you can't be friendly.* "And where are you from?"

"Well, I'm actually from Atlanta, but I spend a lot of time in the L.A., San Diego area. Mexico. Southern Arizona."

Arizona. Red felt herself tense up a bit, but tried not to show it. Now he was getting too muthafuckin' close to where she was running from. "Oh? Is that for business?"

"Yeah," he said.

"What business?"

"I'm an entrepreneur."

Entrepreneur? she thought. *As in hired gun?* She looked beyond his shoulder and saw a few other passengers along the rail farther down. She was relatively safe. "That's actually kind of vague, Robert. What's your line of business? Or is that an embarrassing question?"

Robert sized her up for a long moment. He seemed to be deciding what to tell her, or how much. "I'm an importer and distributor."

Again, too close to home. Too close to Bacon's line of work. Still, he just didn't look like the kind of nigga who'd know Bacon. No prison ink, no hard look in his eyes. "You import and distribute. I see. I've known people in that same general line of work."

"Oh? And what did they import and distribute?"

"What do *you* import and distribute?"

Robert laughed. "Things vital to U.S.–Latin American relations."

"Bananas?"

"Sure, let's say it's bananas. And maybe we can discuss what you do over drinks."

"Hmm, well make mine a margarita, and I'll tell you anything you want to know."

"Margarita. Yeah, let's get into that south of the border mood."

They went to one of the inside bars and got to know each other. She told him she was in real estate and had some other business ventures going. She had to be at least somewhat honest so that she could answer any specific questions realistically. However, she didn't want to say she was in publishing because she wanted to steer away from any titles that might identify her or people she was connected with. Robert was a fine-looking man and seemed like a nice guy, but she still wasn't letting her guard down.

For his part, Robert continued to speak in vague terms about his business. And every time she pressed him, he turned the topic back to her. He was definitely into something interesting. She wanted to know more. So, when afternoon turned to evening, and he invited her to dinner, she couldn't turn him down. He took her to one of the cafés onboard, rather than to the formal dining room where they would have to juggle their table assignments and, in all likelihood, would still have to sit with other travelers.

Over lobster and chardonnay, Robert seemed to grow more and more interested. Red began to think he wasn't gay after all. And when dinner ended, and he invited her dancing, she thought things were really going somewhere. He was rubbing his hands all over her. Front and back. And then he invited her to his stateroom for a drink.

His accommodations were twice the size of hers. He brought out a couple of snifters and poured each of them an Appleton Estate's premium dark rum. They sat at the little bistro table by the porthole.

Red tipped back the snifter and took in a mouthful of the rum, savoring the sweet, molasses taste. "So, you got the most expensive stateroom on the ship, and you drink eighty-dollar rum. This import thing you do must be working out."

"Of course," he said with a shrug. "Cocaine is a very popular product."

Red raised her eyebrows. "Oh, so now you feel all trusting."

He gestured at her from head to toe. "Well, now that I've satisfied myself."

She thought about it for a moment. "Oh," she said. "So all that stuff on the dance floor. You were checking for a wire?"

He smirked. "I hope I didn't come across as too forward."

"Don't you think that's a bit paranoid?"

"Let's just say I've attracted the attention of certain entities that would like to know more about me. Which is also why I'm looking for someone to be my—shall we say, import assistant."

"And you think . . ." Red pointed to herself. "You just picked me out of the crowd?"

"Not at all. I've spent half the day sizing you up. You're articulate, intelligent, nicely dressed, but alone. You're also adventurous, but cautious when you talk about yourself, which tells me you probably have something to hide too."

Red swirled the rum in her snifter and watched the light dance in it. So, it had all been a job interview. Again it proved to her that she couldn't trust anybody's motives. At least this time nobody was trying to burn her. "So what would I . . . That is, what exactly does an import assistant do?"

"I'd want you to help me get some pieces across the border into the U.S."

"Pieces?"

"Kilos. Several. I'm not a huge importer, but I've been bringing up enough coke each month to provide me with a very comfortable life." He gestured around the luxury stateroom. "As you can see."

"And you always just pick somebody at random to help you?"

"No, like I said, I didn't pick you at random. But even so, I'm having to change things up a little. I would usually fly it in myself, or have one of my people drive it across the border. But the heat is on just now. I'm afraid the feds might have my planes targeted and might know my regular people. I have a scheduled delivery to make and my connect in Mexico doesn't like schedule changes."

Red shook her head. "Hold on a second. You want me to go with you to Acapulco, then drive a car all the way back up to the border and cross into San Diego or some shit?"

"No, it's not like that. It's folks in the U.S. I'm worried about. My connect has got Mexico wired. He's in Acapulco, but I'll fly us from there to Agua Prieta, just this side of the Arizona border. Nobody will hassle us. You leave the airport alone, so nobody sees us together, and you just drive a couple of suitcases up to Douglas. I got some people up there who'll take if off your hands."

"And what if I get stopped?"

"Look, I told you, I've checked you out. You can handle yourself. And you're an elegant-looking young lady dressed in Fendi. They won't stop you."

"Won't, or probably won't?"

"Ninety-nine point nine percent won't."

"Yeah, and see, there's that other point one percent."

"Sure. That's what you get the five grand for. One day. Five grand. Nothing to it."

Five grand. That sounded right to her. But a drug mule? Is that what she wanted to be? She thought about Beverly Hills and the slice of it that she wanted to break off for herself. She would do what she had to do to make that goal a reality. On the other hand, she wasn't ready to end up back in the U.S. just now.

"But see, I gotta be in Mexico right now. That's the thing."

"You will be. You need to pick up the money, drive it back across, and then I'll fly you back to Acapulco. I have to get back on this ship and disembark in L.A. when this is all over. I told you I have people watching me."

Five grand. It was a lot of money. But Red didn't want a lot of money. She wanted a whole muthafuckin' shitload of money. She sipped her rum and looked into Robert's eyes. Already she was beginning to formulate a plan.

Two days later the ship docked in Acapulco at dawn. Robert had no intention of letting Red meet his connect, so he told her to meet him two hours later. She took a taxi to the small airport and told the driver to find hangar three as Robert had instructed. When the car pulled up, Robert was standing outside the hangar. He opened the cab door for Red, paid the driver for her, and escorted her up the steps into a small Bombardier jet.

As the thing streaked up into the sky, her heart beat a little faster. It wasn't the exhilaration of the ride that got to her, but the situation she was in. Taking off from Acapulco with a load of cocaine, a man she barely knew at the plane's controls, trusting in whatever corrupt Mexican officials his people had paid off, getting ready to drive the drugs across the border right back into the state she'd run from. It was surreal. *Girl,* she thought. *You done lost your muthafuckin' mind.*

When they landed in the small Sonoran Desert town of Agua Prieta, Robert handed her a set of car keys. "Okay, you got two Samsonites strapped in by the door. Souvenirs on top, the bad thing below. Take those and go—"

"You're not coming with?" said Red.

"I told you, I got people watching me. They could have folk hanging around these border towns. If they see us together, I guarantee you they'll search every inch of you and your car."

She closed her eyes and nodded.

"Don't freak out. I'm gonna sit right here in this plane. No-body's gonna see me. You'll be just fine."

"Okay. So I take the suitcases and . . . ?"

Robert handed her a set of car keys. "It's the Volvo by the hangar."

"Volvo?" said Red. "You couldn't hook me up with something a little more fly than that?"

"Trust me. You want to be driving a nice car, but not flashy. The car says you're respectable, stable, safe."

She nodded again, a bit too enthusiastically. "All right. You're right. That's good."

Robert took hold of her hands. "Hey," he said gently. "Calm down. Okay? You drive to the address I give you in Douglas and let my people unload the shit and load the cash. In an hour, you'll be back here, I'll put five grand in your pocket, and I'll fly you back to Acapulco. Simple."

Red took a deep breath and smiled. "I'm ready."

She left the airport in the Volvo and watched carefully to make sure Robert didn't have anybody following her. No doubt his people on the U.S. side knew the car she was driving and would stop her if she didn't go where she was supposed to on the other side of the border. That was fine. As long as she could steal a few minutes in Agua Prieta.

She stopped at the first *pharmacia* she came to and jumped out of the car. She ran inside and bought two jars of powdered lactose, a sheet of plastic, a pair of scissors, and some tape. Then she found a relatively secluded spot a few blocks away, brought one of the suitcases to the backseat, and went to work. Robert expected her to do the entire run in an hour, so she didn't have time to do a good job. She mixed the lactose into four packages worth of coke, extending them to five. She repackaged everything, then put the suitcase back in the trunk and headed for the border.

Just as Robert had said, she attracted no particular attention. She drove to the address she had in Douglas, a garage on a quiet side street. Four heavily inked Mexican men surrounded the car immediately.

One yanked the driver's door open and leaned down. "You should have got here fifteen minutes ago. Where you been, *putita*?"

"Robert said I wouldn't have any trouble at the border. Guess he didn't put bein' wrong about that in his timetable. And I ain't no *puta*, nigga."

The man laughed. "You had trouble at the border?"

Red stood up out of the car and let the men get a look at her fine shit. "Nothin' I couldn't talk my way out of."

He looked her up and down and nodded. "Okay, *chica*. So, you got nine pieces in the trunk, huh?"

"I don't know what I got in the trunk, but Robert told me it was ten."

"Bullshit, bitch," said one of the other men, a little guy.

Red felt the palms of her hands start to sweat. Maybe it was too bold a play. She didn't know these people, how they did business, what they expected from each other. She was playing it off-the-cuff, desperate for as much money as she could get.

"Hey," said the first man, glaring at his friend. "Can you count?"

"Yeah, I can count."

"Then open the fuckin' suitcases and count."

The little guy took the keys from Red and headed for the trunk, muttering to himself as he went. "Yeah, I'll count the fuckin' shit, *ese*. Better be the right fuckin' count, too." Then he turned to Red. "Don't matter how much is in here, *puta*. We was told nine, and that's how much money we got."

"Look, muthafucka," said Red. "I just drove the fuckin' car. I ain't got no power to negotiate. I'm just the hired help."

The little guy popped the trunk. Red heard the zippers of the suitcases, then saw the souvenirs go flying in all directions. Then the little guy started muttering again as he counted the packages. "Hey, Hector," he said coming out from behind the car. "It's ten, just like the *puta* said."

Hector turned to Red and glared at her.

Red's knees went weak and she decided this was a bad muthafuckin' idea. She started to backpedal. "Look, if y'all niggas ain't got the money for ten, I'll take one back with me. Ain't no thing."

"Call Robert," said the little guy.

"Look, what's the big deal," said Red. "I'll just take one back."

Hector turned to the little guy and held up a hand. "No phone calls, *cabron*. You know the rules."

Then the two of them lapsed into Spanish. "If we don't take all of it, Robert's gonna be pissed," said Hector. "What's he gonna do with a stray key down there."

The little one shrugged. "He can just deal it down there."

"No, he ain't no street dealer, fuck head."

"Then he can give it back to the big guy for the next time."

"Are you stupid? You want him to go back to the big guy and say he fucked up a delivery? He got the count wrong? They don't like that kind of shit, man. You know that."

Hector looked at his watch. "Fuck, man," he said, still in Spanish. "We're already running late thanks to this fucking bitch."

Red fought the urge to look at her watch, not wanting to give away the fact that she knew Spanish.

Hector shook his head. "All right," he said in English. "Go in the back room an get another thirty."

Thirty? thought Red. *I'ma get thirty K out this bitch, plus the five Robert already promised me.* She had to struggle to keep from laughing.

CHAPTER THIRTY-SIX

*A*fter crossing back into Agua Prieta, Red stopped at the same spot where she'd cut the coke. She counted thirty grand out of one of the suitcases and tucked it into her large Louis Vuitton.

When they landed back in Acapulco, Robert gave her $5,000 and a phone number. "You have to remember that," said Robert. "Don't write it down anywhere. That could be just as bad for you as it could be for me. Call me next month, and we can do this again."

"I definitely will," said Red, already slinging the Louis Vuitton over her shoulder. But she had no intention of ever seeing Robert again. She wasn't going to make a career as a drug mule, and she'd gotten the score she'd wanted out of this deal.

She took a cab back to the cruise ship and threw her shit together as quickly as she could. She knew Robert would have to take care of his post-flight checklist on the plane, and she was going to be off the ship well before he returned. Hector had said phone calls were off the menu, but she didn't know if maybe they had some way of communicating, and she didn't want to find out.

She took another cab to a spot three blocks south of the Calinda Beach Hotel and walked from there. She stopped at a tourist shop on the way and bought a cheap beach bag. The adrenaline was still pumping through her veins when she checked into the hotel and the quality of the room only brought her to a bigger high. This place was tight. Nicer than any of the places she'd stayed since being on the run. Or maybe it was just the adrenaline and the thirty-five grand in her bag that made it seem like that. Anyway, this was *the* place to escape to. She stepped out onto the huge, tenth-floor balcony and looked down at the beach. The room was nice, but she wasn't gonna keep her ass inside when the beautiful Mexican beach was right below her. The people below were either chillin' in beach chairs, or up doing shit—jogging, throwing a football, swimming. Whatever they were doing, they looked happy. But in a few minutes she'd be the happiest bitch down there.

She quickly unpacked a few things, including the Parah Noir bikini she'd been wearing the day she left her crib in Scottsdale with Catfish on her tail. She stripped out of her street clothes, pulled on the bikini, and admired herself in the mirror. *Chase my ass out into the desert, huh, muthafucka?* she thought. *Well, look at me now. I'm still here, and I'm still the shit.*

She slipped into a pair of Liz Claiborne leather flip-flops, stuffed the $35,000 into the cheap beach bag, and headed for the elevator. No way was she leaving her hard-earned cash in the room, and no way was she walking down an Acapulco beach with a Louis Vuitton bag beggin' to get snatched by some street kid.

On the beach she found an empty lounge chair to lay out in. Immediately, a brown-skinned kid clad all in white from the hotel's beach bar came to take her drink order. That sounded good. She needed something to take the edge off, bring her adrenaline down a notch, but she also wanted something sweet. And after all the shit she'd been through, she deserved it. "I'll tell you what," she said to the bar waiter. "I'm in the mood for a Key Largo."

"Right away, ma'am," said the skinny boy, and he hurried off.

Five minutes later he returned with an ice cream soda glass filled with the ice-cold, frothy orange concoction, a bright red umbrella leaning against the rim. *Red.* It was a sign. It said, *You've arrived. This is where you're supposed to be.*

The cold glass felt good in her hand. She took the first sip through the straw and tasted the rum as she looked out across the wide beach and the smiling people with nothing on their minds but fun in the sun. *This is me,* she thought. *This is my life. And this is what my life is gonna be from now on. You heard me, all you raggedy ass Motown niggas? Try to take Red down. Now ya'll muthafuckas see who's winnin'.*

She finished the Key Largo and felt the buzz from it. That edge was definitely falling away. She patted her tummy and pinched a bit of flesh. She knew it was a fattening drink. *Do I have room for another?* she thought. Then she smiled. *Hell, yeah!* She got the bar kid's attention and sent him on his errand of mercy.

Halfway through the second drink, she was drifting into a more relaxed mood. More thoughtful. It was a nice buzz, but *thoughtful* wasn't what she'd been aiming for. She realized how troubled her thoughts had been since leaving her crib in Scottsdale. But then again, who the fuck could blame a bitch for worrying when fools like Catfish and Black kept popping up out of nowhere?

Phoenix, Vegas, Beverly Hills, now Acapulco. As she listened to the waves crash on the beach and felt the heat of the sun soaking into her skin, she realized how tired she was of running. She felt safe here. She had a cold drink in her hand, a buzz in her head, and thirty-five grand tucked under her lounge chair. Did she really need to go back to Beverly Hills? The money she had still wouldn't be enough to do it up large in a town like that, but in Mexico, she could make it happen. And with her intelligence, her skills, her fluency in Spanish and English, and her entrepreneurial talents she could start any number of businesses down here and crank her life back up to the level she was used to in Scottsdale within a couple of months.

And there was one other item of business she needed to take care of that would bring her even more money that she could use to get her shit set up right. Triple Crown Publications. She'd been so busy trying to stay one step ahead of various muthafuckas that she hadn't had time to even think about her books. And she couldn't have done any real business with her publisher anyway, because she hadn't known when she'd have to take off running again. Now she felt safe, and she was ready to settle down. For the time being, at least. It was time to reach out and touch Kammi Johnson.

She finished her drink, left the empty on the arm of the lounge chair, slung her bag with the thirty-five grand over her shoulder, and headed back to her room to change into some street clothes.

Before pursuing her writing and calling Triple Crown, she did a little research. She found a bank on the other side of Acapulco to which she could have money wired in the name of Lisa Lennox. She felt relatively safe in Mexico, but she wasn't about to receive money in her real name and not at the Calinda Beach even under a fake name. She didn't want any electronic shit hanging out there that could be traced to her.

She thought about the bug Quisha had found in her crib

back in Motown. She didn't know how they might do it, but she wasn't going to risk anybody tracing a business call back to her room, or even to the lobby of the Calinda Beach. It was getting on into late afternoon in Western Mexico, but it was barely after lunch at Triple Crown. She had plenty of time. She also realized it wouldn't be wise to carry her cash all over town. She popped down to the hotel gift shop and bought a small, locking suitcase. Back up in her room, she transferred the money to the case, then took it down to the front desk and asked them to hold it in their safe. The concierge escorted her to the vault, let her watch him put the case inside, then gave her a claim check.

Out on the street she enjoyed the sights and sounds of Acapulco as she looked for a pay phone from which to place her call. Street vendors hawked various items, from cheap sunglasses and sunscreen to iPods and cell phones. Even the kids were getting their hustle on. She smiled as she watched the young ones— some of them no more than five or six—work the crowds. *Shawties know what's up,* she thought. *They're gonna do just fine.* She thought back to her own childhood, the lessons she'd learned on the street, the shit she'd survived at home, and the determination that got her up out of there.

She stopped at one of the street vendors and bought a phone card and a disposable cell phone. She would use the card to make regular calls, but keep the cell phone for emergencies. She strolled down the street a little farther until she found a nice little beachside bar. Inside, she ordered a Corona and hit the pay phone.

"Triple Crown Publications is the blueprint," said the receptionist on the other end of the line. "How may I direct your call?"

"Good afternoon," said Red cheerily. She was almost startled to hear that tone in her own voice. It was the first time she'd felt carefree since Catfish had shown up on her doorstep in Scotts-dale. "I need to speak with Kammi Johnson, please."

"Certainly. And may I say who's calling?"

"You may. This is Lisa Lennox."

"Oh, yes, Ms. Lennox. I recognize your name. One of our au-thors, correct?"

"That's right."

"Looks like Kammi's just getting off another line. I'll go ahead and connect you."

Red waited a few seconds, then Kammi picked up the call.

"Lisa Lennox," she said, a smile in her voice. "It's good to hear from you. Where've you been?"

"Hi, Kammi. It's good to talk to you, too. Where've I been? Hmm. Good question. I guess it'd be easier to tell you where I haven't been."

Kammi laughed. "Okay, so, busy, in other words."

"Girl, I have had so much going on, you wouldn't believe it if I told you."

"I'm sure you're accomplishing great things with all your hard work."

Well, thought Red, *I've managed to keep my ass from getting shot, beat, or otherwise put in the ground. I guess that's a pretty big accomplishment.* "I'm getting there," she said. She took a sip of her beer and looked out the window at the tourists stroll-ing by.

"That's good to hear. And to what do I owe the pleasure of your call today?"

"Couple of things. First, I wanted to give you a new location to send my royalty checks and correspondence to."

"That's good," said Kammi. "Because the last check I sent to your PO box in Arizona came back as undeliverable. And you haven't been answering your phone."

"I know. I'm so sorry I wasn't in touch before this. The rent on the box ran out and I've been running around so much it just slipped my mind to get it renewed."

"Oh, that's fine," said Kammi. "Okay, I've got a pen. What's the new address?"

"If you can, I'd like you to tear up that check and just wire the money to my name, Lisa Lennox, at the Banco Nacional de Acapulco."

"Oh!" said Kammi. "Acapulco now. Look at you!"

"Well, you know. I decided to take a vacation. Figured I de-served it." Red didn't want to give her the impression she had relocated to Acapulco. No telling who might come around asking questions. In a week or so she'd get back up to Arizona or SoCal and set up a fake address to which her shit could be forwarded. For now, as far as anybody knew, she was down south for a few days.

"Oh, you do deserve it," said Kammi. "What's the point of being successful if you can't enjoy it?"

Red smirked. "Indeed."

As she gazed out the window, something caught her eye on the far side of the street. Two people, hand in hand, strolling down the sidewalk. But there were too many people in the way for her to get a good look at them. She stepped to her left as far as the phone cord would allow, but she still couldn't see their faces.

"Okay," said Kammi. "Let me just update all your contact info. Do you have a phone number where I can reach you?"

Red strained to see the couple. "What's that?"

"Phone?"

"Uh, I'm calling from a pay phone," she said absently.

"Yes, but I mean, is there a phone number you'd like me to keep on file for you?"

"A number of files?"

"Uh, no, I mean, is there a phone number where we can reach you. Something you'd like us to have in our records."

The couple on the other side of the street had moved on, out of Red's view. She snapped back to reality. "Oh, I'm sorry, Kammi. My phone number?"

"Yes."

"Yeah, let me get back to you on that. I'm just here chillin' for right now. Let me call you when I get back to the states in a few days. How's that?"

"Oh, sure," said Kammi. "No problem. I'll be looking forward to hearing from you in a week or so."

"Right. Thank you so much, Kammi. I appreciate all you've done for me."

"Believe me, we appreciate all you've done for Triple Crown."

"Good. Let's keep moving forward together. I'll talk to you soon."

Red hung up the phone before Kammi could say good-bye. With her fist around the neck of the Corona bottle, she ran out into the street and looked in the direction the couple had gone. They were nowhere in sight. *Couldn't be,* she thought. The guy was Q's height and his build. And he was walking with a cane. And with the limp she'd given him. She closed her eyes and shook her head, trying to blot out the memory of Q shot and bleeding on the floor, the smoking gun in her hand, the percussion of the bullet ringing in her ears.

And the woman? She could have sworn that bitch was Chass. But that couldn't be. *Mexico was supposed to be our place,* she thought. *Mine and Q's.* She shook her head. *Okay, Red. You been under a lot of stress, girl. Don't start seeing things. You're just starting to get your shit back together. Move forward. The past is the past. Don't dwell there.*

But the pain of seeing Q was almost too much for her, even if it was just in her mind's eye. Q with another woman. Q with a bullet in him. She stood in the middle of the street and guzzled half the beer as she tried to fight back the tears. Then she went back into the bar to make another call.

"Hello?" said the familiar voice on the other end of the line, hesitant, almost hostile.

"Quisha?"

"Red? Is that you?"

Red giggled like a school girl as she connected with the person who may have been her only real friend in the world at that point. "It's me, girlfriend."

"Goddamn, Red. You like a ghost, disappearing and reappearing and shit. And what the fuck is this unknown number bullshit you're calling from?"

"You alone?"

"Well, hang on a second."

Red heard a door open and close, and then she could hear the sounds of traffic.

"I'm over at my sister's place," said Quisha. "But I'm alone now. What's up, fugitive?"

"I'm calling you from Mexico. And that's just for you and you alone."

"I got your back, girl. You know that."

Red leaned against the wall by the pay phone and took another swig of beer. It was a relief to be hanging with a real friend, even if they were a couple thousand miles away from each other. "I do know that, Quisha. You my girl. And, yeah, I'm south of the border. I been running, but I think I've found a place to chill. For a while anyway. You never know what's gonna come your way in this life."

Quisha scoffed. "Shit, I heard that, baby girl. But you doin' okay?"

"I'm all right. But listen, what's the 411 back in Motown?"

"Aw, girl, don't tell me you're feeling homesick for this bitch?"

"You know. Just like to keep up on shit."

"Well, I'll tell you one thing. Foxy rolled back up in Divas after her trip to Cali talkin' 'bout how she saw your ass out there."

"Oh, she did, huh? Yeah, I ran into her when she was out there on her vacation with her girlfriends."

"Girlfriends?" said Quisha. "Naw, baby, she didn't have no bitches with her on that trip. She was flying solo."

"What? Why the fuck was she tellin' me she was on some kind of girl's holiday?"

"I don't know. But she was out there alone for a few days and came back looking like she got bitch slapped good and hard."

Red laughed. "She and I got into it."

"Oh, do tell."

"She wanted to throw down with me right there on the sidewalk on Rodeo Drive."

"Girl!"

"I told her she wasn't man enough to go toe to toe with me."

Quisha howled with laughter. "Brought that bitch down out whatever cloud she livin' on! My girl!"

"Bitch better not try to brawl with me. But, listen, you heard anything about Q, by chance?"

There was silence on the line. For a moment, Red thought she might have lost Quisha in some piece of shit international connection.

Finally Quisha answered her. "Aw, damn, girl. You ain't heard?"

Red swallowed hard, knowing bad news was on its way. "Heard what?"

"Yeah, Foxy was going on and on about that at Divas, too. She brought everybody up to speed on the history between you and Q. Took great pleasure in your misfortune."

"What, Quisha? Tell me."

"Q and Chass."

"Nuh-uh."

"They got married."

Red closed her eyes tight and gritted her teeth.

"Red?" said Quisha.

"I'm here."

"I didn't want to be the one to break that to you."

"What Foxy say?" Red heard her voice quiver a little when she spoke.

"Naw, Red, you don't need to be dwellin' on that shit."

"What she say, Quisha? I wanna know."

Quisha sighed into the phone.

"I'm serious, girl," said Red.

"Damn, you a glutton for punishment."

"Just tell me."

"Foxy said you shooting Q was the best thing ever happened to him, 'cause it drove him into the arms of a good woman for a change."

"That stupid ass bitch," said Red. "I shoulda beat her ass down when I had the chance."

"I'm sorry, girlfriend. Sometimes, you just got to move on. And now's that time."

Red wiped a single tear off her cheek and stood up straight. "Yeah," she said. "Time to move on."

CHAPTER THIRTY-SEVEN

*D*etective Thomas walked out of a café in a strip mall a quarter of a mile from Red's house in Scottsdale. He'd been canvassing the area, showing Red's picture to everybody he could, but with no luck. He squinted in the hot Arizona sun and slipped on his sunglasses. He sat on a bench and shook his head. If he didn't come up with something, he was fucked. He had no doubt Agent Holt would stab him in the back with Detroit PD Internal Affairs.

He reached into his pocket for his ringing cell phone and flipped it open. "Thomas," he said.

"Detective Thomas, you ready to do some business?"

"Who's this?"

"This Black."

Muthafucka, thought Thomas. *Here we go with act two of the Motown gangsta show.* "Been waiting to hear from you, Black. Where you been?"

"Never mind all that cop bullshit. Holt say you and me supposed to hook up. You ready?"

"Like I said, I been waiting to hear from you. Where you at?"

"Man," said Black, frustration creeping into his voice. "I'm where I'm supposed to be, doin' what I'm supposed to be doing to get myself out this shit Holt dropped me in. Now you gonna listen to me, or what?"

Thomas was starting to feel his own frustration. "I'm sitting here with the phone to my ear, aren't I? Can I listen any better than that? You got some shit to say, say it."

"Yeah, I got some shit to say, muthafucka. I got a line on where Red at. Now, you wanna work with me on this shit? 'Cause right now I don't know if I can trust your ass. You give me too much more static, I'ma take care of this shit my own self."

Thomas stood up off the bench and started walking out his anger. "You don't know if you can trust me? Muthafucka, how the fuck am I supposed to know if I can trust you?"

"I called you, didn't I?"

"After leaving me waiting on your ass forever. What's that shit all about?"

"I been working trying to come up with something on Red 'cause I didn't want to come to you empty-handed. I know how po-po do if they don't get what they want from a nigga. Look, you and me both want Red's ass. I almost had the bitch in Vegas, but she give me the slip. It's gonna take both of us working together to put the noose on that bitch neck. You feel me?"

Put the noose on that bitch neck. Whether Black meant that literally or not, it was starting to sound better and better to Thomas. And Black sounded like a man on a mission. Catfish had been as flaky as any dumb street thug he'd ever crossed paths with. And he'd dealt with plenty of those in his career. But he liked the way Black carried himself. He even liked the man's anger. He was taking this shit seriously. And he was right, he *had* called even after Thomas had almost given up hope of hearing from him.

"All right," said Thomas. "You want Red, I want Red. You know where she is, I need to know where she is. So let's do this thing."

"Now hold on," said Black. "I don't want no misunderstandings here that's gonna get you all uptight, make you wanna mess with a nigga. I know what city Red supposed to be in. You and me got to go down there and hunt for her."

"Down there? Down where?"

"Mexico, nigga. We goin' to Acapulco."

"Acapulco? You sure about that?"

"Now, see? There you go tryin' to hold me accountable and shit. I just told you I know where she *supposed* to be at. My girl Foxy ran into Red in L.A. Red told her she was headed to Acapulco."

Thomas thought about it for a minute. It made sense. Red was running out of places to go north of the border. If she really wanted to get away, why not Mexico? She also might be trying to find her way into Bacon's connect down there. Thomas also thought there was a good chance that Catfish had headed that way too, either to chase after Red, or to hook up with the black tar down there himself. If he could catch up with both Red and Catfish, he could save his ass with the feds and the DPD.

"Yeah, all right," said Thomas. "So where you at now?"

"I'm still in Vegas, nigga. But I'ma catch the next plane down to Acapulco. You grab a flight outta Phoenix, and I'll meet you down there."

It didn't take Thomas long to pack up his shit, check out of the hotel, and get to the airport. Within a couple of hours he was on a flight to Acapulco. He got there just before dark. While he waited at baggage claim, he flipped open his phone and found the last received call. He called Black, who said he was already checked into a place called the Hotel Fiesta Inn.

"All right," said Thomas. "I'll be there in forty-five minutes or so. First I'm gonna stop by the police station and let them know we're in town."

"All right."

"You heard?" said Thomas. "I'm going to give them your name, say you're working with me."

"Yeah, I heard. Why you trippin'?"

"I just want you to know if you got any thoughts about that black tar, that'd be a bad idea."

"Naw, muthafucka. I'm just trying to get clean with your cop thinkin' ass. And the feds. Don't you worry 'bout me. I'll put my shit together another time."

Thomas flipped his phone shut just in time to grab his bag off the carousel. He snapped out the handle and began maneuvering it through the crowds of American and European tourists, eager to get to the cab stand.

He stuffed his bags into the backseat, not trusting a Mexican cab driver enough to be separated from them even for the time it would take to get to the police station. The driver was a fat guy in his sixties. The interior smelled of gasoline, and Thomas wondered if the thing was even roadworthy. He dusted off the little bit of high school Spanish he remembered. *"Yo buscando por la policia,"* he said.

The old man looked over his shoulder at him, then pointed out the window at the sidewalk. "There's a cop right there," he said.

"You speak English?"

"Yeah. Better than you speak Spanish, I think."

Thomas smirked. "No doubt. Take me to the police station."

The driver pointed out the window again. "This guy's not good enough?"

"Nope," said Thomas.

The driver shrugged and pulled away from the curb.

Taking in the scenario Thomas thought of the complexities

of his decisions. Twenty minutes later Thomas paid him for the ride and walked into the station with his rolling suitcase and his carry-on. He leaned the handle of the suitcase against the front desk and reached into his back pocket for his badge. "My name's Detective Thomas. I'm here on business from the Detroit Police Department. I need to check in with you."

The desk officer, a gangly guy with a uniform at least one size too big for him, shrugged, then turned and shouted over his shoulder in Spanish.

A minute later, a plainclothes cop appeared at the desk. "Good evening, Detective," he said. "You need to speak with someone in English?"

"Yeah," said Thomas.

"I speak it. But just don't use too many of the American slang words." He smiled. "I only know the dirty ones."

Thomas smiled and shook his hand. "I'll keep that in mind."

"Come on," said the cop, motioning for Thomas to follow him deeper into the station. "My name's Detective Reynaldo Guzmán."

Thomas found himself in a big room with several desks amid a swirl of activity. He took a seat across from Guzmán and tossed a picture of Red onto his desk. "You seen her, by chance?"

The detective picked up the photo and studied it. "I seen women like her in my dreams," he said, then he shook his head. "But, no, sorry."

"Yeah, well, she's wanted by the Detroit Police and the FBI. I think she might be in your town so I'm gonna take a look around for her. She might also be trying to make contact with a supplier of black tar heroin."

Guzmán looked around the office, startled, then leaned forward toward Thomas. "That's a sensitive subject around here," he whispered. "There could be some guys right in this room who work for such a supplier."

Thomas looked around, but it seemed that everyone was too busy with other things to have noticed the exchange. "Sorry," he said. He was about to tell Guzmán about Black, but realized maybe he shouldn't if the cartel had ears in the room. Black was not a CI exactly, but if he could help him track down Red, he owed it to the man to keep his name from getting out.

"You got a cell phone number I can call?" said Thomas. "In case we need any help with the lady?"

Guzmán scribbled something on a slip of paper. "I just ran out of business cards." He tossed the paper to Thomas. "The first number is the phone here on my desk. The second is my cell phone. And if you decide you really don't need to take her back with you, just slip that paper to her. Tell her I know a couple of Mexican restaurants in the area."

Thomas chuckled as he folded the paper and stuck it in his shirt pocket. "I'll do that." He stood and shook the man's hand again.

Back out on the street he hailed another cab and told the driver to take him to the Hotel Fiesta Inn. It was fully dark now, and Thomas took in the sights and sounds of a party town coming alive for the evening. He checked out some of the fine local señoritas, as well as the ladies vacationing from north of the border. *I gotta remember this place,* he thought. *If I manage to save my job and ever get to the point where I can collect a pension, I'm coming back.*

Once he'd checked into the hotel, he threw his shit in his room and went straight to Black's. Black answered the door looking tired, or sick.

"You okay?" said Thomas.

"Yeah, I'm all right," he said. "What side the hotel they put you on?"

"What side?"

"Yeah, the front or the back?"

"Uh, the front, I guess."

Black shook his head. "Goddamn. Check this shit out." He led Thomas out to the balcony, which overlooked a dark expanse. "You believe this shit?"

Thomas peered into the darkness. "What is that?"

"I know, right? I'm in Acapulco, and they gave me a room overlooking the fuckin' golf course. I mean, Acapulco about the beach, right? I can't even see the ocean from up in this bitch. I look like I play golf to you?"

Thomas tried not to laugh. "Yeah, you look like about a five handicap."

"What, muthafucka? What you mean, handicap? I ain't no handicap."

"Relax, my man. It was a joke. We ain't here to play. We got work to do. So you got any ideas about where Red might be hanging out?"

Black led the way back into the room and dropped into a chair. "Man, if I know that bitch—and I *know* that bitch—she out partyin'. Only problem is, in a town like this with so many clubs and shit, where we gonna start lookin'?"

"Maybe we're looking at this the wrong way," said Thomas as he leaned against the dresser, arms folded across his chest. "You said you know her, right?"

"Yeah."

"Well, maybe instead of chasing her down like a rabbit, we should lure her in. Sweet talk her."

Black thought about it for a minute, nodding his head slowly. "Yeah, I feel you."

"How can we reach out to her?"

Black smiled, "I might know a way."

CHAPTER THIRTY-EIGHT

*A*s long as they were in the Fed's pocket, Black and Thomas decided they didn't have to eat on a budget. They weren't going to go down to a corner market and buy shit to fix in the room. Instead they ordered up room service. They discovered the hotel kitchen did killer chile rellenos, which they washed down with Dos Equis.

Even before they'd finished eating, Black broke out his laptop and logged onto Facebook.

"Don't get too pushy with her," said Thomas around a mouthful of food. "Finesse."

"Yeah," said Black as he typed *Raven Gomez* into the search box. "Bitch gonna see some finesse if I get hold of her."

Thomas took a sip of beer and watched as Black tapped away at the keyboard. He'd thought many times of what he would do if and when he caught up with Red. Black obviously had enough hatred for her that he could do her harm. As for himself, Thomas wasn't sure. While he was on her ass in the U.S., he had intended to play it by the book. But this was Mexico. The Wild West. South of the boarder—south of the rules. He thought about how Red had dropped him in the shit with IA in Detroit. Fucked him bone dry, videotaped it, and charged him with rape. She was a heartless, dirty bitch. He felt the pulse in his temple pound as he thought about it, then took another swig of beer and moved in behind Black to read over his shoulder.

After a few minutes of typing, Black looked over his shoulder. "What you think, Mr. Detective? That smooth enough?"

"Looks good. And you know her better than I do."

"That's right, I do." Black stopped to shovel the last couple bites of chile rellenos into his mouth. "I'ma tell you right now, Red got a lot of backbone, but she all alone down here. And she a Motown girl. This a different culture for her. All this *mas cerveza, por favor* shit—she don't know that."

"I thought she knew Spanish," said Thomas.

"Yeah, she do. She do. But I'm not talking about the language, I'm talking about the vibe. She don't know how these Mexican niggas roll. Right about now, she wantin' to see a familiar face."

Thomas settled into a chair. "I hope you're right. For now, I guess all we can do is wait."

"For real," said Black, and he clicked "send."

Red lay in bed, fully clothed, staring up at the ceiling. She'd given up self-pity many years ago. That never got a bitch anywhere. And she'd always been going places. But hearing the news about Q took the wind out of her. What the fuck was she doing down here? She'd made all her moves, been so smart, so far ahead of everybody else, and look what it got her. A bag of cash, one single, solitary friend, and a crick in her neck from looking over her shoulder.

Nuh-uh, she thought as she sat up. *Enough of that shit. The time to move on is now. Things are gonna come together for me down here.*

She hopped up out of bed and powered up her laptop. She had to start researching her business opportunities down here. Real estate was a likelihood. She knew that game and figured there were plenty of possibilities in the area. She could sell Mexican villas to wealthy Americans and Canadians. She could handle rentals for seasonal visitors and businesspeople. Hell, she could even develop resort real estate. There had to be a piece of that kind of business that she could break off for herself.

She found a wireless connection and opened a Google search. She was about to type in *Acapulco real estate,* but then she decided to do something else first. She opened her Facebook page. She had a few new messages, including one from somebody she thought would never message her again—Black.

She put the pointer over Black's message and let her finger hover over the touch pad for a moment. Did she really want to read that shit? She could predict what it was—hateful bullshit, maybe even death threats. Or it could be some taunt about how Q had left her for Chass. She was about to skip over it, but she just couldn't resist seeing what shit the fool had to say.

She opened the message and began to read. She couldn't believe her eyes.

Hey Red!

Can we chill for a minute? I been trying to get with you, but we keep getting our wires crossed. That first time I saw you in Vegas, I know I musta scared the shit out of you. I was scared myself at that moment. I guess you figured out I was running from Five-Oh. They shot my nigga Trap. Believe that shit? They was gonna shoot me too, but I bolted.

And then when I saw you in the casino, I probably looked like I was sneaking around, but you know I didn't recognize you at first. Damn, girl! You looked so different. I was like—who that? She look like Red a little, but, naw, couldn't be. Sorry I scared you.

But you know what, girl? With Bacon out the way, and Trap out the way, I'm trying to get paid from that black tar connect they had. But I can't do this shit alone. I ain't trying to be partners with Bacon or Catfish or none of them other niggas. I tried that with Trap, but he started trippin' at the first sign of trouble, got his self killed. Nearly got me killed.

But you solid, girl. I know you can handle yourself, whatever kinda shit go down. You proved that to everybody. And on top of all that, I know you don't need no man to take care of you, but in a game like this, you could always use some muscle. And you know I throw down with any muthafuckin' nigga. 'Sides, I always felt something special for you. You know that.

Reason I'm saying all this is I'm down in Acapulco scoping shit out, trying to get with that connect. Now, don't trip, but Foxy told me you might be down here, too. I'ma tell you what. We could make some shit happen down here. I'm talkin' 'bout *real* money. Kind of money set us up for life, we do this right. You know these Mexican niggas think we need them, but they need us just as bad. You know I can hook up some distribution up north. Now that Bacon out the way, they need that shit. And I know you know Spanish, and I don't. You can actually talk to these niggas. Better yet, you can understand what they sayin' when they talkin' to each other.

I ain't askin' for no commitment, but we should just talk. That's all I wanna do is talk. Just talk to me, Red.

Holla back.

"Muthafucka," said Red out loud. She shivered and had to look over her shoulder to make sure nobody was there. No matter how far she ran, or where she ended up, there was always some Detroit nigga rollin' up on her.

She leaned back in her chair and shook her head. Black. She had to smile when she thought about him. He was a fine nigga and the kind who stood tall through all kinda shit. Unlike Catfish, he had a brain in his head. And unlike Bacon, he *could* be a gentleman where a lady was concerned. But could he really be getting with Bacon's connect? Did he have the business structure that Bacon had? Could he move black tar? It was absolutely true that there was a vacuum in Detroit. Any number of niggas wanted to step in and fill it. Trap for one. And now he was dead? Goddamn! If Black could pull it off, hooking up with him could be a smart move.

But could she trust him? Was he really just trying to get a better look at her in the casino that night? That was bullshit. She didn't buy that for a second. But if Black was on his own now, he might be seeing the potential of making a big play. And it was true, she did know the language down here and he didn't. And the money? Without even trying, her mind shifted gears and started formulating plans to extend distribution, improve deliveries, negotiate discounts. Shit, a couple of years in that business could buy her a Park Avenue penthouse will all the trimmings. It was the kind of money that could make even Q jealous.

All Black wanted to do was talk, he said. She had the disposable cell phone. What could it hurt? She typed her number into the message field, then clicked "send" before she had a chance to change her mind.

Thomas was in the bathroom taking a piss when he heard Black shout. "What?" he called over his shoulder.

"Bring your ass in here, nigga. You ain't gonna believe this."

"Can I finish pissin' first?"

"Piss all you want, Popo, but you gonna shit when you see this."

Thomas shook his dick out and stuffed it back in his pants. "What?" he said as he hurried out of the bathroom.

Black leaned back from the computer. "Check it out."

Thomas leaned over and read the screen. He stood up straight and smiled at Black.

"Those digits gonna change everything for us," said Black.

"That's all she sent? Just the phone number?"

"That's all she need to send." He reached for his phone. "Now you just don't say nothin', 'cause I'm supposed to be here alone."

"Don't worry, my man. Just do your thing."

Black punched up the number and hit "talk."

It rang a couple of times, then he heard Red's voice. "Black?"

"Oh, damn, girl," said Black. "It's good to hear your voice."

"I'm not sure I should be saying the same to you."

"I know, I know. We been into some crazy shit, the both of us. You know I been on the run, same as you, for a while now."

"You been on the run?" said Red. "Why?"

"I told you, girl. Them Vegas cops shot Trap. He was in the driver's seat, and I was sitting right next to him. Nigga fell out right in my lap. I got the fuck outta there running for my life. I guess they still got paper out on me. Description and shit. They trying to find me for sure."

Red tried to hear something in his voice that wasn't just right. "Well, I'm sorry about Trap. That's some nasty shit."

"For real. But being down here in Mexico gonna work out just about perfect. I can be out the country, and work on this black tar business at the same time."

"You got any idea where to start with that shit?"

"I got a couple of ideas," said Black. "But, really, I just want things to be good between you and me. I want to prove to you that you can trust me and take me at my word. 'Cause we gotta work together if this shit gonna happen big like I know it can."

Red put her elbow on the dresser of her hotel room and rested her chin in the palm of her hand. "Now, how you gonna prove that, Black?"

"I feel you. But maybe we could do it like this. There's a place down by the beach called the Galerias Diana. It's right on that main street, Costera Miguel Alemán. They got a big-ass movie theater up in that bitch. You meet me there, it's out in public, we surrounded by people, but we can whisper to each other, too. Like being in private and in public at the same time. The address is 1632. They's another one on the same street, so don't go to that one by mistake."

"So you want to take me on a date to a movie."

"Yeah, I guess you could say it that way. Look, you can drive around all over the place, come up from whatever direction you want. Even if I'm looking out for you, I won't know where you comin' from."

Red thought about it for a minute.

"You there, girl?" said Black.

"Yeah, I'm here. What time?"

Black looked at his watch. It was about eight thirty. "About an hour. Say nine thirty."

"I'll be there," said Red, and she hung up the phone.

Black flipped his phone closed and tossed it on the dresser. "Oh, damn!" He stood up.

"What?" said Thomas.

"We got that bitch. Movie theater in one hour."

"She sound committed?"

"Mm," said Black. "She sound wary, but she gonna show up. You got an extra piece?"

"Extra piece?"

"Yeah, I couldn't risk bringin' nothin' down on the plane, but you being popo, I figured you ain't had no problem with that."

"You want me to give you a weapon?"

"Man, I just told you she sound wary. I bet she strapped."

"You think you're gonna get in a shootout with her in a movie theater?"

Black hung his head to the side. "I think if she strapped and she get nervous, she might pull her piece on me. I ain't trying to get my ass shot off by that bitch."

It wasn't a bad idea. Thomas had no doubt Black would drop a trigger on her if he had the chance. And if he did, that would save Thomas the trouble of having to justify shooting her himself. He dug a snub-nosed .38 out of his suitcase along with some ammo and handed it to Black.

"Damn. This some old school shit, right here." He smiled at Thomas. "This your cold piece?"

"It's not registered, if that's what you mean."

"Yeah, that's what I mean, partner."

"If you wind up having to use it, make sure you're at close range, and don't hit any civilians."

Black nodded. "Oh, I'll be close up on the bitch. No doubt."

It almost sounded like Black had already made up his mind what he was going to do when he saw her. And Thomas didn't say anything in response.

They got to the movie theater at a quarter after nine. Black bought a ticket and went into the lobby to wait for Red. Thomas took over the watch and waited across the street, keeping an eye on the front of the buildings for Red's arrival. When she went in, Thomas would hurry across the street and come up behind her in the lobby. He and Black would both grab her. That is, if Black hadn't already shot her by the time Thomas got to them. Either way would work out.

From down the block, Red watched as Black entered the building containing the theater. Nobody went in with him, and he didn't seem to have a tail. But the muthafucka had glanced over his shoulder just before he went inside. Maybe he'd been looking for a tail, too. Or maybe he'd been checking to see if she had arrived. But something about it just didn't feel right. Something about that glance. And his body language. He was too smug. Not happy, not excited, not nervous. Just satisfied. Like he knew something nobody else knew.

Nope, she thought. *This ain't cool*. Red hailed a cab and headed back to her hotel.

As he stood in the shadows and watched the front door of the building across the street, Thomas saw a cab pass. As it went under a street light, he could see the passenger in the back seat clearly. It was Red. He waited for it to pass, then he stepped out into the street and tried to hail a cab to follow her. But a drunk couple that had just stumbled out of a bar took the next one. And three college age American kids took the next. By that time, Red was long gone.

Muthafucka, thought Thomas as it started to rain. He jogged across the street, badged the girl at the ticket window, and went into the lobby.

Black's eyes got big when he saw Thomas, thinking that the cop was about to blow the set up.

Thomas shook his head and waved him off. "No good," he said.

"No good? What you mean?"

"I saw her. She rode by in a cab. She ain't comin' in."

CHAPTER THIRTY-NINE

Q watched Chass dancing in front of him in the club. There was no denying that she was a fine lady and had some moves, both on the dance floor and in bed. He half-danced across from her. He'd left the cane at their table, but now the pain in his leg and hip were taking the fun out of watching Chass, and a wave of dissatisfaction washed over him. Finally he forced a smile and reached out to grab her. He pulled her to him and wrapped his arms around her.

"I'm starved," he said into her ear over the noise of the club.

Chass looked at her watch. "Well, no wonder. It's almost a quarter after nine. We've been having way too much fun."

They'd started the evening with drinks in a bar with a jazz guitarist. Chass had stuck to soda water, and Q had tried to keep his drinking in check out of respect for her. They'd shared an appetizer, but Chass had been so mesmerized by the music that she'd insisted they go dancing before they got to dinner.

Chass cocked her head. "At least I've been having fun. Are you okay?"

Q hated that question. Nothing drove him nuts more than a woman asking if he was *okay*. He took a deep breath and forced himself to stay calm. "I'm fine, baby. Just hungry, that's all."

Chass gave him a devilish smile. "We could order room service."

Q realized that if he went back to the room, he could get into the mood for sex without too much trouble. But at that moment, it was the furthest thing from his mind, and he really just didn't want to think about it. "You know what?" he said. "I heard about a nice restaurant in the Calinda Beach Hotel up the street. I want to take you there."

Chass pouted. "You want to go there instead of ordering room service?"

Q laughed mechanically. "I'm really hungry, baby. And I heard they do steak like no place else in Acapulco."

"Oh," she said, teasing. "You're in the mood for meat, huh. That's funny, because so was I. Until you started talking about restaurants."

"I promise, you'll get your full serving later on. Right now, I need some calories before I fall out." He took her hand and led her back to the table where he collected his cane. Without sitting down, he picked up his glass and tossed back the last of his Jack on the rocks. Chass had joked that it wasn't a very Mexican drink, but he had wanted his booze without any nonsense.

It took Red an hour to get back to the Calinda Beach Hotel. She'd told the cab driver to take her out to the airport. Then she'd gotten a different cab from there back into town. She'd changed cabs two more times before finally arriving at the Calinda Beach.

She was sure she hadn't been followed, and she was also sure Black didn't know where she was staying. If he did, he wouldn't have come up with a plan to lure her out to a place where he could ambush her.

If that was what he was doing. She didn't know anymore. After running for so long from so many people, she could no longer tell if she was smart, or just paranoid.

Before going to her room, she decided to stop at the restaurant and get some food in her stomach. And a drink or two. She wasn't sure whether she needed to clear her head, or numb her brain, but she definitely needed to come down off the jitters she'd gotten after seeing Black.

The hostess sat her at a small table in the corner. She ordered two fresh chicken tamales with guacamole and a margarita. She'd barely put the second bite of food in her mouth when she heard a voice that caused her jaw to freeze. She looked up and saw Q holding a chair for Chass as she sat at a table not twenty feet from her.

"Okay, now the steak is gonna take a little while to cook," he said as he made his way to the other side of the table using his cane. "So we need a couple of appetizers to start out." He settled into his chair and immediately opened his menu.

Chass was all smiles as she read her own menu. They were dressed for the club, and the lawyer bitch looked like she'd been having a good time. Q seemed more thoughtful. Red wondered how much pain he was still in from his injury. They ordered appetizers. Q ordered a Jack on the rocks. Chass ordered soda water.

Red realized she wasn't chewing anymore and spit her food back out onto her plate. She took a gulp of her margarita to rinse the bad taste out of her mouth. Her first instinct was to get up and march over to their table. But what would she say? She considered trying to sneak out of the restaurant before they saw her.

But their table was between Red and the door. How would she get past them?

That's ridiculous, thought Red. *Why should I slink around? I made my apologies to Q. He knows how I feel. And, if Chass doesn't know how I feel about her, she has no business pretending she's smart.*

She downed the rest of her margarita and stood up. After all the shit she'd been through, she wasn't going to let this go by. She strolled over to their table, taking it slow, wanting to see how long it would take them to notice her.

When she was still ten feet out, Chass looked up. At first she seemed unable to believe her eyes. Then she glared at Red.

"What's wrong, honey?" said Q.

"Honey?" said Red, now stepping directly to the table. "Is that what she is to you now?"

Q turned and looked at her. His jaw dropped. "What . . . ? How the . . . ?"

"How can you even keep your appetite sitting across from this bitch?" asked Red.

Chass stood up. "My God," she said. "How on earth can you walk over to this table and dare to speak to him after what you did?"

"I've spoken to Q about all that happened. He knows what's in my heart."

Chass looked like she was about to be sick, but instead, she drew back her arm and slapped Red across the face.

Red staggered back, surprised. She picked up a drink from the next table and flung it in Chass's face. Chass screamed as the alcohol stung her eyes.

"Muthafucka," shouted Q as he stood up.

Red turned to him. "Q, I need you to know—"

But Q wasn't about to listen to anything from Red. He reached out and grabbed her around the throat with both hands.

"I oughta kill you right here and now, you nasty bitch. I should put you outta everybody's misery."

Red felt her throat close up, and she struggled to breathe. She looked into Q's eyes, and he returned her gaze. Soon she felt his grip loosen, and she pulled away.

"Get the . . ." said Chass, still trying to blink and rub the drink out of her eyes. "Get the manager."

Red stood her ground and held Q's gaze. "You ought to kill me? Is that what you said?"

Q stared back at her, jaw clenched.

"You can't kill me, baby. You still love me."

"I—" said Q. But he couldn't find the words.

"You know you do," said Red. "There's a passion you and I shared that she can never give you. You just been killing time with her. Waiting for this moment."

Chass struggled to her feet, eyes watering. She grabbed Q by the arm and began to tug him toward the door.

Q barely managed to grab his cane as he was pulled away.

Red stood there looking after him as he glanced back over his shoulder to make eye contact one last time before reaching the door.

CHAPTER FORTY

*R*ed stood in the middle of the restaurant watching the door close on Q and Chass. The lively chatter of the diners had descended into a shocked murmur. She looked around. Some people were staring at her, mouths open. Others were looking away, too embarrassed for her to make eye contact.

"Hey," said the young American woman at the table she was standing next to. "That was my drink."

Red turned to her. "Oh, you want a drink, bitch?"

The woman's husband, boyfriend, pimp, whatever the fuck he was, stood up. "I don't know who you think you are, lady," he said. "But—"

She felt a hand grab her upper arm. She was about to throw a punch, but when she looked over her shoulder, she saw that she was in the grasp of a 6'4", 250-pound Mexican dude in a dark grey, three-piece suit.

"I'm sorry, ma'am, but I'm going to have to ask you to leave," he said. He actually didn't seem the least bit sorry.

"Oh, you kickin' me out, huh?"

The man rolled his eyes. "I'm trying to do this the easy way. We can do it the other way if you want."

Red held his gaze for a moment longer. Then she jerked her arm out of his hand and started for her table.

"Ma'am, the door is in the other direction."

"I'ma get my purse," she spat over her shoulder. "*If* you don't mind. Muthafucka!" She scooped the Prada clutch purse off her table and turned to the door.

Out on the street Red gritted her teeth and blinked away the sting in her eyes. She wished she could rewind the last few minutes. She wanted to go back so Q could play it out differently. In the replay, he took Red's face in his hands and kissed her, instead of grabbing her by the throat and trying to strangle her. Or maybe Chass slapped her, and Q jumped up to put his hands around *her* throat. Or, when Chass was trying to drag him out of the restaurant, he broke away from her and told her it was over.

Could this night get any muthafuckin' worse? she thought as she turned and started down the sidewalk.

She walked for several minutes, bumping into partiers as they tumbled out of the bars and clubs, full of laughter. She hadn't even gotten to eat her dinner—hadn't eaten in hours—and she was starved. But she was sick of Mexican food, sick of Mexico altogether. She wanted a fuckin' cheeseburger. That's what she wanted. Did they have any real American cheeseburgers in this bitch?

Then she saw the next best thing. A place called Giuseppe's. It didn't seem like the cheeseburger kind of place, but at least it wasn't Mexican. She stepped inside and was magically transported to Italy. There was Italian music playing. Murals of northern Italian landscapes covered the walls. And the smell was definitely Italian food.

For the second time that evening, she found herself telling a hostess she needed a table for one. Just one. Just little ol' Red, that's all. Single. Solitary. Solo. Alone.

She was seated at a small table by the kitchen. Waiters rushed past the kitchen door was constantly in motion, and the clatter of dishes and bluster of a dictatorial chef almost drowned out the cheerful music. If Q had been with her, he'd have demanded another table. But what the fuck did Red care? It wasn't like she'd be carrying on any romantic conversations. All she wanted to do was get some muthafuckin' food in her stomach.

As the hostess walked away from the table, Red saw an elegantly dressed American woman in her mid-30s. The two spoke for a moment, then the hostess returned to Red's table. She was blushing a bit, and as she began to speak, Red realized that English was a struggle for her.

"Please," said the girl, gesturing for Red to stand up. "Sorry for a table. Better is over here."

Red shrugged and stood. She followed the hostess across the room to a table by the window. Red could see the moonlight reflected in the Pacific and the silhouettes of palm trees swaying in the breeze. *Very romantic*, thought Red. *Just what I need right now.* But she forced a smile and thanked the hostess just the same.

She started with some red wine, and, by the time her food came, she was on her third glass. As she dug into her dinner, she realized she'd picked the right spot. The rich eggplant parmigiana almost melted in her mouth, and the Italian bread was so soft and delicious that she could have made a meal out of that alone. Before she finished, she ordered a fourth glass of wine. And then, of course, she figured she deserved the tiramisu and a cappuccino.

As she was finishing her dessert, the nicely dressed woman appeared beside her table. Up close, Red could see that she was beautiful, and not dressed on a budget. The diamond earrings looked like Cartier, the dress was Bulgari, and the watch was Piaget.

"Was your dinner satisfactory?" asked the woman, displaying a smile full of perfect white teeth.

After four glasses of wine, Red was feeling no pain. Still, she was not in a social mood. "Fine."

The woman nodded through the window. "I trust the view here is more to your liking than the one by the kitchen."

Red rolled her eyes. "Fabulous."

"My name's Candace Forbes. If I may I say, you're a very lovely woman. Very striking." The woman extended her hand.

Red looked at her hand, but didn't shake it. "That's nice of you to say, Candace, but to tell you the truth, I've been harassed enough today."

"Oh? I'm sorry to hear that, but I assure you, I have no such intention." She pulled out the chair across from Red and sat down.

"You must be one of the regular customers here, huh?" Red asked.

"I do eat here regularly, but I'm not a customer. I'm the owner."

"Oh, I get it," said Red. "I'm paying in cash, if that's what you're worried about."

"Believe me, the question never crossed my mind. In the kind of work I do, I have to be able to read people. I read you as something quite special."

"You have to be able to read people in the restaurant business?"

"Oh, God no," said Candace. "I don't *run* this place, I just own it. My real businesses are in New York."

Red's interest was piqued. "Oh," she said. "I'm sorry. I didn't mean to be rude. My name's Re—uh—Regina Morales. Pleased to meet you." She shook hands with the woman.

"I didn't take you for rude. I see you as a woman with a great deal of strength and independence who's been carrying some heavy responsibilities of late. We all have to let our hair down once in a while."

"Really?" said Red. "You can tell that just by looking at me?"

Candace looked into Red's eyes. "Let's see. You're from a big city. Northern. You have an entrepreneurial spirit. You're in upper management, if not a business owner yourself. You're used to juggling a lot of projects at once. You hate compromise but have had to make many in your life. But that last one was a gimme. We *all* have to do that, dear."

Red nodded slowly. "Okay, Candace. I'm impressed. You see all the trouble I've had with men, too?"

Candace laughed. "Strong women *always* have trouble with men. It's part of that compromising issue we have."

"Is that what it is? I always thought my standards were either too high or too low."

"Hmm. Your standards can never be too high when it comes to men. More wine?"

Red picked up her wine glass and swirled the last drop. "Sure, why not?"

"You were drinking . . . ?"

"Your house Bardolino."

"Let's switch to something a little nicer." Candace raised her hand and beckoned a waiter, who hurried over to the table. "Let's have a carafe of Famiglia Anselma Barolo. Yes?"

"Right away, ma'am," said the waiter.

Red and Candace talked well into the evening. The restaurateur's primary line of work was in PR and event promotions in New York. She worked with high-end clients and high-end happenings, including what she called *specialty events*. These were exclusive parties—some of which were themed—that catered to eccentric tastes. She declined to name anyone who might have attended such events, but she assured Red that her clients included A-list celebs, Wall Street moguls, and heads of state. It was that kind of work that allowed her to *play* at the restaurant business, and she did a lot of playing. In addition to Giuseppe's in Acapulco, she owned restaurants in Moscow, Berlin, and Madrid, and would soon be opening a place in Paris.

Tipsy as she was, Red revealed more about herself than she would have sober but not enough to get her in trouble. She mentioned her real estate business in Detroit and her publishing ventures, but all that paled in comparison with Candace's successes. Of course, if she could have told the woman about all she'd really done, it probably would have knocked her out of her chair, but Red didn't want to shock her. Not yet, anyway.

It wasn't necessary. Candace knew Red was a hustler, though she might not have put it in those terms. "A woman of your experience and determination could go far in Mexico," said Candace. "Take it from me."

"I've thought about that," said Red. "It seems like a place with some great opportunities, but to tell you the truth, I can't stay here. Things that have happened in the past couple of days . . ." She shook her head. "I won't go into all that. But let's just say, certain events have poisoned the well for me here. I thought I might be here for a long while, but I already need to get out."

"Well, Regina," said Candace. "I'll tell you honestly, a woman like you can create her own success wherever she goes. Though it never hurts to have a friend in the right place." She reached into the pocket of her blazer and handed Red a card. "I'm leaving for New York tonight. If you're ready to make a change—I mean a *big* change—think about paying me a visit there."

Red rubbed the card between her thumb and forefinger and looked at Candace. "Actually, I *will* think about that."

"I think it may be time for you to leave Mexico, Detroit, and everywhere else behind. They call it the Big Apple for a reason, you know. Come see me and find out why."

Candace stood and got the attention of the waiter. She pointed to the table. "This is all on the house."

"The wine?" said the waiter.

"The wine, the dinner, everything."

"Yes, ma'am," he said.

Candace shook hands with Red. "Regina," she said. "It's been a pleasure getting to know you. I hope to hear from you soon."

"Thank you," said Red. "I believe I'll be in touch."

Red watched through the window as Candace climbed into the passenger seat of a Range Rover. As soon as the door closed, the car was off, headed toward the airport. Red looked at the card in her hand. *Candace Forbes,* she thought. *Now that's the kind of life I could enjoy living.*

CHAPTER FORTY-ONE

*M*aybe I should have included Detective Guzmán in our little caper last night," said Thomas.

He and Black had spent the morning trying to get a lead on where Red's cab might have taken her. What they found was that many of the taxis in Acapulco were operated by gypsies. They didn't use dispatchers, they didn't have medallions, and they didn't keep records.

Now Black and Thomas were on foot, making their way through the streets of Acapulco on their way to a burrito stand Black had heard about. According to Black, they were supposed to have the best burritos in town. Thomas was skeptical that some roadside stand in Acapulco could have good food. But since he'd hooked up with Black, he'd come to have a grudging respect for the man. He was a stone gangsta, but he kept it tight. The nigga walked it like he talked it, and didn't get into the kind of bullshit nonsense that had seemed to be an essential part of Catfish's personality. It was a good trade—Catfish for Black. So if the man wanted a burrito, what the fuck? Thomas could go along with that.

"The fuck you talkin' about, call Guzmán?" asked Black.

"All I'm saying is that if we had a few locals with us last night, we could have had Red. They could have pulled that cab over and put the bracelets on the bitch right then and there."

"Naw, man," said Black. "We don't need no Mexican po-po fuckin' with our shit on this. Red is *our* business. As long as we on that bitch, I say we do it ourselves. If it go past that into that black tar bullshit, then maybe we get your nigga Guzmán in on it."

Thomas glanced at Black, trying to gauge what he was thinking. It didn't take a genius to figure out that Black still had blood in his eyes. Without any local cops around, it would be a simple thing to drop a hammer on the bitch and say she had a weapon. In a town like this, even if her *weapon* wasn't recovered, it wouldn't really matter. What happened in Mexico stayed in Mexico. When they delivered the corpse up north, they could tell the tale any way they wanted.

"But, you know," said Black. "She was there. It wasn't like she just told me she was gonna be there and then didn't show up. She came to the muthafuckin' meet. We almost had her."

"I know," said Thomas. "But something spooked her."

"You think she might coulda seen you?"

Thomas shook his head. "No way. I was across the street and in the shadows."

"I say I just call her again." Black put his thumb and pinky finger up to the side of his face. "Be like, *Yo, girl. I waited for you for like a hour. I thought we was gonna sit down. Talk it out. 'Sup with you, girl?*"

"It's worth a try," said Thomas.

"I'll sweet talk her. Don't you worry, partner. I'll sweet talk her. You bet I will."

"The point is, we need to get this bitch," said Thomas. "One way or the other."

"I feel you, partner."

"I mean, if we can't pull this shit together, my career's fucked. They will do me quick as look at me. I go out with no pension, nothing."

"Who the fuck you tellin', nigga? That Agent Holt mutha-fucka want to throw my black ass inside. And he got some heavy shit on me. I ain't trying to do no hard time, man." Black gestured to the city around them. "And I can't retire down in this bitch. Can't speak the language, don't understand what the ladies of the pole be saying when they bend down to pick up my pesos, can't tell what's in the muthafuckin' food."

Thomas laughed. "Aw, you could live down here. You'd get it all figured out."

"Yeah, you never know," said Black. "We might roll up into this burrito place, they be a nice little señorita waitin' on us, and the food be primo. That's all a nigga need, right?"

The clack of high heels on the sidewalk approached them from behind, coming up fast. A slender young lady with a nice round ass hurried past them, arms swinging purposefully.

"See, like that one," said Black, pointing to the girl. "That's a nice piece of pussy right there."

Thomas held a finger to his lips to hush him.

"She don't know what the fuck we saying, man. I guarantee you, she don't speak no English."

Maria smirked and rolled her eyes as she put on a little more speed and left the two Americans behind. Ordinarily, she might spend a few minutes embarrassing them, but she didn't have time now. She had a meeting to get to—a money meeting. She was proud of the way she'd hooked Catfish and his friend, Ernie Banks. She could tell they were angry to begin with. But business was business. Her loyalty was valuable to them. Without it they had nothing.

In fact, with Juan as suspicious as he was, they might not have survived their first meeting with him had she not offered her services. So, adding it all up, they owed her for their lives, their relationship with Juan, and the steady stream of black tar he would provide. How much was all that worth? Besides, after paying her ten percent, they'd still have enough to live in luxury. So she really wasn't demanding so much.

She turned down a side street, dodging slow-witted tourists, checking her watch to make sure she wasn't too late. Not that it mattered. They would wait for her. And it wouldn't be a long meeting. They just needed to discuss a few details that they couldn't get into in Juan's house. Details like the number of the bank account the Americans were going to wire her money into, how they were going to do the accounting, and how frequently they needed to make the payments. Just a few simple math problems. And then she'd be set for life.

CHAPTER FORTY-TWO

*W*here that bitch at?" said Catfish, fidgeting in his chair at a table in the back of a near-empty cantina. "Bitch wanna get paid, she best be on time."

Banks shook his head and chuckled. "Nigga, why you trippin'? This Mexico. Everything more laid back down here. Chill."

"Man, you takin' this shit awful light. This Mexican ho playing us. Then she keep us waiting on her ass on top of it."

Banks took a sip of his Corona. "I'm figuring all this shit is gravy. Every nigga in Motown knew Bacon had this connect. And every goddamn one of them muthafuckas wanted to step in and fill the void when his ass got put away. We the ones got here first." He spread his hands. "So? It's all good, right?"

"I don't like no bitch trying to manipulate me." He turned and looked directly at Banks. "You know who she remind me of?"

"Who?"

"Red."

"Man, leave that be. She gone. She in the wind, partner. That shit is over."

"Nuh-uh," said Catfish. "I'ma keep my eyes and ears open for her. She pop her head up, I'ma be there. And Maria? This mutha-fuckin' Mexican shawty? Somebody need to put they act right on her ass, too."

Banks chuckled again. "Oh, and you the man to do that, huh?"

"What? Nigga, you know I don't play."

"Whatever. Anyway, for now, we need the bitch, so don't go fuck nothin' up."

They heard the front door of the place open and looked up to see Maria strolling in. It took a moment for her eyes to adjust to the dimly lit room, but then she spotted her new partners and hurried back to the table with a big smile on her face.

Banks gestured to an empty chair as she approached. "Have a seat, girl."

"We been waitin' on you," said Catfish.

Maria sat down and put her purse on the floor next to her. "I hope you were enjoying the beer while you waited," she said.

"Yeah," said Banks. "It's cold."

She bounced in her chair a little, adjusting herself. "Yes, and it's so hot outside. Perhaps someone will offer me a cold beer, no?"

Banks got the waitress's attention and ordered a beer for Maria and another round for him and Catfish.

When the waitress returned, Maria lifted her bottle. "Here's to partnership and wealth."

Banks smiled and clicked bottles with her. Catfish followed suit grudgingly.

"We're all going to be very happy in a short time," said Maria. "Where do you think I should live? I've heard Chicago is very ex-citing. You have been there?"

"Yeah, I been to Chicago," said Banks. "That town is tight. They got a lot of Mexicans there, too."

"Can I live in the Sears Tower?"

Catfish laughed. "Sears Tower ain't condos. Just offices."

"Where can I live?"

"Get yourself a place in the Loop, baby," said Banks.

"The Loop?"

"Yeah, you could get yourself a big loft up there. That'd be off the hook. You'd be havin' all kinda parties and shit."

Catfish glared at Banks, but the man just kept on and on. Like Maria was his little sister or something. The bitch was trying to rip into their business and that muthafucka was laughing and joking with her. Catfish just sat there saying nothing while the two of them went on and on. Musta been twenty minutes.

Finally Catfish couldn't just sit there quiet anymore. "So, is this supposed to be a business meeting or what?"

Maria looked at him. She seemed genuinely surprised at the change in the meeting's tone. "You want to talk business?"

"Hell yeah, I wanna talk business. You think I wanna sit up in this bitch all day? We got better shit to do than this."

Maria smirked and took a sip of her Corona. "Do you know how to say *beer* in Spanish?"

"The fuck?" said Catfish. "We didn't come here for no Spanish lesson."

Maria looked at Banks.

"*Cerveza,*" said Banks.

"That's right. *Cerveza,* with a Z."

"So?"

"That's the number of the back account you'll wire my money into. Like on a phone, each letter corresponds with a number."

Catfish reached across to Banks. "You gotta pen?"

Maria laughed. "You don't write that down. Are you stupid?"

"What, bitch?"

"If you're too stupid to remember the word *cerveza,* I'm sure your partner can."

"You ain't never been with a man strong enough to teach you respect?"

Maria wasn't smiling anymore. And she wasn't scared. She was angry. "Are you man enough to teach me. Do you think you are?"

"I'ma teach you what it feels like to take a bullet in your face," said Catfish, and he raised up, bringing his gun out from under his shirt.

"Aw, muthafucka," said Banks.

"Gentlemen," said a voice from across the room.

They all turned, startled by the voice they recognized.

Juan strolled across the floor toward their table, his boys at his side carrying the same shit they had in their first meeting— an AK and an Uzi.

Catfish didn't flinch. Outgunned though he was, he was ready to get busy with his nine. He spoke to Banks without looking at him. "Bitch set us up, nigga. I knew she was bad news. A scandalous bitch, just like Red."

Juan planted his feet ten feet from the table. He shook his head and wagged his finger. "I think you set yourselves up. When my friend Alberto told me the three of you were meeting in his cantina, I had to come and see for myself. It's hard for me to believe that the DEA would send a catfish to try and hook me."

Banks was frozen in his chair. "Man, we ain't no DEA."

"No," said Juan. "You're DOA."

"Now, hold on a second," said Banks. "You checked my shit out. You know I'm for real."

"Yes, I can see that you are entirely honest. You come here to meet with my little friend in secret? You have a strange way of proving your value as a business associate."

"Man, we ain't no federales, I'm telling you right now. Your girl here, she was trying to cut herself in for a taste."

Juan raised his eyebrows. "Using what as a bargaining chip? She is offering you something I cannot?"

"Naw, man, it ain't like that." Banks was still seated, but he could see Catfish out of the corner of his eye. That nigga was standing tall, ready to go out in a blaze of glory and take one of them two Mexican muthafuckas with him. He tried to envision a move. If he didn't get cut in half by the AK in the first two seconds, he might be able to dive for the floor and come up firing his own nine. If Catfish dropped one of the bodyguards, he might be able to get the other one and Juan. But in his heart, he doubted either he or Catfish was going home. This was something right outta *Scarface*. Or more like *Butch Cassidy and the Sundance Kid*. All south of the border and shit.

Then someone else came through the door. Catfish wasn't about to take his eyes off Juan, but he recognized the voice, and he definitely heard what the nigga was saying.

"Now, you know that's bullshit. I never did one thing to make Red think I was interested in her."

Then Catfish did turn, because he couldn't believe his muthafuckin' ears. There, walking into the cantina, big as life, was that Detroit nigga, Q. "Ah, hell no!" said Catfish.

Juan turned to the new arrivals as well, hearing English, seeing a large black man who carried himself like he was from the street. It was a setup. The Americans were closing in. He reached inside his coat for his own gun and shouted to his boys. *"Matalos!* Kill them!"

Q heard the shouts and saw a man with an automatic rifle wheeling around towards him. Instinctively he grabbed Chass

be-
had
d the
ish yell
do about
t. And then

fu

the

the ta

rolled c

was screa

up. But he

The man stoo

after another. I

into his right shou

practically taken his a

spattering the chair, the wa

"I'm hit," he screamed. "E,

trigger on his nine, but his right I

reached for the gun with his left hand

he looked up. The muthafucka with the

over him, smiling.

Muthafucka, thought Q when he heard the screams. *That's Catfish. The fuck is he doing down here?* And then he heard the sirens. The tires screeching outside. The car doors opening and slamming.

"Policia," said somebody with a bullhorn. And then the cop was shouting orders.

Q crawled over to Chass and helped her around the end of the bar. "You okay, baby?" he said.

"Oh, my God," said Chass, her voice strangled with panic. "What the hell is going on?"

"The cops are gonna come through that door blastin' any second," Q shouted over the gunfire. "Just stay down. Whatever you do. Just—stay—down! You heard?"

flung her out of the way like a rag doll. He dropped to the
or as he heard the first burst of gunfire. An AK-47. What the
ck did they walk into? He reached for his piece, but it wasn't
re. He hadn't been carrying since the day Red shot him.

E, blast them muthafuckas," shouted Catfish. He upended
ble for cover. But he knew it wouldn't stop an Uzi. He
ut to his right and started blasting with his nine. Maria
ming. He wanted to shoot her just to shut her the fuck
kept firing at the Mexican with the heavy firepower.
d like a statue. He squeezed off one short burst
Muthafucka had skills. Then Catfish felt fire rip
lder. He looked over and saw that a burst had
rm off. Blood was shooting everywhere,
ll, the floor.

I'm hit." He tried to squeeze the
and didn't work anymore. He
d. Just as he got a grip on it,
Uzi was standing right

eams. That's

And then something hit the door. A boot. A battering
Something. And the door exploded inward and was practic
ripped off its hinges. The gunfire became more intense.

Banks crawled across the dusty floor of the back room
hind the bar. He had no muthafuckin' idea how or why Q
shown up in that place at that moment. But he was gla
nigga had distracted Juan and his boys. He heard Cat
that he was hit. But there wasn't a damn thing he could
that. He got through the back door and got to his fee
he ran. And he didn't look back.

CHAPTER FORTY-THREE

*T*homas sat on the wooden bench and swiped his hands together to get the burrito crumbs off. Then he cocked his head and turned to Black. "You hear that shit?"

Black hung his head and shook it. "Man, that sound like a AK."

"Fuckin' Acapulco. Beach, beer, and bullets."

Black laughed. "Sound like it ain't too far away either. I still got your cold piece on me, but if that shit start gettin' closer I say we run."

"Hell, yes," said Thomas, standing up now and looking in the direction of the noise. "I spend a lot of time on the shooting range, but I ain't gonna test my skills against some cartel muthafucka with an automatic rifle."

His phone rang and he flipped it open. "Thomas."

"Detective Thomas," said the voice on the other end. "This is Detective Guzmán. You still looking for those American gangsters?"

"I am."

"I think I might have something for you. I'm on my way to a shootout in progress at a cantina not far from your hotel."

"You kiddin' me?"

"Nope. Witnesses said there were some American black guys in the place with guns. We got cops there now, but the situation is not contained, so approach with caution."

Guzmán gave him the address and said he'd meet them there. Thomas flipped his phone shut and jumped up off the bench. "Come on, we gotta hit it."

"What?" said Black, falling into quick step beside him.

"That gunfire over there is us. American gangsters in a cantina. Got to be Catfish."

Black reached under his shirt and pulled out the snub-nosed .38. "I thought we just agreed to run *away* from this shit. Now we marchin' right into it."

"Put that thing away," said Thomas. "They got cops on the scene, and I don't want to get shot by them before we can even identify ourselves."

"Damn." Black tucked the piece back into his waistband. "I ain't trying to get shot by no Mexican popo."

They broke into a jog and arrived at the cantina just as Guzmán was getting out of his car. Uniformed cops swarmed around the entrance to the restaurant.

Guzmán grabbed a uniform and pulled him aside. He talked to him for a minute, then turned and led Thomas and Black around the corner.

"Okay, so there are a number of people inside, some of them might be innocent civilians, so we can't go too heavy."

Thomas noted the amount of gunfire the cops were pouring into the place and wondered what qualified as *heavy* in Acapulco.

"We got one or two dead," said Guzmán. "We're not sure. But

there are at least a couple still alive in there. One of them is Juan Pintero. He's a bad fucker. That black tar you're interested in?"

"Yeah?" said Thomas.

"Juan Pintero runs all that shit."

"What can we do to help?"

"You armed?"

"Yeah." Thomas pulled out his nine millimeter. Black showed him his .38.

"What the fuck?" said Guzmán, looking at the snub nose. "That thing's no good in a shoot-out like this. It's only for up close. One on one."

Black sneered. "Yeah, that's what I heard."

"Okay, listen, you get a clean shot with that, use it. But don't take any chances."

Thomas and Black moved into position at a frosted window on the side of the building. Thomas jimmied it open and had Black boost him up. "It's a restroom," he said. "Come on, push me through."

Black helped him through the window, then climbed in after him. They stood at the door of the restroom and listened. The gunfire had fallen off. The AK-47 was still alive, as was somebody with a handgun. Nobody was firing wildly.

Thomas turned to Black. "Those are carefully placed rounds. These guys have their shit together."

"All right," said Black. "So we gonna have to make this count."

"Okay, now you cover me, but you stay out of the gunfight."

"I'm here, ain't I?"

"Yeah, but that six-shooter you got won't do you much good out there."

"I'ma be careful. Don't you worry."

Thomas nodded. "I just wish they'd take out that muthafucka with the AK."

"Well, look, partner. He concentrating on the front of the place. He ain't thinkin' 'bout nobody comin' out the bathroom."

"True dat. But when we go through this door, stay against the wall. Otherwise you're stepping right into the crossfire from the cops. And watch out for ricochets."

Black smiled and nodded. "Oh, yeah. I see a ricochet coming at me I'll make sure to duck."

"Oh, now you're a funny nigga, huh?"

"Come on, man," said Black. "Let's do this thing."

Thomas turned the doorknob slowly and eased the door open.

He could see the room clearly. There was a nicely dressed man with a handgun sitting behind a table. Next to him, a big guy with an AK-47 was on one knee, stock to his shoulder. Thomas stepped out and drew a bead on the dude with the AK. He had a clear shot and was about to drop the hammer. Then the well-dressed dude caught him out of the corner of his eye and turned. He shifted his aim to him and fired at his chest, but hit him in the throat. The nigga with the AK spun on him. Two hard, loud pops rang out next to Thomas. The AK clattered to the floor. The gunman fell on his side, lifeless.

Thomas turned. Black was grinning from ear to ear, looking down at the smoking weapon in his hand. "Naw, nigga. This thing ain't no good in a gunfight. Not at all."

CHAPTER FORTY-FOUR

*G*uzmán!" shouted Thomas. "Guzmán!"

He heard the screech of a bullhorn, then the detective's voice. "Detective Thomas."

"Yeah," shouted Thomas. "It's over. Shooters are down. Come on in, but don't let any of your peeps blow our fuckin' heads off when they come in."

Thomas heard Guzmán shouting orders. A few seconds later he came through the front door of the cantina, cautiously, gun at the ready. He looked around, kicked the weapons away from the fallen gangsters, then holstered his piece.

He shook his head at Thomas and Guzmán. "What the fuck did you do?"

"We took care of business, partner," said Black, still smiling.

"Detective Thomas, you took out a guy with an AK-47 using only an automatic handgun."

Thomas shook his head and pointed to Black. "He did it with the snub-nose."

Guzmán looked at Black and his jaw dropped. "Remind me never to get in a gunfight with you, my friend."

"No doubt," said Black.

The Mexican detective turned and addressed the other cops in Spanish. They all looked at Black, smiling. They exchanged impressed looks with one another and nodded.

After Guzmán looked around the cantina, he called Thomas over to the heap of furniture near the back wall. "Is this one of your gangsters?" he asked, pointing to the floor.

Thomas looked down and saw Catfish lying in a pool of blood. "That's the man I was looking for," he said.

"You can take him back with you if you have a garbage bag to scoop him up in."

"Guzmán," shouted one of the other Mexican cops behind the bar.

Thomas followed the detective and found himself looking down on Chass Reed and Quentin Carter. "What the fuck are you two doing here?"

Q looked up. "This was supposed to be our honeymoon."

"Hey, Q," said Black, smiling. "Congratulations, dog." Then he pointed to one of the gunmen on the floor. "Muthafucka with the AK? I took him out with a little snub nose .38."

"You with the police now?"

Black turned serious. "Naw, man. I'm down here looking for that bitch Red. You know we *all* want that bitch to go down."

Q tried to use his left arm to push himself up off the floor, but a sharp pain tore through it. He looked down and saw that he'd been shot in the arm. "Muthafucka," he said.

Chass jumped to her feet. "Oh, Q! Sit down, baby. I don't want you passing out."

Q allowed himself to be guided to a chair, even though he knew he wasn't about to pass out.

"Oh, my God," said Chass. "Somebody get a doctor."

Guzmán held up his hands to calm her. "Don't worry, Se-ñora. Help is on the way." He turned to Q. "You okay?"

"I'll live," said Q.

"Yeah," said Guzmán with a wink. "Not only that, but you're gonna be swimming in pain pills." Then he moved off to speak with his officers.

Q looked over and saw the worried look on Chass' face.

Chass shook it off and turned to Thomas. "Detective, did I hear right? You're down here looking for Red?"

"Among other things. But I'll leave you two alone. I'm sure that's not something you can help us with."

"Oh, but I can," said Chass.

Q held a hand up to try to quiet her, but she went right on.

"My sources confirmed that she's staying at the Calinda Beach Hotel."

"What?" asked Thomas. "Are you sure about that?"

"Yeah, I am. And I may be an officer of the court, but frankly, I don't care if you take her back to the U.S. or throw her in a Mexican jail and leave her to rot down here."

Thomas grabbed Black by the sleeve. "Come on," he said.

They started running for the door.

"Hey," shouted Guzmán. "Where you going? I have to get statements from you two."

"We'll swing by the station later," said Thomas.

Out on the street, he immediately started looking for a taxi. "Oh, so now you don't want no Mexican cops helpin' us grab Red, huh?" said Black.

"Shit, if we can catch her in her room, we got her cornered. She'll have no place to go but off the balcony. And I wouldn't be too broke up about that. As long as the floor she's on is high enough."

"Now you talkin'," said Black.

It didn't take long to find an empty cab. Thomas told the driver to take them to the Calinda Beach Hotel.

In front of the hotel, they bolted from the cab before it came to a complete stop. Thomas threw money at the driver and didn't wait for the change.

He fished the picture of Red out of his pocket and showed it to the desk clerk along with his badge. "She may be registered under the name of Red or Raven Gomez."

The clerk looked at the picture and shook his head. "No Gomez. But she looks a little like another guest."

"What guest? What's the name?"

"Lisa Lennox."

"American girl?" said Black.

The clerk nodded.

"Room key," demanded Thomas, holding out his hand.

The clerk handed him a card key. "Seven twenty-one," he said.

Thomas and Black raced to the elevator and hit the button.

"Yeah," said Black as the elevator started to move. "Fall from the seventh floor just about do the trick."

When the doors opened, they crept down the hall, guns drawn. Thomas slipped the key card into the slot on the door to 721, watched the light turn green, then opened the door. He rushed into the room with Black right behind him.

They stood in the middle of the room for a moment and looked around. Nothing and nobody. The bed was unmade, but there was no luggage, no clothing, nothing.

Thomas went into the bathroom. "Shit," he said.

"What you got?" said Black.

Thomas tossed him a towel. "It's almost dry. And no water drops on the bottom of the sink. She left last night or very early this morning."

"Muthafucka," said Black. "That slippery bitch."

CHAPTER FORTY-FIVE

Three Months Later

*R*ed popped out of the back of a cab in front of a building on Fifth Avenue. It was one of those gray, drizzly Manhattan days, but she was all smiles as she weaved in and out of the heavy pedestrian traffic on the sidewalk, eager to get inside before the rain really started coming down.

She took the elevator to the seventeenth floor and entered the offices of Royal Enterprises. She liked the name. After all, Regina, her new first name, meant *Queen*. And she felt like royalty. She was back in the legit life, though she'd pulled a few illegal strings to solidify her new identity after the legal name change to Regina Morales.

Her receptionist looked up from the front desk and smiled. "Ms. Morales, Candace Forbes called again. She's flying in from Paris and wants to know if you'd like to have lunch tomorrow."

"Of course. Make a reservation at Kiki's, and in case she calls back before I get a hold of her, tell her I'm all hers."

She breezed into her office and opened the blinds on the canyons of Manhattan. Water droplets dotted the window, but the view was still amazing. She never tired of looking at it.

She had put her ill-gotten gains to good use. There were two Gomez Realty offices in New York—one in Chelsea, and one in a recently revitalized section of Brooklyn. With the help of Candace Forbes, she'd discovered that she, too, had an eye for talent. And she'd recruited a number of dynamic Realtors for her offices.

She'd also developed a couple of talents in the literary department under the auspices of the Gomez Literary Agency. One was still a little raw, but had great promise. The second, Annette Beal, was a budding superstar. Red had just developed an auction for Annette's first novel, and the price was already into the high six figures with two bidders yet to be heard from.

Her own books were doing well, and Triple Crown Publications was sending her fat royalty checks.

But Red kept herself insulated from those businesses. Gomez Realty and Gomez Literary Agency were owned by two separate Bahamian holding companies. Gomez was a common name, but she wanted a buffer between her former last name and her current life. Even the holding companies were in the name of Regina Morales.

What the new name gave her was anonymity. She'd finally given all those Detroit niggas the slip and was a new person. She'd heard from Quisha that Q and Chass had been caught up in a shootout in Acapulco, but that Detective Thomas had rescued them. Catfish, on the other hand, had died in that same shootout. She was not shedding any tears for him. Black had been seen around Detroit, walking around a free man. Word was he was spreading some story about how he'd killed some drug cartel muthafucka who was hooked up with the CIA. And to keep from having the embarrassing story get out, the Agency had cut a deal with him to keep him out of trouble with the feds. Sounded like street thug bullshit to Red. Probably he'd cut a deal with the feds themselves, but he didn't want any of his Detroit niggas knowing that. As long as he stayed in Detroit, what the fuck did she care?

All her businesses were going well, but those were just side hustles. Red's main business was something she'd thought up with Candace, who had introduced her to some of her high-powered friends. Candace had the special events market sewed up, but Red developed a service in which she would get things done for a client. That included anything from locating a one-of-a-kind classic car and negotiating a fair price for it, to arranging ultrasecret, bicontinental rendezvous between celebrity cheaters who were constantly watched by the paparazzi. Such services commanded a price that paid for the Fifth Avenue office, as well as a luxury apartment on Central Park West, practically right across the park from her office.

She managed to put all the letters of her life's story together. Her life was working. But as she stood there looking down into the living streets of the Big Apple, her sweet smile slowly turned to a bitter frown. She'd managed to put all the letters together. Except one: and that letter—or rather, lover—was Q.

She still had that picture in her mind of the last time she'd looked into his eyes. Chass was practically dragging him out of that restaurant in Acapulco. He had looked over his shoulder. She kept that memory in her mind like a snapshot. But the picture wasn't set. It was just a little out of focus. She wasn't sure what those soulful eyes of his were saying. Was that a sneer on his face, or a look of longing? Was his jaw set in anger, or was he straining his neck to try to keep her in sight as long as he could?

Red sighed and turned away from the window. She dropped

into her desk chair and buried her face in her hands. She would never know the answers to those questions. She'd covered her trail too well for him to follow her. And she could never risk reaching out to him. Even if he did have feelings for her, if Chass caught wind of anything, she'd unleash the hounds of hell, and Red would have to run all over again.

Her intercom beeped. "Yes?" she said.

"Ms. Morales, I have Annette Beal on line one."

"Thanks," said Red, and she snatched up the phone and punched the button for line one. Annette was about to be a superstar novelist, and Regina Morales couldn't let the ghosts of Red Gomez interfere with business.

"Hey, Annette," said Red in a cheery voice as she wiped a single tear from her cheek. "How's my girl?"

CHAPTER FORTY-SIX

*D*etective Thomas sat at his desk eating a Big Mac and gazing out his window at a gray Detroit drizzle. He got back on the job a week after returning from Mexico. He'd had to attend another IA hearing and listen to all their bullshit. Roylon Shaw, his attorney, had gone on and on about lack of evidence, extenuating circumstances, distinguished service in a foreign country, the bringing to justice of a drug kingpin, etcetera. That shit burned his ass. He knew what the truth was. He didn't need to sit through some tired ass hearing to understand it. The Detroit PD shouldn't have needed all those formalities either.

But Shaw had done his job. Agent Holt had come through for him too. With Catfish coming off the plane in a box and Juan Pintero dead in Acapulco, Holt had gotten everything he wanted. Thomas knew Pintero's death didn't end the black tar trade; all it did was create more of a vacuum. Somewhere in Acapulco, various factions were fighting for control of Juan Pintero's share of the market. All over Motown, niggas were scrambling to find their way into that connect. Nothing had changed. Not one muthafuckin' thing. All that had happened was that Agent Holt got to wave a report around that said a major Mexican drug dealer had been killed in a shootout with operators under his supervision.

The straw in Thomas's drink squeaked as he adjusted it in the plastic cap and took a sip. He used his tongue to dig bits of Big Mac out from between his teeth and his cheek. Then he took another bite.

He didn't care about any of that bullshit anyway. What he'd hoped to do in Mexico was chase down Red. And that hadn't worked out. Detroit PD didn't seem concerned about the fact that she'd slipped through their fingers. Why should they? The bitch had only framed one of their detectives for rape. And probably gotten away with murder. Who the fuck cared? They gave him a pat on the back for mopping up Catfish and Pintero, and that was that.

Raven Gomez was a cold case. He'd spent a few weeks on it when he got back to town, but higher-ups had told him to move on. There was plenty of crime in Motown. They couldn't worry about one bitch who didn't seem to be messing with anybody or anything in their town any longer.

Thomas stuffed the last bite of burger in his mouth and sucked his fingertips. He took another swig of Coke and got back to the bottomless stack of work on his desk.

"Detective Thomas," said a voice.

He looked up from his desk and saw a female uniform coming towards him with a cardboard file box.

"You the one working on Ra—Rowen—shit, I can't even read my own handwriting."

"Let me see," said Thomas. He took the transfer slip off the top of the box and read it. "Raven Gomez?"

"Is that what that says?" she asked. "Okay. Yeah, you working that one?"

Thomas looked at the stack on his desk. The stuff his commander had told him to dig into. The stuff he was supposed to be working on instead of Raven Gomez. "Yeah, that's mine," he said.

The officer dropped the box on the corner of his desk. "There you go. Just sign the slip for me."

Thomas stood and flipped the lid off the box. "What's this?"

The girl laughed. "You supposed to be a detective? It's a box of evidence."

"Excuse me?" said Thomas, glaring at the young cop.

She blushed. "Sorry, Detective. It's a box of evidence. I was told to deliver it to you."

"Where'd it come from?"

"Evidence control. I guess you were supposed to get it a while back. The transfer slip is dated like four months ago, but it says *Recipient N/A*. It don't usually say that unless the receiving officer is retired. Or maybe on disciplinary leave or something."

Thomas sat back down in his chair. "You mean to tell me this box has been sitting in evidence control for four months, I been back at my desk for *three* months, and nobody thought to deliver it to me?"

The girl shifted her feet. "Uh—I just—I mean . . ."

"Never mind," said Thomas. "I'll take it." He scribbled his signature on the transfer slip and handed it back to her.

"Goddamn," he said out loud after she'd left. "Muthafuckin' Detroit Police."

He tilted the box toward him and began combing through the contents.

His commander wandered into the office and strolled past Thomas's desk on the way to his own. "What's that?" he asked.

Thomas played it cool. "Some bullshit burglary case. Store inventory shit."

"Mm," said the man, completely disinterested.

Thomas continued to look through the files. One was marked *Triple Crown Publications*. He pulled it out. His chair creaked as he leaned back in it, opening the file. Some kind of papers relating to authorship of a book. Royalty statements, contracts, addenda to contracts, account information. And on all the papers was a name that seemed familiar to him. He flipped open his phone and punched up a number.

"Who dis?" said Black.

"This is Detective Thomas."

"My nigga. My wild west partner. What's up?"

"Black, lemme ask you something?"

"Yeah, man."

"Does the name Lisa Lennox ring a bell with you?"

"Lisa Lennox? Yeah, I heard that name."

"Is that the name Red was using at the hotel in Acapulco?"

Black snapped his fingers. "It sure 'nough is, partner. I knew I heard that somewhere. Why? She ain't popping her head up, is she?"

"Not sure. I just found some papers with that name on it." He looked over his shoulder. His commander was on a phone call of his own. Thomas bowed his head and lowered his voice. "Officially, I'm off that case. If I come up with something, I may need a kind of unofficial partner. You up?"

"Damn, son, you know I am. If it puts me face-to-face with that bitch."

"Okay. Let me check this shit out and I'll call you back." Thomas flipped his phone shut, then opened it up again.

He looked at the number on one of the official forms in the file and dialed it.

"Triple Crown Publications is the blueprint," said the bright voice. "How may I direct your call?"

"This is Detective Thomas of the Detroit Police. I need to speak with someone there about one of your authors."

The receptionist put him on hold. Two minutes later, the call was picked up again.

"This is Kammi Johnson, can I help you?"

The name *Raven Gomez* didn't appear on any of the documents, but Thomas was used to dealing with bureaucracy and knew how to bluff his way through a situation like this. "Yeah, Ms. Johnson, I think you can. This is the Detroit Police. Detective Thomas. I'm looking at a box of evidence here that contains some material from your company relating to a Raven Gomez." He paused and waited.

"Yes?" said Kammi.

"And Raven—or, well, I mean Lisa Lennox—but it's the same person . . ." He held his breath.

"Yes?"

"Yeah. So, when you correspond with Raven under the name Lisa Lennox, where do you send to correspondence?"

"I'm sorry?"

"Well, I mean, you do stay in touch with Raven, correct? Lisa Lennox? How do you communicate with her?"

"Well—we don't give out that information. It's confidential. What's this regarding?"

Thomas kept it reined in, but put a little edge into his voice. "Did you hear me say I'm with the Detroit Police Department? This is regarding a police matter."

"I'm sorry, but I still can't violate her confidentiality. I can call Ms. Gomez and ask her to call you."

"Oh, that'd be a good idea. Except that she's a fugitive wanted for questioning about her involvement in a capital crime. So if you're telling me that you're gonna call her, I may as well just roll out to your place right now and put the cuffs on you for aiding and abetting. How's that sound?"

He could almost hear Kammi swallow hard over the phone. But she paused.

It was time to crank up the bluff. He picked up a piece of blank paper and rattled it in the phone. "I'm not gonna bother to read you the court order, I'm just gonna give you the short version of what it says. Says if you don't give me what I want, you go to jail for contempt of court. Your business closes down for a day. Or two or three. Your phones go unanswered. The press runs a story about your failure to cooperate in a capital case . . ."

"All right, all right," said Kammi. "I've got a phone number and address for her."

Thomas smiled as he took down the info she read him.

He hung up with Triple Crown and immediately called Black. "Pack a bag," he said. "We're going to New York."

CHAPTER FORTY-SEVEN

*T*he next morning Black met Thomas in the airport at check-in. When he saw he hadn't checked his suitcase yet, he dragged him out of line and away from the crowds.

"Hey, partner," he said. "You being a cop and all, you get to put your piece in your checked bag, right?"

"Yeah," said Thomas. "I'm not rolling up into New York naked."

Black nodded. "I feel you. I need you to tuck something in there for me, too."

"You kidding?"

"Naw, man. Unless you want me to tote that snub-nosed revolver of yours again."

"You did okay with it last time."

Black beamed. "True dat, nigga. But, you know, I need my real shit this time."

"What are we talking about?" said Thomas.

"I don't want to pass it to you here, but I got me a Glock .357

and a Sig Sauer .38. We go back out to the parking lot, away from the cameras and shit, I'll let you carry 'em for me."

Thomas hesitated. On the one hand, it did make sense for Black to be armed with something more than a six-shooter. But carrying a couple of automatic handguns for him was almost like giving him approval to do something with them. Something serious. Considering the fact that Thomas wasn't even supposed to be on this case anymore, if Black's weaponry ever found its way into any kind of reports—police reports, lab tech reports, eyewitness statements, any of it—things could get ugly. Still, the man had stood tall in Acapulco, and Thomas couldn't deny him the respect he'd earned.

They went back out to Thomas's car and got in the backseat with the suitcase. Thomas stored the ammo separately from the guns themselves, zipped the case up again, and they headed back to the check-in desk.

From LaGuardia they took a taxi into Manhattan and checked into the Skyline Hotel in Midtown. It was the cheapest place they could find—they didn't have the feds, or even the DPD, picking up the tab on this trip.

In the room, they unpacked their guns and laid out their plan. Thomas would dress in jeans, a Tommy Hilfiger shirt, and a Yankees cap. At Red's door, Black would stand to the side, and Thomas would play delivery driver, cap low over his eyes so she couldn't see him through her peephole.

"And then what?" said Black, lying back on the bed.

"And then what, what?"

Black sat up. "Naw, man. I got to know. I mean, you *know* how I want this shit to go down. I need to know if we on the same page."

Thomas thought about it, then shook his head. "In the first place, I'm a cop, muthafucka. You can't ask me a question like that. And I can't answer it. Second, this is something we have to play by ear. If there's somebody in the apartment with her, then we got to back off. We aren't gonna be shooting up the whole muthafuckin' building just to off this bitch. And we aren't gonna have any witnesses pointing fingers at us when NYPD rolls up."

"All right," said Black. "We clear on that. But we get up there, and everything look good—"

"Yeah?"

"All I'ma say is, you need to look away, you look away."

Thomas didn't say a word.

They wasted no time getting over to Red's address. Thomas badged the doorman and said they needed access to the building. He was carrying a clipboard and a small, empty cardboard box.

"Who you going to see?" asked the man.

"Confidential," said Thomas.

The guy hung his head. "You know, that ain't a NYPD badge."

"That's because I ain't NYPD."

The inexperienced doorman gave him a tired nod and waved him through the lobby to the elevator.

Coming out of the elevator on the fourteenth floor, Thomas pulled the cap down over his eyes. Black reached under his shirt, put his hand on the Glock, and hung back a few steps. When Thomas rang the bell at Red's door, Black pressed himself up against the wall and waited. Nothing. Thomas rang again and still got no reply.

Thomas moved back toward the elevator, waving for Black to follow. On the way down to the lobby he shrugged. "Maybe she works days now."

"So, we come back after dark."

They went back to the hotel. They decided to wait until very late, around two in the morning. That would give Red plenty of time to finish work, do her socializing, then get home and get to bed.

"Then the delivery man shit is out," said Black. "Ain't gonna be no delivery man knocking on her door at two in the morning."

"Good thinking," said Thomas.

He pulled out his laptop and got to work. In just a few minutes he had a fake name badge that bore the name of Red's building and identified him as part of the maintenance crew. He put it on a thumb drive, took it down to the concierge, and had him print it out on blue paper.

After having their plan all laid out, the men ate, watched TV and waited.

After closing up shop, Red headed down to the KGB Bar on Fourth Street in the East Village. The former headquarters of the Ukrainian Social Party was a literary hangout. There were no readings scheduled that night, but she was sure to run into some writers and she was always looking for opportunities to network. Also, she liked the red décor of the place. But no one else got that. Known around town as Regina, she wished she had someone to share her inside joke with, but there was no one. She ate at the bar, starting with the borscht and moving on to the *buzhenina*—baked ham.

After dinner she went mobile, table hopping and buying drinks for several people. She recognized a bestselling author she'd seen in there before. He wasn't very social and seemed to show up only to say, *I belong in literary circles, but I'm too important to actually talk to anyone.* There were younger writers there as well, including an Ethiopian woman who was doing something she called *immigrant urban*. Red had seen some of her stuff. She was talented and Red made a special effort to spend time with her.

At about half past one, Red said good-bye to her friends and new acquaintances and hailed a cab.

What Red didn't know while she was making friends was that her enemies, Thomas and Black stepped out of their hotel and into the late night bustle of Manhattan. There was still a lot going on, but it was fairly easy to get a cab. They gave the driver the address and sat back as he weaved in and out of traffic, cussed out other drivers in whatever his native language was, and used his horn more than his brakes.

When Red was just three blocks from her building, she remembered she needed to stop. "Oh, wait," she said to the driver. "Can you circle back to that market? I need to get some milk."

The man, a Pakistani, seemed annoyed. "There's another place two blocks up. It will be quicker."

"Are you sure? I don't remember a place two blocks up from here."

"My shift is almost over. You're my last fare."

Red cocked her head. "So, you're saying there's a place two blocks up, or your shift is over?"

"My wife is waiting for me."

"So, you're not going to stop?"

"My wife has not been feeling well."

"Look, if you're not gonna stop, just come right out and say you're not gonna stop."

The man looked at her in the rearview mirror. "I'm not going to stop."

"All right, muthafucka, just pull the fuckin' cab over."

"You don't want to go home?"

"I want some muthafuckin' milk for my breakfast. And you ain't gettin' a tip either."

"No tip?" asked the man half indignant and half hurt.

"No!"

He looked at her in the rearview again. "If I go back will you give me a tip?"

"If you go back to the store?"

"Yes."

"If you go back and wait for me, and then take me home, I'll give you a tip."

"A good tip?"

"Yeah, muthafucka, I'll give you a good tip. Now will you go back? I'm too tired to walk."

He held up a finger. "And you must stop calling me mother-fucker. I don't like being called motherfucker."

Red laughed. "All right," she said, exhausted. "I'll stop calling you muthafucka."

Black and Thomas climbed out of the cab in front of Red's building and badged the doorman. It was a different guy now, and Thomas had to go through the same bullshit about how he knew he wasn't NYPD. Again, they took the elevator to Red's floor and soft-footed it down the hall. Black pressed himself against the wall. Thomas pulled down the visor of his Yankees cap and clipped his homemade maintenance ID to his shirt. Then he rang the bell.

Red paid her cab fare and tipped the driver ten dollars. Why the hell not? She'd had a productive evening and the guy had made her laugh, even if he *was* a muthafucka.

With her half gallon of milk, she stepped into the elevator and punched the button for fourteen. She leaned against the back of the elevator and closed her eyes. It had been a long day and she was looking forward to climbing into bed. When the elevator came to a stop she opened her eyes and started to push herself off the back wall. And then the doors opened, and she was looking down the hall at two men standing right outside her apartment. One was reaching for something under his shirt. She blinked. It was Black. And the other guy was Detective Thomas. They didn't see her.

What the fuck? she thought. For a moment she froze, and then she gathered the presence of mind to reach out and push the button for the lobby. She held her breath until the doors had closed again and the elevator started down.

CHAPTER FORTY-EIGHT

*W*hen she reached the lobby, Red had to force herself not to run. She walked past the doorman, still carrying her half gallon of milk. Suddenly, she was right back in flight mode, not knowing who she could trust. Did the doorman know Detective Thomas was looking for her? Had they told him on the way in? She glanced at him as she walked past, and he gave her an odd look. That was it. He had to know something was up. And then it dawned on her. She was walking out of her building carrying the same half gallon of milk she'd just walked in with. It just looked funny. The doorman wasn't out to get her.

But Black and Thomas were. Furthermore, Black had been reaching for something under his shirt. A cop and a thug? That wasn't official police business. That was some heavy shit. And she had to get away from it now. She kept it casual going through the front door, but as soon as she was outside, she took off running. She had to make it to the corner of the building and up the alley. She couldn't stay on Central Park

West. Not out in the open. They could be coming down any moment.

Why is this muthafuckin' shit happenin' to me again? she thought. Caught flat-footed without any real cash on her, without a gun to defend herself. Once again, she'd gotten too confident. Too settled. And she was once again bewildered by how they'd found her.

She was about to take a sharp left into the alley when someone stepped out of it onto the sidewalk. She literally ran smack into him. A big man. Powerful. When she hit him she lost her grip on the milk and it went flying. When it hit the sidewalk, the plastic ripped apart and the milk went everywhere.

"Oh, my God," she said. "I'm sorr—" And then she looked up into the man's face and realized who it was. "Q?"

At first, she thought maybe he was with Thomas and Black. Maybe he wanted her dead, too. But when she heard the tone in his voice, she knew that was not the case.

"Damn, girl. Where you runnin' off to in such a panic? You look like somebody's chasing you with an axe or something."

"Oh, my God, Q." She grabbed him and pulled him around the corner back into the alley. "Q, what the fuck you doin' here?"

"What do you *think* I'm doin' here? I came to see you."

"What? Well, how did you find me?" *How are* all *these niggas findin' me all the time?* was what she really wanted to ask.

"I followed the trail."

Red looked over her shoulder and realized they were too close to the mouth of the alley for her comfort. She pulled him farther back, away from the street. "Followed the trail? What trail? Starting where?"

"Starting where? You muthafuckin' kiddin' me? Starting with Foxy. Where else?"

Red dropped her head and shook it. "Foxy. That skanky ass ho. Why is that bitch always in my business?"

She looked up to see that Q was trying not to laugh. "What?" she said.

He shrugged. "I don't know, girl. I don't know why Foxy is in your business. I don't know why you do what you do. I don't know why the world keeps spinning us around and throwing us together. But it does."

Red gazed up at him for a long moment. "Throwing us together?"

"Now hold on," he said. "I don't mean that the way it sounds."

"No? Then how did you mean it?"

"I didn't come here to get back with you. But I didn't come here to kill you, either. So, I don't know. Maybe we're evening out. Maybe everything's just—you know—it is what it is. I just wanted to see you. I wanted to let you know that I know you been through some shit, and I don't believe you meant to shoot me. You *said* you were trying to shoot Bacon."

She nodded. "I was, Q. That's the truth."

"And I believe that now." He looked up into the sky above the narrow alley and sighed. "Sometimes I wonder how all this shit would have turned out if you'd managed to shoot the mutha-fucka you was aiming at to begin with."

She put her hands on his chest. "Q, you have no idea how many times I've asked myself that same question. How many times I've wanted to rewind it and do it over again."

"Yeah, well, you don't get no do-overs behind a trigger. That shit's forever."

But what if it had *been different?* she wanted to ask him. *What if Bacon had gone down and you'd been the one left standing? Would we have been together? Would we be together right now?*
"Yeah," she said, looking away. "That shit's forever."

"Anyway. We've gone past that. It's behind us." He spread his hands. "You noticed?"

"Huh?"

"No cane. I'm doing all right."

"Oh, God, Q, that's great."

"Yeah. I still get a little stiffness sometimes, but I'm making it."

"I'm happy for you."

Q nodded. "Anyway, I wanted you to know, that—well—we good. You and me."

She stared up at him for a moment, and he seemed to be on the verge of saying something more. Or of kissing her. Or grabbing her and taking her away from all the bullshit in her life.

But then he took a step back. "All right, then," he said. "I'ma bounce. But you take care of yourself, girl."

"I will, Q. You do the same."

And then he backed out of the alley into the bright streetlights, waved to her one more time, and he was gone.

Red turned away from the street and covered her face with her hands. Her moment of hope was gone, and now it was back to reality. Back on the run. Back in the bullshit she'd made of her life. She drifted back into that fantasy she'd had many times. That fantasy that she now knew Q shared with her. What if she'd put Bacon down that day and left Q standing? What if she hadn't acted such a fool to him so many times before that? What if she were in his arms right now, someplace far away? What if he loved her the way she knew she still loved him? What if all those things were true, instead of the fact that she now had to gather up her strength and run again?

She leaned against the wall of the alley and, just for a moment, just before she took off into the night, she rested, gathered her strength, and allowed herself to dream.

*I*n the city behind her, Red heard the hustle of the street. The traffic, the sirens, the radios playing the wild, exotic music of the passing cab drivers. She had a little money in her purse. She could get to the other end of the alley and hail a taxi on Columbus Avenue.

And just as she was about to put one foot in front of the other and put her shitty little plan in motion, she felt a hand grab her around the upper arm. And then an arm reached in front of her and wrapped around her neck.

"Raven Gomez," said the familiar voice of Detective Thomas. "You and I got a score to settle."

"What?" she screamed. She reached up with her hands and tried to pull his arm away from her throat. "What the fuck are you talking about? I'm not Raven Gomez."

"Goddamn, you scandalous," said Black stepping into view. "We got you dead to rights, and you saying you not who you are."

"I don't know that the fuck you're talking about. My name is Regina Morales. You can check my ID. It's in my purse."

"Look," said Thomas. "You can call yourself Raven Gomez, or Regina Morales, or Lisa Lennox, or the Queen of muthafuckin' England for all I care. All I know is that you're the bitch who set me up for a rape charge and hung me out to dry."

When Red spoke again her voice was more strangled as Thomas tightened his grip. "I don't know who the fuck you niggas are, but you best get the fuck off me. I got friends. You heard? I got friends."

Black reached up and grabbed her face. "You done used up all your friends, bitch. Ain't a soul in the world give a fuck about you."

"You niggas are making a big muthafuckin' mistake. I'ma give you one more chance to get the fuck off of me."

"Listen to this bitch," said Black, laughing. "You gotta hand it to her, she got some balls."

"You had to know it was gonna end this way some day," said Thomas. "Didn't you?"

Black let go of her face and came up with his Glock. "Let's do this thing," he said. And he looked farther up the alley to find an even more secluded spot.

"Hey," said Red. "You trying to get paid? Is that it? We need to talk about cash, we can talk about cash."

"No more talking," said Thomas, and he began to walk her back towards Black.

"Stop muthafuckas!" yelled a voice from behind them all.

Thomas swung Red around, not letting her go.

Q stood with his gun leveled, taking a careful bead on Thomas's face.

"Q," said Red. "Thank God!"

"Q?" said Thomas. "What the fuck are you doing?"

"I'm tellin' you and your partner to put your guns down and let her go."

"You have got to be fucking kidding me! Do you not owe us your life, my man?"

"Do I?"

"We stepped in and shot it out with those cartel muthafuckas in Acapulco. You and Chass might not have come back from your honeymoon if we hadn't stepped in there."

"True dat," said Q. "Now get your hands off the lady."

"Lady?" asked Black, his own gun raised. "Ain't no lady here."

Q shifted his aim to Black. "I remember that shooting you did in Mexico. That was luck, nigga. You know you don't want to shoot it out with me."

"You got him, Black?" asked Thomas.

"Got him? Maybe. But I can't lie to you partner. If he get a chance, this nigga gonna smoke us both. For real."

"Just go back to Chass," said Thomas. "Go home to your wife."

"Not gonna happen," said Q.

With Thomas's arm still wrapped around her throat, Red looked into Q's eyes. He wasn't going back to Chass. Was he serious? Or was he just trying to bluff these niggas into backing off?

"Let her go," said Q. "And, Black, you put that piece on the ground."

"Muthafucka," said Thomas. "Red, you are one slippery, muthafuckin' bitch." He slowly released his grip on her.

When she had enough slack, Red slipped out from under his arm and moved cautiously toward Q, making sure not to block his line of fire at Black.

"Red, you all right?" Q asked her.

"I'm—yeah—I'm okay." She turned back and saw that Black was carefully placing his weapon on the ground.

"Now you, Detective," said Q. "Take your gun out real nice and slow, lay it down."

Thomas did as he was told.

"Red, go around me," said Q. "Go around me and get us a cab."

Red staggered out to the curb and raised her arm.

Q looked at Thomas. "Now both y'all niggas start walking to the back of the alley. Don't let me see you turn around."

When Red had a cab she called to Q. He tucked his nine into his waistband and hurriedly followed her into the back seat. "JFK," he said to the driver.

"Which side?" asked the driver.

"Departing flights."

"Now, why you strapped?" said Red. "I thought you gave that up."

"I did for a time. But the day after I saw you in Acapulco, I walked into some bad shit."

"I heard there was a shootout."

"You heard right. And I promised myself I was never gonna be caught without my gat."

Red leaned into him. "Ain't I the lucky bitch, then?"

Q laughed as he put his arm around her. "Girl, you are without a doubt, the luckiest muthafucka I ever heard of in my life."

Red relaxed into the heat and solidity of Q's body. She was on the run again. But this time, she had a good man to run with. This time, things would be easier. Q was a big baller. He was the perfect match for her. And she knew that together, they could do anything.

ACKNOWLEDGMENTS

To My Lord and Savior for his forgiveness, mercy, and favor.

My editorial team at Atria Books (Ms. Malaika Adero and Todd Hunter) and my staff at Triple Crown Publications. Michael Ward, you have been such an anchor. May your dreams come true.

To my pastor, Dalyn L. Dunn, for being a man of God, a man of service, style, and good taste ☺, and also for being just a phone call away for me. This year was rough, and you showed me how to walk the walk. To my first lady, Dawn, who shares her husband openly. You are a beautiful woman who I admire.

And, to the brother of all brothers, Cedric (Benzo) Stringer. How lucky am I to have such a great big brother and all the perks that go along with it?!

To my extended fam: Margaretta Wright, what a strange niece you are! You never ask me for anything. What's wrong with you? Love you for that and keeping me hood!

Tanille Jackson, welcome to my family and thank you for assisting me with Triple Crown Publications. It's a lot of work and most people don't know that.

To my angels, I need you now: Martha Jane Kitty, Margaret Wright, Mary Lilley. Rest in peace.

Last, but never least, to my readers and supporters all over the entire world.

What is understood doesn't need to be spoken on.

My sons' father, E. Steve Berry, you are mine and I am yours.

To our kids Valen and Victor: it gets greater later!